PRAISE

Hummingbird Lane

"Brown's (*The Daydream Cabin*) gentle story of a woman finding strength within a tight-knit community has just a touch of romance at the end. Recommended for readers who enjoy heartwarming stories about women overcoming obstacles."

—*Library Journal*

Miss Janie's Girls

"[A] heartfelt tale of familial love and self-acceptance."

—*Publishers Weekly*

"Heartfelt moments and family drama collide in this saga about sisters."

—*Woman's World*

The Banty House

"Brown throws together a colorful cast of characters to excellent effect and maximum charm in this small-town contemporary romance . . . This first-rate romance will delight readers young and old."

—*Publishers Weekly*

The Family Journal

HOLT Medallion Finalist

"Reading a Carolyn Brown book is like coming home again."
—*Harlequin Junkie* (top pick)

The Empty Nesters

"A delightful journey of hope and healing."
—*Woman's World*

"The story is full of emotion . . . and the joy of friendship and family. Carolyn Brown is known for her strong, loving characters, and this book is full of them."
—*Harlequin Junkie*

"Carolyn Brown takes us back to small-town Texas with a story about women, friendships, love, loss, and hope for the future."
—*Storeybook Reviews*

"Ms. Brown has fast become one of my favorite authors!"
—*Romance Junkies*

The Perfect Dress

"Fans of Brown will swoon for this sweet contemporary, which skillfully pairs a shy small-town bridal shop owner and a softhearted car dealership owner . . . The expected but welcomed happily ever after for all involved will make readers of all ages sigh with satisfaction."

—*Publishers Weekly*

"Carolyn Brown writes the best comfort-for-the-soul, heartwarming stories, and she never disappoints . . . You won't go wrong with *The Perfect Dress!*"

—*Harlequin Junkie*

The Magnolia Inn

"The author does a first-rate job of depicting the devastating stages of grief, provides a simple but appealing plot with a sympathetic hero and heroine and a cast of lovable supporting characters, and wraps it all up with a happily ever after to cheer for."

—*Publishers Weekly*

"*The Magnolia Inn* by Carolyn Brown is a feel-good story about friendship, fighting your demons, and finding love, and maybe just a little bit of magic."

—*Harlequin Junkie*

"Chock-full of Carolyn Brown's signature country charm, *The Magnolia Inn* is a sweet and heartwarming story of two people trying to make the most of their lives, even when they have no idea what exactly is at stake."

—*Fresh Fiction*

Small Town Rumors

"Carolyn Brown is a master at writing warm, complex characters who find their way into your heart."

—*Harlequin Junkie*

The Sometimes Sisters

"Carolyn Brown continues her streak of winning, heartfelt novels with *The Sometimes Sisters*, a story of estranged sisters and frustrated romance."

—All About Romance

"This is an amazing feel-good story that will make you wish you were a part of this amazing family."

—*Harlequin Junkie* (top pick)

THE
Paradise
Petition

ALSO BY CAROLYN BROWN

Contemporary Romances

The Party Line

The Sawmill Book Club

Meadow Falls

The Lucky Shamrock

The Devine Doughnut Shop

The Sandcastle Hurricane

Riverbend Reunion

The Bluebonnet Battle

The Sunshine Club

The Hope Chest

Hummingbird Lane

The Daydream Cabin

Miss Janie's Girls

The Banty House

The Family Journal

The Empty Nesters

The Perfect Dress

The Magnolia Inn

Small Town Rumors

The Sometimes Sisters

The Strawberry Hearts Diner

The Lilac Bouquet

The Barefoot Summer

The Lullaby Sky

The Wedding Pearls

The Yellow Rose Beauty Shop

The Ladies' Room

Hidden Secrets

Long, Hot Texas Summer

Daisies in the Canyon

Trouble in Paradise

Contemporary Series

The Broken Roads Series

To Trust

To Commit

To Believe

To Dream

To Hope

Three Magic Words Trilogy

A Forever Thing

In Shining Whatever

Life After Wife

Historical Romance

The Black Swan Trilogy

Pushin' Up Daisies

From Thin Air

Come High Water

The Drifters and Dreamers Trilogy

Morning Glory

Sweet Tilly

Evening Star

The Love's Valley Series

Choices

Absolution

Chances

Redemption

Promises

THE Paradise Petition

CAROLYN BROWN

This is a work of fiction. Names, characters, organizations, places, events, and incidents are either products of the author's imagination or are used fictitiously. Otherwise, any resemblance to actual persons, living or dead, is purely coincidental.

Text copyright © 2025 by Carolyn Brown
All rights reserved.

No part of this book may be reproduced, or stored in a retrieval system, or transmitted in any form or by any means, electronic, mechanical, photocopying, recording, or otherwise, without express written permission of the publisher.

Published by Montlake, Seattle

www.apub.com

Amazon, the Amazon logo, and Montlake are trademarks of Amazon.com, Inc., or its affiliates.

EU product safety contact:
Amazon Media EU S. à r.l.
38, avenue John F. Kennedy, L-1855 Luxembourg
amazonpublishing-gpsr@amazon.com

ISBN-13: 9781662514371 (paperback)
ISBN-13: 9781662514388 (digital)

Cover design by Mumtaz Mustafa
Cover image: © Jacinta Bernard / ArcAngel; © G. Yancy / Getty

Printed in the United States of America

This one is for the women who fought the battle for women's rights in the past, and for those who are still on the front lines for all of us.

Chapter One

On a hot late-June afternoon in 1883, when the sun was streaming heat down upon the town of Autrie, Texas, two women stepped off a train. A porter unloaded two trunks onto the platform at the side of the tracks and waved for the engineer to start moving. The wheels of the train generated enough motion to create tiny tornadoes of dirt, and Lily winced when the hot wind blew the dust onto her dark skirt.

Almost as bewildered as she was the day she'd arrived in Spanish Fort with no money, she rolled the kinks out of her neck. Even though she now had money in her purse, and quite a bit more tucked away in the lining of her rolltop chest, the feeling was the same: absolutely bewildered and lost.

"I'm alone," she blurted out, "and there's no one in this town like Miz Raven to rescue us like she did." As soon as the words left her mouth, she wished she could take them back. After all, she was the one who was almost six feet tall, and supposedly had a temper to go with her red hair. She shouldn't be worrying Daisy at this point.

"No, but I'm with you," Daisy said in a firm voice. "We've got each other."

Lily bent slightly and slipped an arm around Daisy's shoulders. Her smaller friend was like a lit stick of dynamite with a short fuse. "Yes, we do, and we *will* remember what Miz Raven told us."

"'Remember, this is an adventure and a new start in life,'" Daisy quipped.

"That's right," Lily agreed, and wished the words came from her heart as well as her mouth. "Who knows? If the chance comes up, we'll even help with women's rights like Miz Raven is going to do in London."

Daisy tucked an errant strand of curly blond hair back into the bun at the nape of her neck. "I'm ready to dive right in whether we get an open door to do so or not. But I have to admit, I already miss the others, and the dust hasn't even settled from the train yet."

"Me too." Lily dabbed at the sweat on her forehead with a lace-trimmed handkerchief. She craved a long, cool bath, with maybe some lavender-scented soap like the kind she favored at the Paradise—the brothel she and the other six women had left behind almost two weeks ago. "We'll hear from them as soon as they get settled, and we are so far from the Paradise that no one will recognize us."

"If they do, shall we shoot them?" Daisy asked with a twinkle in her eyes. "Remember when old drunk Cooter came to the gates and Jems threatened to shoot him?"

"I hope it doesn't come to that, but it's a very real possibility. By now Cooter has probably dropped dead from too much liquor." Lily was glad that a little of Daisy's spunk was rubbing off on her. "Remember, we have to sell the story that we are sisters traveling together. Until now, it has been an adventure for all seven of us on this journey. But it's time for us to forget the past."

"Do you really think anyone is going to believe that we are sisters, or even related? Look at us. You are almost six feet tall, have red hair and green eyes. I barely come to your shoulder and have this mop of blond hair and blue eyes. Maybe we should say we are cousins," Daisy said.

"I agree," Lily said with a nod. "Cousins, then. Do you remember the last words Miz Raven told all seven of us when we mounted up on the horses and rode away from the Paradise?"

"'You are strong. You are independent . . . ,'" Daisy quoted loudly as she popped up on her feet and spoke as if she were delivering a rousing, inspirational speech.

2

The Paradise Petition

Lily wrapped her arms around her short friend and gave her a quick sideways hug. "'And you have the ability to change the world.'"

Daisy raised a fist to the sky. "And we will do just that right here in Autrie, Texas. Get ready, folks—we have arrived."

"Amen, cousin. Preach on." Lily giggled and then checked the time on her gold pocket watch, a gift from Miz Raven on the morning they had left town. "Two o'clock. We shouldn't waste time. Maybe someone in the train depot can help us get our things to a hotel." She cocked her head to one side and listened intently. The noise of the town reminded her of bees buzzing around a hive, but she could hear something else, and it seemed to be coming closer and closer. She turned to see a wagon pulled by four horses coming their way. A tall, dark-haired man sat on the buckboard, and he flashed a bright smile when he was close enough.

"You ladies need some help?" he asked. "That was the last train of the day, so the stationmaster has most likely already left."

"Yes, we do," Daisy answered.

"Where are you going?" he asked.

"To the nearest hotel," Lily replied.

"I'm going that way, and I'll be glad to take you." He hopped down off the buckboard and hoisted the first steamer trunk onto his shoulders as if it were nothing but a feather pillow, then loaded it onto the back of his wagon. Even in the heat, he wasn't breathing hard when he finished. "But the nearest one is no place for decent ladies like yourselves. I'll drive you to the Crockett Hotel and help you get these trunks inside."

Lily often saw men with big muscles, but very few that towered above her, and none had ever called her a *decent lady*—at least, not since she'd gone to work in the brothel five years ago. Maybe Miz Raven, the very sophisticated madam of the Paradise, was right when she'd said that if the seven women who worked for her got far enough away from Spanish Fort, they could start new lives as proper women.

"My name is Matt Maguire," he said as he placed the second heavy trunk beside the first one.

3

"Pleased to meet you, Mr. Maguire," Lily said. "This is Daisy Lindberg, and I am Lily Boyle."

"Likewise," he said with a nod before he put his hands on Daisy's waist, set her on the buckboard seat, and then did the same for Lily.

Lily had never had a man pick her up without at least a little groan. Or have enough wind left in him to whistle as he hopped up onto the buckboard. A shiver skipped down her spine, and more sweat popped out on her neck at the same time. "Do you do this kind of thing for a living?"

"No, ma'am." Matt flicked the reins to get the horses moving. "I just came into town to get a few supplies for my ranch and visit awhile with my Uncle Elijah, who runs the wagon yard."

"You must live fairly close, then?" she asked.

"About two hours west as the crow flies or on horseback, but it takes a little longer to get from there to town in a wagon," he answered. "What brings you ladies to Autrie?"

"We are going to put in a seamstress shop," Daisy answered from the other end of the buckboard.

"The ladies will definitely like that," Matt said. "I'll tell all the folks out at the ranch that there's going to be a place to have their clothing made right here in Autrie."

"We will also make men's shirts." Lily noticed that even though Matt's chambray shirt was faded and had a few stains, few women wouldn't see anything but the way his broad shoulders and chest stretched the seams, as well as the buttons.

Matt tried to steer the horses around a hole big enough to bury a full-grown possum in, but the back wheel slipped right down into it. Had Lily not grabbed Daisy and jerked her back, she would have been thrown out into the road.

"Sorry about that," Matt said. "We're almost there. The main street of town is always busy, but the spring rains made a lot of holes in the road."

Lily's head felt like it was on a swivel as she tried to take in the shops on both sides of the street. "How big is this place?"

"The town itself has about eight hundred people. There's two churches, one at either end of the main street. The school is that way, close to Preacher Jones's place of worship." He nodded straight ahead. "It goes all the way to the eighth grade. 'Course, we've got our own little building where the children can learn out on our ranch. Post office is to your left, and as you can see, there's a general store, several saloons, and that big place is the courthouse. One hotel is also a bar, and"—he lowered his voice to a whisper and kept his eyes straight ahead—"shady women work there. That's why I said I'd take you to the Crockett. It's respectable. Where do y'all come from?"

As she tried to banish thoughts of Matt's shoulder against hers, Lily held on to Daisy even tighter when they hit another hole in the road.

"Up in the northern part of the state. Have you lived here your whole life?" she said, once the ride had smoothed out.

"I was born out on the ranch when less than fifty people lived in Autrie. The railroad caused the growth," Matt said.

Lily sensed longing for the simpler days in his tone. "The town we lived in was booming at one time," she told him. "But it's slowly dwindling down to nothing but empty buildings and a few folks hanging on only because that's where they were born."

"I understand that very well," he said. "I liked it better when there were fewer people to contend with around these parts. Used to be, there wouldn't be a half-dozen wagons or people on the street when I came in from the ranch. I'm glad I don't have to put up with all this noise and hustle every day."

When she and her friends went to town for supplies, Lily had often seen men with guns strapped to their hips standing outside a saloon in Spanish Fort, as well as the scantily clothed women flirting with them. Evidently, no matter where she went, the people were basically the same—just more of them in a bigger place.

Women hurried from one store to another with their children in tow. They sped past the women who made a living entertaining men as if they might catch some dreaded disease, just like they did with the saloon ladies in Spanish Fort. She had always wondered if, deep down, they really appreciated the women for taking care of the bedroom duties they didn't like.

Matt pulled on the reins to slow the horses so he wouldn't run over three little boys playing Kick the Can up and down the street. No little girls were in the mix. Lily remembered when her brothers could do that very thing and never had to do women's work in the house or the yard. And they got to go to town once a month with her father. Not so with her! She had to stay home and close to her mother to learn the skills of taking care of a house and raising babies.

Lily tucked that memory into the back of her mind and concentrated on reading every sign hanging outside businesses on the bumpy ride from the station to the respectable hotel. She didn't see a single one advertising custom-made clothing and hats, and counted that as a good omen. When Matt stopped the wagon in front of a building that had to be four times the size of the Paradise, she bit back a gasp.

He hopped out and then helped both women down. A hot breeze reminded Lily of the blast of heat she often got when she opened the oven door in the kitchen at the Paradise. The wind set the CROCKETT HOTEL sign in motion, sending a squeaking sound every time it moved. Matt opened the door for her, and she stepped inside the lobby to the murmur of dozens of conversations going on between people sitting around tables covered in white cloths. To her right, a man stood behind a tall desk with a book on a swivel base.

The windows and doors were open, letting in a few flies and some of the dust from the road. Lily brushed away a couple of the insects that landed on the sleeve of her dress, then turned around to see why everyone had left, only to find that they were still there. Apparently, only the conversations had stopped, and everyone in the hotel lobby was staring at her and Daisy. She bit back a soft giggle as best she could—if they knew where she and Daisy had worked the past few years, they would probably run them out of town on a rail.

"There you go." Matt set the first trunk on the floor. Then he hurried back outside and brought in the second trunk.

"How much do we owe you?" Lily asked.

"Not a thing," he said.

"Then thank you, kind sir," Lily said.

"We'll make you a shirt for your help, if you'll stop in at our seamstress shop after we get things set up," Daisy offered.

"That sounds beyond fair." He tipped his hat and disappeared outside.

The clerk cleared his throat and fiddled with his thin, blond mustache. "May I help you ladies?"

Daisy marched up to the counter with her back straight and her head held high. "We need a room for a week."

"One or two?" he asked.

"One will do fine," Lily replied.

He raised an eyebrow. "Will your husbands be joining you?"

"We are traveling alone," Daisy said. "We'll be looking around for an empty business to put in a seamstress shop."

"Sisters?" he asked.

"Cousins," Lily answered, thanking Daisy inwardly for the change of term.

The man handed them a key, told them the price for a week, and flipped the guest book around for them to sign. "That's room 214. If you need someone to take your trunks up for you, that will be an extra dollar."

Daisy took the money from her purse and handed it to him. "Thank you—and yes, we do need the services of the porter. Plus, we would like some hot water brought up to our room each evening. Do we pay for that now, or can you add it to our bill and we'll take care of it when we leave?"

He nodded toward the book. "Once you sign in, I can run a tab for you, and that can include any meals you have in the dining room."

"Thank you," Daisy said.

Lily stared at the ledger book for what felt like a full minute. Did she sign her full name, Abigail Carolina Boyle? She had simply been known as Lily for so long that she was taken aback for a moment.

Daisy looked down at the ledger, dipped the pen in the ink, and without hesitation, signed *Daisy Lindberg* with a flourish. Lily followed her example and signed *Lily Boyle*. When Miz Raven took her in, she'd had trouble getting used to having a different name, but the madam of the Paradise assured her that she was leaving her past behind her and adopting a new way of life. Now her birth name brought back memories that made her both sad and angry.

Now I'm leaving the past behind again, she thought. *So should I go back to Abigail or stay with Lily?* She figured she'd have to ponder that over the next few days, since the answer didn't fly into the lobby with the next group of winged insects.

The desk clerk frowned. "You sure don't look like you share enough blood to be cousins."

"I was adopted into the family," Daisy lied.

"Well, that would explain it. Thank you, ladies. I'm Frank Calvin. Just let me know if you need anything at all. We serve supper until seven, and then we close the dining room. You can still order tea after that time, but no food."

"Don't look back," Lily said when they started climbing the staircase.

"You mean, as in right now or forever?" Daisy glanced over her shoulder.

"This is a big town, and we're being watched," Lily said in a barely audible voice. "We want folks to see us as independent women, not as scared little country mice because we don't have a male escort."

"Well, let them look. If they are honest, I bet they've got more secrets hiding in their chifforobes than we do in our trunks," Daisy said. "And we'll need to be careful around that desk clerk."

"Why's that?" Lily asked.

"He's got shifty eyes, and I never trust a man with three first names," Daisy declared.

"He just said Frank Calvin." Lily stopped by the door with "214" painted on the outside.

"I'll bet you a dollar that his middle name is Edward or Paul or another first name, too. My dead husband was John Edward Andrew, and he had that same shifty look about him. He'd lie to his own mother to get what he wanted," Daisy hissed.

"I believe you," Lily said as she unlocked the door and stepped into a room even hotter than the lobby. "The fiancé I left behind had three first names, too, and he was horrible."

"We do not need a man to tell us how to run our lives, or to own anything that belongs to us. Miz Raven taught us to outride a cowboy, outshoot any of those gunslingers out there, and outtalk a politician—so stand back, Autrie. Lily and Daisy are here, not Abigail and Ethel."

"What makes you say that?" Lily crossed the room and raised the single window. The wind that blew the curtain back was still hot, but at least it replaced the stale scent that had greeted her and Daisy.

"Abigail and me, with my original name, and all the baggage we had when Miz Raven took us in are gone. We are Lily and Daisy, two independent women who don't need a man to travel with them." Daisy tossed her hat on the vanity and eased down into a rocking chair. "And we are more than cousins. We are sisters of the heart."

"Great speech, and you are right," Lily replied. "We were both adopted into Miz Raven's—if either of us can do anything at all, we owe it to her. Do you really think she's never going to be a madam again?" Lily turned around slowly to take in the whole room: a large bed situated so that any breeze from the open window would flow across it, a dresser, and a vanity with a big round mirror attached to the back of it. "She told me that she got into the brothel business because it was profitable, but she could see that in the coming years, it would die out, and she wanted to go home to London and help her sister with the women's rights movement."

Daisy chuckled, removed the pins from her long, blond tresses, and let her hair fall to her waist. "The process of running a brothel might change, but men will always be men."

"Yep, but who knows what tomorrow might bring?" Lily waved a hand around to take in the whole room. "This is not the Paradise, but it sure beats sleeping on the ground, or propped up in a stagecoach or a train."

Daisy stood up and unbuttoned her jacket. "I could use a nap before we have supper. How about you?"

Lily had already taken off her jacket and slipped out of her skirt before she stretched out on the bed. "Yes, I could. It feels good just to stretch my bones out straight."

She closed her eyes, and an image of Matt Maguire was right there, sitting close to her and causing her to sweat even more than the summer heat. Not even the man she had been engaged to, Phillip Robert Paul, had brought on that kind of feeling—but then, he had been, and quite possibly still was, a brutish fellow when they were alone. She couldn't put her finger on it, but something about Matt screamed that he was a decent sort—at least for one of the male species, and at the very least, he didn't have three first names, so that was a good sign.

A hard knock at the door made Lily sit straight up in bed, her eyes wide and staring across the room. "Who would be coming up here at . . . ," she gasped.

Daisy cracked the door slightly and then opened it wide. "Our trunks are here. The porter just left them by the door," she said and grabbed the leather strap on the end of hers and dragged it into the room. "Just lay back down. I'll drag yours in, too."

"Thank you," Lily said and closed her eyes again. She wasn't even fully asleep when the sharp sound of gunfire startled her and brought her to a sitting position for the second time. "Who got shot? Miz Raven makes the men check their weapons at the door."

Daisy dropped the thin curtain over the window and turned to face her. "I couldn't sleep, so I've been watching the people on the street. Evidently, there was a gunfight out there. Both men are wounded. Here comes a doctor from the saloon next door."

Lily covered a yawn with the back of her hand. "I guess we didn't leave that kind of thing behind in Spanish Fort."

"Don't you know that the whole state of Texas is the Wild West?" Daisy asked with half a chuckle, and stepped back from the window.

She unfastened all the buttons on her shirtwaist and tossed it over the back of a rocking chair in the corner. Then she did the same with her skirt. "I'm going to try to get a nap, but not in all these clothes. My hair will be a mess when I wake up. Will you help me put it to rights before we go to supper?"

"If you will return the favor," Lily agreed. "But don't dress mine too high. I feel like a giant already."

Daisy lay down on the opposite side of the bed and crossed her arms over her chest. "I'll take your height and red hair, if you are giving it away."

"I would give you as much as you want if it was possible, and I'll take a dose of your spunk as payment," Lily said.

"If we could make a deal like that, I'd shake on it," Daisy said.

Lily's eyes grew heavier and heavier, and she finally drifted off to sleep. When she awoke, Daisy was pouring water from the pitcher into a bowl on the washstand. "A lady brought this up to us a little while ago. It's the perfect temperature now."

Lily sat up and rubbed the sleep from her eyes. "I need a washing-up. I feel as grimy as if I'd worked in the garden all day. I've missed our bathtubs at the Paradise."

Daisy finished and moved over to the vanity with the big round mirror above it. "I *don't* miss having to clean those big tubs every morning."

"At least Jems dumped all the water from them for us," Lily reminded her. "I'm glad that Miz Raven took him to England with her. She might need a bodyguard."

"Do you feel like this is all a dream?" Daisy brushed the tangles from her hair.

"Yes, I do." Lily got out of bed and dumped the water in the basin into the slop jar under the washstand before she refilled the bowl. "But I'm always glad to wake up and know that it is real. I'm beholden to Miz Raven for all that she and the rest of the girls in the business taught me about pleasing men, and for the lessons about life, but I'm glad to be done with . . ." She paused.

"Being a soiled dove or a shady lady?" Daisy asked.

Lily shrugged. "Either one or both."

"Me too," Daisy told her as she pulled a white shirtwaist with mutton sleeves and a high collar from her trunk. "This should make everyone in the dining room think we are as pure as the driven snow. The men will respect two ladies in white, and the women will love the new style we are wearing, and will soon flock to our store to have dresses made or to try on the ones that are already made and ready to buy."

"From your lips to God's ears." Lily opened her trunk and removed a shirtwaist similar to Daisy's. "My hair is going to have to be taken down and redone, too. Ugh. I just knew a nap would do that!"

"Twist mine up into a bun at the nape of my neck. That way my hat will fit well. I'll do the same with yours." Daisy handed Lily her brush. "Do you really think we're so far away from the Paradise that no one will ever show up that we knew from Spanish Fort?"

"We might still be in Texas, but it took us two weeks to get here. The chances of anyone traveling as far as we have is slim."

"Right," Daisy agreed. "We are seamstresses, and that's not a lie. We did a lot of sewing at the Paradise."

The Paradise Petition

A soft giggle escaped Lily, and then it turned into full-fledged laughter. Soon, both women were holding their sides and guffawing.

"Miz Raven would fuss at us . . ." Daisy hiccupped. "For behavior unbecoming to a lady."

"We are not at the Paradise anymore, cousin!" Lily said.

That brought on a whole new round of laughter. Finally, Lily got control and said, "We have to stop or I'm going to break one of the ribs in my corset."

Daisy held her side and took a deep breath. "Corset? Hell, I feel like I might break one of my own ribs."

Lily sucked in a lungful of air. "That let out some of my nerves, but there's plenty left in me to dread walking into that dining room."

"Me, too, but we won't let anyone know that," Daisy assured her.

"How did you get to be such a spitfire?" Lily asked.

"I've never been a tall person, so I had to stand my ground. If I'd had your height and that evil look you get when you are angry, no one would have messed with me."

Lily sat down on the vanity stool and handed her hairbrush to Daisy. "I didn't know I had an evil look."

"Oh, honey, you could make a freight train take a dirt road when you look at a person with your *Don't cross me* expression," Daisy said as she brushed out Lily's long, red hair.

Once she had Lily's hair done up neatly, she said, "There you go. Once you redo my hair, we'll be ready. I'm hungry. How about you?"

Lily stood up and Daisy sat down. "I'm starving. I hope they have decent food here in the lobby. Besides the bathtub, I miss having our lunch with Miz Raven and the other girls every day."

"Me too," Daisy agreed. "Good luck trying to tame my hair after I've slept on it. I barely get one section tamed before another one sneaks past me."

"Anyone who wants curly hair should have to deal with it for a whole week," Lily said.

"Just do the best you can, and I'll keep it out of my eyes with my hat," Daisy suggested.

When Lily had finished, she crossed the room and opened the door. "This is a little like the hallway in the bordello, except that we had those lovely red velvet chairs beside our doors."

"Shhh . . . ," Daisy scolded as she led the way to the top of the stairs and lifted her skirt just enough to prevent getting tangled up in the hem as she started down to the dining room. "We don't need anyone knowing our past—and even if this town is bigger than Spanish Fort, you can bet there are gossiping ears around every corner."

When they had both stepped away from the wide staircase, everything went so quiet that Lily figured if a feather had fallen from the ceiling, it would have made a thunderous noise when it hit the wooden floor.

A little girl sitting at a nearby table squealed and clapped her hands. "Daddy, look! Angels are coming down from heaven!"

"No, silly little sister," an older one said with a long sigh. "That's two brides on their way to the courthouse to get married."

"'Silly,' yes," their father said in a booming voice. "But not 'brides,' and you are both being rude. If there was one wedding—much less two—going on today, I would know about it."

"I guess the preacher *would* know," Daisy said out the corner of her mouth.

"How do you know he's a minister?" Lily whispered.

"The collar," Daisy mumbled. "Looks like there's only one table left, and it's next to him and his family. We'll have to be on our best behavior."

When they were seated, the preacher caught Lily's eye and said, "I do not mean to intrude, but are you ladies waiting for your husbands?"

"No, sir," Daisy said with half a smile. "We aren't married. We are cousins." She fought back a nervous giggle. "We are new in town and are looking for a place to put in a seamstress-and-millinery shop."

"Well, then . . ." He visibly puffed out his chest. "I am Preacher Joshua Jones, and I would like to invite you to my church at the west end of the street here in Autrie," he said. "Maybe we can find each of you a good husband and then you won't need to put in that shop. You can do what the good Lord intended for women to do: love and obey their husbands, keep a clean home, and raise a family."

"Thank you for the invitation," Lily said and hoped that her tone didn't say something very different. No use in starting an argument about women's rights in the middle of the hotel–dining room on their first day in town.

"We'll hope to see you on Sunday morning at ten o'clock," Preacher Jones said.

"You are pretty," the smallest little girl said.

"Abbie!" the preacher scolded. "Pretty is as pretty does. What's on the outside isn't as important as having a good heart and a saved soul. Now, let's pay our bill and go home."

"But you said we could have dessert if we ate all our supper. It's my birthday," the other little girl argued.

"Elsie!" he barked.

The child dropped her head and said, "I'm sorry."

"What else do you say?" the woman, evidently the wife, asked.

"Thank you, Father, for the lovely birthday supper."

"That's a much better attitude," Preacher Jones said and then tilted his chin up a notch when he looked over at Lily and Daisy. "Forgive my daughters for their bad manners. They will be punished. Now, Alma, you and the girls go on outside and wait for me."

The mother stood up and whispered just loud enough for Lily to hear, "If you don't want a life of misery, don't ever get married."

"Alma, don't dawdle," he hissed. "That's a bad example for the children."

Lily fought the sudden urge to stand up and slap some sense into that man, even if he was a preacher. She was sure that God wouldn't lay that charge to her long list of sins, but she gritted her teeth and told herself that the time was coming when men like him would have to eat crow. And she planned to be right there to hand them a rusty fork to take the first bite with. Not even the fiancé whom her parents had chosen for her—the man who'd told her she would be turning over her entire life to him, quoted Bible scriptures about women being submissive after he'd raped her—had been that rude to her in public.

"Can you believe that?" Daisy asked.

Lily nodded. "Yes, I can. I've told you my story. I had to run to escape a man just like that fool. Thank goodness Miz Raven was in Spanish Fort the day I landed there with no money and nowhere to go."

Chapter Two

The bright sun coming through the window warmed Daisy's face the next morning and woke her from a deep sleep. She threw her feather pillow over her head and turned over to find Lily sleeping soundly right beside her. The smell of bacon and coffee wafted up the stairs and reminded her of the many, many breakfasts she had served to a client each morning at the Paradise. She would sit across from him in her snow-white dressing gown and share a meal before Jems escorted him with the other six men off the Paradise property and locked the gate behind them.

"Whatever you are thinking about could give you premature wrinkles," Lily said.

Daisy jerked her head around to see that Lily was now awake and propped up on an elbow.

"The Paradise and Jems. I miss him as much as I do Miz Raven," Daisy said with a sigh.

"Do you miss waking up to a snoring man beside you?" Lily asked.

Daisy shivered. "I do not!"

Lily nodded toward the open window with the wind billowing the curtain out. "It sounds like the town is waking up out there, and it's not nearly as hot as it was when we arrived."

"I don't think this place ever went to sleep. The music from the saloon played until dawn," Daisy said.

Lily sat up and then pushed the thin sheet back from her body. "Let's find some breakfast and then go for a walk to see if we can find an empty building for sale or rent, or maybe a house. I don't want to stay in this hotel any longer than I have to. I feel like someone is listening to every word I say."

Daisy slung her legs over the side of the bed and stood up. "Those two precious little girls have been on my mind. I hope that evil man didn't beat them."

"Surely that woman—What was her name? Oh, yes, Alma—wouldn't let him physically hurt them. No mother would do that," Lily said.

"I hope not—but if he did, I hope God strikes him dead," Daisy said as she began to get dressed. "We should do what we can before the afternoon sun heats everything up to a boiling point. We'll want to come back here and have a bit of lunch before we shuck out of as much clothing as we can for an afternoon rest."

Lily poured water into the basin, washed her face, and dressed in her walking suit—a long, dark green skirt over a petticoat, topped off with a lighter green shirtwaist that had a high collar and long sleeves.

Daisy wore a navy skirt with a pale-blue-and-white-striped shirtwaist. "Do we look like businesswomen?" she asked as she gathered up her thick, blond hair into a bun at the nape of her neck and secured her hat with some long pins.

"I hope so." Lily opened the bedroom door. "If things don't work out here, maybe we'll go on to Nechesville with Holly, Iris, and Jasmine."

Daisy followed her out into the hallway and down the stairs. "Or Jacksonville with Poppy and Rose—but I bet that Miz Raven had her reasons for sending us here."

"I hope so," Lily said with a smile. "I'm ready to settle down and—"

"Find a husband?" Daisy teased.

"That is the last thing on my list to want or even to look for," Lily growled.

"Do I hear some spunk?" Daisy asked.

"Your attitude is rubbing off on me."

Frank Calvin waved from the middle of the dining room. "Are you ladies interested in having breakfast? If so, just choose any empty table."

"Yes, we are—and would you know of any places in town where we might put in a seamstress shop?" Lily asked as she crossed the room to a table beside the open window.

"Only store that's empty right now is the old hardware store," he said. "The preacher who was here last night owns it. His father-in-law passed a couple of years ago and left everything he owned to his daughter. Preacher Joshua might sell it to you, but . . ." He paused.

Lily bristled and asked, "But what?"

He fiddled with his thin mustache. "Is it right that you are old maids?"

"I'm twenty-three and Daisy is twenty-four. That hardly makes us 'old maids,'" Lily barked. "But if the property belongs to a woman, why would she have misgivings about selling to other women to put in a legitimate business? A law was passed last year that said a married woman could own her own property."

"Her father died two years ago before that bill was passed." The man then lowered his voice. "I'm not one to gossip, but I don't know how Alma stands that man . . . Enough about that. What can I bring you ladies?" He pulled out a chair for Lily and then one for Daisy.

"That would be great, Mr. Calvin, and thanks for telling us about the property," Daisy said.

"Alma was raised up in that store." He lingered beside their table. "She and her parents had living quarters in the back. I was told there are two bedrooms, a kitchen, and a sitting room. Might work well for y'all if Joshua sells it to you. Would you be interested in the regular breakfast? Bacon, eggs, biscuits and gravy with a side of fried potatoes? Or just the light one of a tall stack of pancakes?"

"Bring us two of the regular. Thank you, Mr. Calvin," Daisy said.

"You may call me Frank," he said with half a grin.

"Sir, we do not know you well enough to call you by your first name," Lily told him.

"Very well." He tipped up his chin a notch. "Hope things go well for you. I have to go wait on our new judge, Mr. Wesley Martin. He was just given the job last year," he said before he hurried off to where a tall, dark-haired man had taken a seat by the window.

"Sweet Jesus!" Daisy gasped.

Lily leaned forward. "What brought that on?"

"If . . . And it is . . . ," Daisy stammered, feeling the blood drain from her face until a certain flicker of courage ignited.

"Are you all right?" Lily frowned.

"Evidently, we did not get far enough from Spanish Fort," Daisy whispered, "but then, maybe . . ."

"I'm still lost." Lily's frown deepened. "Do you see someone in this place that can help us get around the preacher? Or is something or someone else making you talk in riddles?"

"The Lord giveth. I just hope he doesn't take away." Daisy finally smiled. "See that man Mr. Calvin ran over to help?"

"Yes, but what has he got to do with anything?"

"Like I said, we didn't get as far from the Paradise as we thought." Daisy stood up and made her way across the room.

"Hello, do you remember me, Wesley?" she asked.

Lily blinked several times, but the scene didn't change. Daisy had blatantly walked right up to a man's table and was talking to him in a low voice. Thank goodness no one else was in the dining room, or the gossip would spread quicker than a Texas wildfire.

The man's dark brown eyes looked like they might pop out of his skull and roll around on the polished floor like marbles. "Daisy? Why . . . ? How . . . ?"

Lily could see the confusion in his eyes and read his lips. *Oh! My! Goodness!* she thought when she realized he had known Daisy in the past. She leaned forward and strained to catch a word or two of what they were saying.

"I'm going to live here," she whispered.

"As . . . ," he gasped.

"As a seamstress and milliner. My cousin, Lily, and I are looking for a place to set up shop," she said. "I understand the Preacher Joshua Jones has property for sale, but he seems to have reservations about selling to two unmarried ladies."

"You're not going—"

Daisy cut him off with a shake of her head. "Not at all, and I would appreciate it if you didn't ever mention the nights we shared at the Paradise, either."

Lily leaned back in her chair. The past had caught up with them after all, but bold Daisy was in the process of taking care of things.

"So, you want the old hardware store," he asked, "and if I buy it and then sell it to you, neither of us will talk about Spanish Fort, right?"

Lord have mercy! Both she and Daisy could easily end up in jail for blackmailing a judge.

She could hear Miz Raven's voice giggling in her head. *But then he would have to come clean about what his past relationship was to Daisy.*

Lily leaned forward again so she could hear better. Daisy smiled at her motion, and Lily suspected she wasn't as subtle about eavesdropping as she'd thought.

"I've heard that the pious Mr. Jones wouldn't want to sell to a couple of unmarried women."

"I will talk to Preacher Jones today. Come by the courthouse Monday morning," the judge snapped. "Too bad that law hadn't been passed when Alma inherited the store—but then, she would have probably signed everything over to Joshua anyway. He's got that poor woman under his thumb pretty tightly."

"We understand each other perfectly, *Judge*," Daisy said, dragging out the title into several syllables. "And would you mind leaving your newspaper on my table when you leave?"

"Why do *you* want my newspaper?" His tone was so cold that Lily could practically feel the chill reaching across the room.

"So that if anyone sees us talking, there won't be rumors. I'm merely asking for your paper to see if I can find a building listed where we can put in a shop. For now, I'm going to leave you alone before rumors get started."

"I'll see you Monday," Wesley said through clenched teeth.

"What was that all about?" Lily whispered when Daisy returned to their table.

"Judge Wesley Martin will see us Monday morning," Daisy said with a smile.

"I heard enough of the conversation to know that you could spend the rest of your life in jail for blackmailing a judge." Lily clamped her mouth shut when she realized Mr. Calvin was coming across the room with two plates of food.

He set one each in front of Lily and Daisy. "I saw you talking to the judge. Are you related to him?"

Daisy unfolded a napkin and placed it in her lap. "No, and it was brazen of me, but I was asking if we might have his newspaper when he finished with it. I thought there might be a listing for a property or maybe a house for sale. Plus, we like to keep up with what's going on in the world."

"Well, enjoy your breakfast, and good luck on finding a place," he said. Lily bit back a giggle. "And people talk about *women* being nosy."

"Amen," Daisy said and picked up her fork.

Lily's curiosity rose to its highest point, but the dining room was not the place to ask Daisy for a more detailed report of what had really happened with that judge. There was more history, for sure, and it had to do with the Paradise—but Frank Calvin was a busybody.

The Paradise Petition

The judge discreetly laid his newspaper on the table when he passed by, but he didn't say a word to either woman. Still, Lily watched Daisy's eyes focus on him until he was out the door. "Now, what were you saying?"

Daisy nodded toward several more people pushing their way into the hotel. "Not in here. I'll tell you the whole story when we are away from listening ears. I don't see any listings, but let's walk around town and look for any empty buildings."

"Good idea," Lily said.

"But will you please act like you aren't really interested when we peek inside the old hardware store?" Daisy asked. "When we return, we'll tell the nosy Mr. Calvin that the preacher's building won't work."

"And you'll explain everything?"

"Of course."

When they were finished eating, Daisy got to her feet and left the newspaper on the table.

They were halfway down the street when Daisy finally started talking. "Wesley came through with one of the last cattle runs and then stopped by the Paradise on his way back home. He said he was a lawyer, out for an adventure, and it was time to settle down. I thought he was trying to impress me when he said he would probably soon be a judge, so I didn't believe a word of it."

"Did he ever talk about Autrie when he was with you at the Paradise?" Lily asked, remembering a few of the tall tales men had told her when they were allowed to visit the brothel. "I just realized how much those two words are alike."

"He mentioned being the judge of Anderson County. I didn't even know that's where Autrie is located."

"The way you reacted when you saw him, I bet you thought about him a lot, though."

They were right outside the general store when Lily nudged Daisy in the arm and said in a loud voice, "Hello, Alma. Nice to see you again."

Alma stopped and smiled. "I didn't catch your names last evening—and I need to apologize for that tacky remark I made."

"I'm Lily and this is Daisy," Lily said. "You do not owe us an apology. Actually, we're pretty much in agreement with you when it comes to marriage."

"Thank you for that, but I still shouldn't have said that to two strangers."

"Where are your sweet little girls?" Daisy asked.

"Thank you for asking about them, but I have to hurry to the general store. I'm out of flour, and Joshua wants a chocolate cake for supper. If the girls do a good job of dusting the church, he says they can have a slice." Alma's chin quivered as she rushed into the store.

"That was a close call," Daisy said. "But you covered it well, and we know now that he didn't whip those little girls."

"I feel so sorry for her," Lily whispered. "Being put down and living under a microscope like that hurts my heart."

"Mine too. Maybe what we hope to do here will help her to stand up for herself," Daisy said.

"That would be wonderful," Lily said with a sigh. "Now that we're alone, tell me what it was about the judge that made you remember him among all the others?"

"He said that if the situation was different, he would take me home with him. A woman—even a shady one—doesn't forget those things."

"Well," Lily giggled, "I guess it'll be legal if *he* signs the papers, won't it?"

"That's what I thought the minute I realized that Frank Calvin was talking about one of my old clients." Daisy stopped in front of a store and peeked in the dirty window. "This will take a lot of elbow grease, but it would work for sure."

"Plus, we wouldn't have to rent or buy a house," Lily agreed, but then she shook her head and shrugged.

"Why are you saying one thing and acting differently?"

"Look across the street," Lily said. "Isn't that Preacher Jones over there, talking to some other men?"

Daisy raised her voice. "I don't know about this. Maybe we could start out with a smaller place."

"I agree. This place is too big, and it's too close to the saloon." Lily looped her arm through Daisy's, and together they walked on down the street.

"Do you think he heard us?" Daisy asked.

"Have no idea, but he could read our body language for sure," Lily answered.

I'm so proud of you, Miz Raven whispered, so clearly that Lily glanced over her shoulder to see if the madam was right behind her.

They passed by a couple of other businesses and then stopped at the general store, pushed open the door, and went inside.

"Come right in," a woman behind the counter said. "What can I do for y'all this morning? Don't recall having seen you in Autrie before. Are you just traveling through?"

Daisy introduced them and then said, "We are here, hopefully, to put in a millinery and seamstress shop."

"I'm Beulah," the woman said, "and we could sure use a business like that. Y'all stayin' at the Crockett? I heard two women without husbands checked in last night. Autrie eats up gossip like those hotel pancakes with maple syrup. I only know of one property around these parts that's standin' empty, and y'all have about as much chance of buying it as a snowball's chance in hell."

Lily smiled at Beulah's language. Although first impressions might not always be right, she already liked this woman. "Why's that?"

Beulah snarled as if she had gotten a whiff of something bad. Her expression and the look in her hazel eyes gave away her emotions immediately. Lily wondered whether the lady had ever played poker, and if so, whether she had ever won a game.

"It belongs to Preacher Jones," she said and wiped her hands on the tail of her apron as if just saying his name had made them dirty.

"I take it that you and Mr. Jones are not good friends," Daisy said.

"You got that right," Beulah said. "My father died six months ago and left me this store—just like Alma's daddy did two years ago. Only, the law now says that I can own property myself, and it does not go to my husband. That bill hadn't passed yet when Alma's father died, so she had to give her store and inheritance to her worthless excuse of a husband."

"And your husband?" Lily asked.

"He dragged me over to the courthouse to stand before Judge Martin and insisted I sign my inheritance all over to him, and that was a great deal more than just this store. When the judge told him that wasn't legal anymore, he got on his horse and rode out of town. Ten years I was married to that man and put up with his bullshit. My father did me a big favor when he left me this store, and the law did me a bigger one when it said married woman could own property." Beulah stopped ranting and took a breath. "Enough about that. We don't have nearly as many women in Autrie as we do men, so when we get a chance to talk, we usually tell too much. Now, what about y'all? I hear you are cousins, but you sure don't look a thing alike. Where do you come from?"

"We are *really* best friends, but to avoid problems, we tell folks we are cousins," Daisy told her. "And we used to live in Spanish Fort. The good preacher man doesn't need to know that we aren't related, though. He's already looking down on us because we are traveling together without a male escort."

"He even invited us to his church so we could find a husband," Lily said.

Beulah laughed and slapped her leg. "I love it. Cousins you are, then—but back to Joshua. There ain't one thing good about that man, or the one who left me, either. If y'all stick around we will have three independent women in Autrie. If you happen to find a place to buy, go down to the wagon yard to get whatever you need to furnish it. Elijah Maguire is a friend of mine, and he's a sweet old guy who'll give you a good deal. Joshua is so money hungry that he sold everything in the store to Elijah for a lump sum. Most of what he bought is still in his storage shed—beds, stoves, and even one of them fancy sewing machines that came out a few years back. Alma's daddy bought it, and then it just sat there. No one in this town could afford the thing, but a lot of women sure coveted it."

"Thank you for that," Lily said. "And it's sure been nice visiting with you."

"Got anywhere else to go?" Beulah asked.

"Not right now," Daisy replied.

"Well, then, come on back here behind the counter and have a seat. I'll pour us a glass of sweet tea . . ." She lowered her voice. "The iceman came yesterday, so I have a block. I'll chip away some of it and share for the company."

"Can't pass up a deal like that," Daisy said and rounded the end of the counter to sit in one of the three ladder-back chairs.

"Give me a minute," Beulah said. "Anyone comes in, just tell them to look around until I get back. Y'all want a little kick in your tea? I always take one in mine."

"What is that?" Daisy asked.

"Just a splash of good whiskey—not that cheap stuff that the owner of the saloon passes off as liquor," Beulah said with a twinkle in her eye.

"Sure, why not? I'm going to prowl a bit just to see what all we can buy from you when we get settled into our new shop," Lily said.

"Help yourself, and I'll be mighty glad for the business," Beulah said.

Daisy stood up and joined Lily to check out the pots and pans, the grocery supplies, and even noticed that Beulah had fresh, homemade pies for sale on one shelf.

Lily leaned forward and sniffed a warm apple pie. "Let's buy this one and take it up to our hotel room for a snack this evening."

"Think we can eat two pies before they go bad?" Daisy picked up a chocolate cream along with the apple pie and carried them both to the counter.

"If we skip supper in the dining room and just have pie this evening and maybe for breakfast, I bet we can eat both of them with no problem." Lily shooed away a fly and went back to her chair. "I miss Holly's cooking at the Paradise."

"Me, too, but Poppy could do better on blackberry cobbler," Daisy said. "Holly always got too much flour in the filling and it was as thick as jelly. But I bet you don't miss men like old Cooter, do you?"

"I do not!" Lily declared.

"Did I hear something about blackberries?" Beulah brought three tall glasses of cold sweet tea from a back room. "I've got a whole thicket of those things out behind the store. I make cobblers for sale on Saturdays, and they go first thing in the morning. If you want one, I'll be glad to set one aside for you anytime. Did y'all have a seamstress shop in that town you came from? I don't remember the name."

"Spanish Fort—and we did a lot of sewing for the ladies we knew," Daisy said. "We want to buy the two pies we've set on the counter."

"I'll start a tab for you. You can pay me by the month or else we can use the barter system and you can do some sewing for me," Beulah said. "I love to bake and cook, but anything that has to do with a needle and thread drives me up the wall."

"That sounds great." Lily took a sip of her tea. "This does have a little kick, but it tastes really good, and to have ice is a real treat."

She and Daisy had never been invited to have tea with a store owner back in Spanish Fort. No, sir! There, they were looked at like they were lower than dirt.

"Amen to that. Something cold to drink on a day like this is special," Daisy added. "And to answer your question, we decided to come to a bigger place and offer our services to more people."

"I'm glad you did, and I hope you find a place. If I had more room, I'd let y'all set up shop right here," Beulah said with a wink. "Us unmarried women have to stick together."

"Have you lived here your whole life?" Daisy asked.

Beulah nodded. "I've always lived here." She chomped on a small piece of ice. "The best part of my morning tea is the taste and coldness of the ice. Right after the war, my parents moved from down around the coast. This place was just a settlement then. Daddy put in this store, and I was born in the living quarters through that door back there. Mother died of a fever when I was ten. Daddy raised me right here in this very building. I married at seventeen. All I ever knew was menfolk telling me what to do. Now I'm my own boss, and I love it."

"Do you know Alma?" Lily asked and told her about the incident in the café.

Beulah set her tea on the counter. "She was my best friend when we were girls—we walked to school together every day and were in and out of each other's stores all the time. We used to read any old newspapers that we could find, and made plans to fight for women's right to vote. But all that changed when we both got married. Alma had it worse than I did because her folks more or less made her marry Joshua. He was a new preacher in town back then, and he seemed like a good man. After all, he is a man of God, right?" Sarcasm dripped from her words, and she slammed a fist into the palm of her other hand. "Wrong!"

"Your folks didn't make you marry your husband?" Daisy asked.

"No, but they were sure glad to see me settled down and not talking about doing things women shouldn't." Beulah took a drink of her tea. "My husband, Orville Walters, was a carpenter and helped build a lot of the homes in town. He even built me a nice little place about a quarter of a mile out of town with a garden spot and a place to raise chickens. My job was to take care of that, make sure his supper was on the table when he came home, do my wifely duties in the bedroom, and have babies."

"Like all of us," Daisy agreed with a nod.

Beulah lowered her voice to a whisper. "I never did have babies, and he blamed me for that. I also must not have been good at the bedroom duties, because after a couple of years, he wasn't interested in that anymore. I figured he was spending time with the soiled doves at one of the saloons or the hotel down the street from here, but by then I didn't care. Lord . . ." She paused and took a sip of her tea. "It's good to have some women that I can talk to. Since Orville left, most men forbid their wives from having anything to do with me."

"But you're the only general store in town," Lily said, sliding a long sideways glance over at Daisy. Without saying a word, they understood each other perfectly. Both of them knew how so-called decent women felt about them.

"They have to buy stuff from me, but they sure don't like that I'm outspoken and don't take bullshit off the men just because they wear pants," Beulah said.

Lily liked this woman more with every passing minute. "Amen to that."

"I have missed Alma so much, but we do what we can," Beulah said.

"Oh?" Daisy asked.

"I put sheets of paper and a pencil in Alma's sack when she leaves, along with the letter that I write a little in every night between her visits. Then she can bring me a letter when Joshua lets her come to town. He would punish her if he found out, so . . ." Beulah put a finger over her lips and went on. "A good wife is submissive and never questions her husband. Don't y'all know that?"

"I'd rather be called an old maid," Daisy declared.

"Amen," Beulah said. "I would have rather been an old maid than a married woman."

Matt Maguire pushed the screen door open and stepped inside the store. "Mornin', Miz Beulah."

"Same to you, Matt." Beulah picked up her tea, finished off the last drink, and set the glass on a shelf under the counter. "I thought you bought everything you needed for the next month yesterday."

"I did, except I forgot to get a twenty-pound bag of sugar, and my mama would make me turn around and come back if I didn't bring it home. It's blackberry season, and she's making pie filling and jelly. When I remembered it, you were already closed, so I spent the night at Uncle Elijah's," Matt explained and tipped his hat toward Daisy and Lily. "Mornin', ladies. Did you get settled in at the hotel?"

"Yes, and thank you again for your help," Lily said.

Beulah picked up a stubby pencil and a receipt pad. "Sugar all you need, Matt? Want it on your bill?"

"Yes, ma'am, and that should do it," he said. "I'll sell off some stock next month and be in to pay you what I owe."

"I'm not worried," Beulah said. "You always have been good for what you owe."

"Y'all all have a good day, then." He hoisted the bag of sugar onto his shoulder and left the store.

"That was unusual," Beulah frowned. "I've never known Matt to forget anything."

"We should be going, too." Lily wondered if Matt forgot stuff on purpose. That thought made her blush, and she hoped that Beulah and Daisy figured it was because of the heat. In reality, seeing Matt again had caused the same reaction she'd had when she sat so close to him in the wagon. "Thank you for the tea, and especially for the ice."

"It was a small price to pay for a visit," Beulah said. "Y'all come back anytime, and let me know when you get your shop open. Like I said, I love to cook and bake, but I hate to sew. I will be your first customer, and I'll be glad to put any of your creations in the store to sell as ready-mades."

"We appreciate that," Daisy said.

As soon as they were outside, Lily said, "Sure seems like there's some dissatisfied women in Autrie. Do you think Miz Raven knew that when she sent us here?"

"Miz Raven knows everything," Daisy said with a chuckle.

Chapter Three

"It's been years since I've been to Sunday-morning services in a real church," Lily said as she and Daisy got dressed in their white outfits that morning. Just thinking about sitting on a hard pew for an hour—or maybe more—and listening to a preacher scold about all the sins that could take a person to hell made her wish she was back at the Paradise.

Daisy frowned and checked her reflection in the mirror above the vanity. "Me, too, and to tell the truth, I'm not looking forward to going today. But it's a good way to fit into the community. I appreciated the little services we had on Sunday afternoons at the Paradise. I liked them a whole hell of a lot better than sitting on a pew with proper women."

"Preach on, sister," Lily said with half a giggle.

"Don't say that," Daisy said. "We had friends, a lovely place to live, and we learned a lot. Not only about men, either. Holly taught me to play the piano, and we found out that you have a lovely singing voice."

"Did you ever feel guilty about the men?" Lily asked.

Daisy shrugged. "Why should I? We got *paid* to make those men happy. When I was married, John just told me how worthless I was as a wife because I didn't give him a son, and he said it was his God-given right to slap me around when I didn't get his chicken fried just right. That wasn't abuse—it was teaching me to be a better wife, according to him. And I didn't get a dime for any of the hard work I did. I was glad when he died, even if I didn't have a place to live anymore."

"That's why we want to fight to make things better for all of us women," Lily reminded her. "Let's have breakfast, go to church, and get told how many hours we need to be on our knees to repent for all our sins. Do you think that the men we made happy have asked forgiveness for their part in those same things?"

"Oh, no!" Daisy said as she opened the hotel door. "Men are born with halos and wings. They fall under that old saying 'Boys will be boys.' But women have to work hard to get any respect at all."

Lily went ahead of her and stomped down the stairs, not caring who heard as her mood began to match Daisy's. "We will take our place in this world, even if we have to get it an inch at a time."

"Quite literally," Daisy agreed with a stony expression. "And I'm ready to take the first step if you are."

"What if we get run out of town for it?"

"There's lots more places we can go."

"Good mornin', ladies," the manager said and waved from across the room. "Y'all have a seat anywhere you like."

"Good mornin' to you, Mr. Calvin," Lily said and chose a corner table.

She had barely gotten settled into her chair when Beulah came through the door, waved, and marched across the room. "I was hoping I might run into you." She pulled a hankie from the long sleeve of her dress and dabbed the sweat from her forehead. "It's going to be a hot one, for sure—but then, this is July in Texas. We'll be lucky to get a little breeze through the church windows. I wanted to catch you before you decided which church to attend, and to invite you to go with me. It's not the one where Preacher Jones rants about hellfire and brimstone. Afterwards, will you come home with me for lunch?"

"Thank you for the invitation, and we'd love to accept—but first let us buy you some breakfast," Lily answered, glad that she and Daisy didn't have to choose where they were going that morning.

"That's great. I will appreciate the company," Beulah said with a nod. "But I've already had my breakfast. I might have a cup of coffee with y'all, though."

"Don't you know that decent women drink tea, not coffee?" Lily asked.

"And they don't take a little kick in their tea, either," Beulah winked. "But then, who said we are decent, right?"

Daisy cut her eyes over at Beulah. "We also like coffee so much better than tea."

"Then let's give the gossipers around here something to talk about," Beulah said. "And just so you know, Frank is the biggest one in the whole county."

"Glad to know," Lily said. "But we kind of figured that out the first day."

Daisy scanned the room to be sure Frank wasn't in hearing distance. "And sometimes a cigar is nice with that cup of coffee, especially if you put a shot of whiskey or rum in it."

"I have a few puffs every evening after I close up," Beulah chuckled. "I knew when y'all walked into my store that we were going to be friends."

Frank straightened his bow tie and came over to their table. "Three regular breakfasts?"

Lily shook her head. "Nothing that heavy for me today. I would like a stack of pancakes and a cup of coffee."

"Same here," Daisy said.

"And just coffee for me," Beulah added. "I had my breakfast at home."

"But . . . ," Frank sputtered. "Are you sure you don't want a nice cup of tea?"

"No, we want coffee," Beulah declared. "It will help us stay awake during the hour-long sermon."

"Okay, but . . ." He hurried off to the kitchen with a disgusted look on his face.

"You likely just joined my ranks as a troublemaker," Beulah said. "Folks are already calling y'all 'the Ladies in White,' but not even wearing those pretty outfits is going to make you angels if you defy tradition and have meals and drink coffee right out in public. Without men. To add fuel to the fire, Preacher Jones is going to be so mad when you don't come to his church that he'll spread ugly stuff all over town about you."

"So, the religion in Autrie is split?" Daisy asked.

"Yes, it is. And never the twain shall meet. Joshua preaches hellfire and damnation. Most of the time, Preacher Tobias talks about loving your neighbor, but I doubt that many folks can find very much love for Preacher Jones. That's what he likes to be called, but I call him by his first name. That makes him so mad that he seldom comes into my store." Beulah threw back her head and guffawed.

According to Miz Raven, ladies did not laugh in public. Even with her training, Lily couldn't hold back a small giggle. "Do you make him angry on purpose?"

Beulah leaned forward so far that her ample bosom touched the table. "You bet I do. If he steers clear of the store, then I can manage to pass letters back and forth to Alma. Speaking of letters, y'all need to go let Stanley—that's the postmaster—know you are here. That way he can hold mail for you."

"Thank you." Lily thought back to the time when she ran away from home, and wondered if, even one time, her parents had tried to find her. She answered the question in her mind with a subtle shake of her head. They would have been so disappointed that she hadn't married Phillip, they would have washed their hands of her. And the ground would part, fire would boil up out of the hole, and the devil would come and drag her down to hell if any of her relatives ever found out she had worked at a brothel.

If I ever have a daughter, she will make up her own mind about who she marries—or even if she decides to never take that step, she thought. *And my sons will be taught to respect women and let them be independent.*

❖ ❖ ❖

About halfway through the sermon, Daisy was reminded of how hard church pews were. Men with their sons who were over twelve sat on the right side of the sanctuary. Of course they would. That would be a subtle sign that the women were less than them. They all sat up straight and tried to look bigger and taller than they were, maybe to look more important to the women who were trying to make younger children behave on the other side of the center aisle. All the guys had to do was pretend to listen, while the ladies' jobs were to keep babies and toddlers quiet, too. Poor little darlings were dressed in their Sunday best. They had to be miserable when the sun was straight up and heating what little air flowed through the building. They were probably wishing they could just be left alone in their crib, wearing nothing but a diaper.

Lily nudged her and then bowed her head—very dramatically. Daisy looked around to see what was going on and saw a man toward the front of the men's section stand up to pray. Evidently, the service would soon be over after a short benediction had been delivered. Not so! The man gave thanks, from the time God created dirt all the way to appreciating the sunshine that day. Daisy figured the previous summers had fried his brain, if he could give thanks for the broiling-hot July sun. Her neck began to sweat and itch, but ladies did not scratch in public—especially not in church.

"Amen," he finally said.

Daisy raised her head and faced the window to get all the good she could out of the gentle breeze that flowed through the sanctuary. She was glad that most of the men had had their weekly bath the night before, or else the wind would have brought the smell across to her. She had definitely had her fill of that scent in the past. After she had given her client for the night a bath, cut his hair, shaved him, and fed him a nice supper, he was a lot more presentable and in a much better mood.

"Whatever were you thinking about?" Lily whispered as she stood up.

"Anything at all to keep from wiggling around worse than a five-year-old kid," Daisy groaned.

"We have gotten our dose of Jesus for the week," Beulah announced. "Let's go home, shuck out of these hot clothes, and have some lunch."

"What was that?" Surely Daisy had misunderstood her new friend. She and Lily had brought nothing else with them to change into, and ladies—especially those who were guests—did not go to the dinner table wearing anything less than proper attire.

"We're not going to run around naked," Beulah chuckled. "I'll explain about the clothes when we get home."

Matt Maguire held up traffic when he stopped in the narrow center aisle to allow the ladies to go ahead of him. "Gonna be a hot one, isn't it, Miz Beulah?"

Beulah wiped beads of sweat from her forehead with a hankie. "Always is, in July. Has the heat dried up all your pastures yet? And what are you doing back in town so quickly?"

"I've still got some green grass in areas, thanks to the river," Matt said. "A little rain through the summer *would* help out. And it is my turn this week to spend the day with Uncle Elijah. Claude will probably be here next week."

"I'd forgotten whose turn it was," Beulah told him. "A bit of rain—even in the form of a storm—would help everyone. Tempers get testy when it's this hot. We have more shoot-outs during times like this than when the temperature is down around the freezing line."

"Yes, ma'am," Matt agreed with a nod. "Ladies." He tipped his hat toward Lily and Daisy.

"Mr. Maguire," Lily said over her shoulder, but Daisy noticed she stole glances at him when he crawled up onto the buckboard beside an older man.

Daisy nudged her with an elbow. "I saw that, and I don't blame you. He's one fine-lookin' fellow."

"'Lookin' is all there will ever be," Lily declared as soon as he was out of earshot.

"Why's that?" Beulah asked.

"I'm not interested in finding a husband," Lily informed her.

"Smart woman." Beulah led the way for the three of them to meander through the wagons that filled the whole lot in front of and beside the church.

"Miz Beulah," a familiar voice said.

"Judge Martin," she said. "Think we might get some rain in the next few days?"

"One can always hope and pray," he said.

"I would like you to meet my friends, Lily and Daisy," Beulah made introductions. "They are hoping to put in a seamstress and hat-making shop. Do you know of any businesses or buildings that might work for that?"

"I'll keep my eyes open," he answered. "I would offer you a ride home, but since my fiancée, Sally Anne"—he locked eyes with Daisy—"couldn't attend services this morning, I rode my horse rather than hitching up the buggy."

"Thank you," Beulah said with a smile. "It's not that far, and after sitting so long, it's good to have a little walk."

"So, he's engaged?" Daisy wondered if he'd told his bride-to-be that she was the love of his life.

"Yep," Beulah answered. "Sally Anne is one of the richest ladies in the county. He'll do well to marry her."

A vision of his strong muscles and tight abdomen filled Daisy's mind. Her job at the Paradise was to make him feel good, but by the end of the night, he had left her with feelings she had never had before—and probably never would again.

Just before the three women went inside the general store, Lily dabbed at the sweat traveling in what seemed like rivers from her face to her neck and on down her corset. Her shirtwaist and undergarments would definitely have to be washed that night and hung up to dry. She blamed all the heat on the weather, but if she was honest, that was only about half of the reason she was perspiring—the other part could be attributed to her thoughts about Matt Maguire.

"Makin' you sweat, is he?" Beulah giggled and motioned for Lily and Daisy to follow her through the store and into the living quarters.

"I'm not sure if it's him or the heat," Lily confessed, "or maybe a combination of both. Tell me about him."

"He lives on a sheep ranch. Some folks call it a sheep *farm*, but I always say that if there's animals—be it cows, sheep, or goats—it's a ranch. It's north of town, and Elijah Maguire, the fellow who owns the wagon yard, is his uncle."

"I see," Lily said.

"Elijah turned the family ranch over to Matt and his cousin Claude a while back. The two of them are doing a fine job of keeping it going. They try to spend time with Elijah on Sundays, so they come to church with him, and then they have dinner together at the café down from the hotel. Other than that, I only see him when he comes in for supplies," Beulah told her.

"Is he married?" Lily asked.

Beulah motioned for them to follow her down a short hallway and talked as she walked ahead of them. "No, he is not. Good lookin' as he is, you'd think that some woman would snatch him up, but all the ladies at the ranch are kin to him, and he's not around town long enough for anyone to lay a trap for him." She slung open a creaky door and stood to the side. "This is my spare bedroom, and today it belongs to y'all. I've laid out a night dress for each of you. Sunday afternoons is my time to shed all these clothes and relax. I thought you might like to do the same, but if you don't want to do that, then there's no pressure. I'll meet you in the kitchen for lunch in a few minutes. Afterwards, we will take a nice nap to get away from this heat for a spell and then visit the rest of the afternoon." She closed the door and left them alone.

"What does this remind you of?" Lily asked as she unfastened a whole row of buttons down the front of her snow-white shirtwaist.

"The morning after, when we would lounge around in our robes after our clients left and get ready for the next night," Daisy answered.

"Then we would all put on our white dresses and sit on the porch until Jems let the next seven men in the gates. I was terrified that first night I had a customer," she admitted.

"Did you cry?" Daisy asked.

Lily shivered at the memory. "A little after the feller left the next morning, but it wasn't as bad as when my fiancé forced me to submit to him."

"How did you ever agree to work in a brothel after that experience?" Daisy asked.

"Miz Raven." Lily folded her skirt and shirtwaist and laid them on the bed. "If you'll remember, neither of us really had a customer for two weeks after we moved into the Paradise. Holly and Rose and the rest of the girls did a lot by talking to me about things. All young women should talk to a shady lady before they get married. Women should not even let a man court her with no more knowledge than I did. If I ever have a daughter"—she slipped the longer of the two thin cotton nightdresses over her head—"I'm going to be sure she understands everything before she goes to bed with a man."

Daisy nodded in agreement as she buttoned the front of a similar thin, flowing dress. "And that she never has to submit to any man, and she can control the bedroom scene as well as he can."

"Amen to that," Lily said.

Beulah eased the door open. "Lunch is on the table when y'all are ready."

"Coming right out," Lily called and sniffed the air.

"I don't know why you're sniffing—I don't smell anything cooking, and I'm a little nervous about this setup," Daisy said in a low tone. "And just so you know, I did not put on my shoes or stockings after I got dressed in this wonderful, cool nightgown."

Lily padded barefoot across the room and opened the door the rest of the way. "Me, either, and something does seem odd about this kind of Sunday dinner. Maybe I was wrong about Beulah being a good woman for us to be friends with."

Not one scent floated out from the kitchen—no roast beef, chicken, or even coffee—which made Lily wonder what exactly they were having. The pancakes she'd had for breakfast had long since failed her, and she was starving.

Beulah nodded toward the chairs around a lovely table set for three with what had to be her best dishes. "Hot, heavy food in this weather didn't sound good, so I made a cold gazpacho soup, egg salad sandwiches, and a vegetable tray. I sliced up a loaf of bread and have fresh butter and strawberry jam. Then we have a key lime pie for dessert. And ice in our sweet tea. How does that sound? I hope you aren't disappointed."

"This looks absolutely beautiful," Lily said as she sat down in one of the chairs. "And I was actually dreading having to sit up straight in my hot outfit and eat a big lunch."

"Me too," Beulah said.

"How did you do all this in the time it took us to get dressed?" Daisy felt a little better about the situation.

"I got a lot of the stuff ready last night and shoved it in the icebox; then I went ahead and dipped the soup before I called y'all," Beulah said. "My mama was a great cook, but she was always picking up more recipes and ideas from other folks that drifted in and out of Autrie. A family from Spain settled here for a few months and taught her to make this cold soup. I believe we've been thoroughly blessed enough at church this morning, so let's just eat."

Lily dipped into the soup, took a bite, and said, "This is like what Miz Raven made on hot days, only a little spicier."

"And who is that?" Beulah asked.

"A lady that we lived with," Daisy said in a hurry. "She was a very good friend."

"Why didn't she come here with you?" Beulah asked.

"She was from England, and she decided to go back," Lily explained. "She was an advocate for women's rights, and they're really making some progress over there."

"I'm glad you mentioned that," Beulah said. "I'd like to start a women's auxiliary group here, associated with both churches. We can make embroidered pieces like tea towels and pillowcases to sell at next year's Independence Day celebration, and work on them while we talk at the meetings, with money to go to the schools and churches and, ideally, mostly used for our bigger causes."

Lily laid her spoon down and picked up her sandwich. "Do you think you could raise enough money for all those things?"

"Of course, but our time together would be a place for oppressed women like Alma. A little time each week to get away from their husbands, good or bad, and visit with other women. And believe me, there is a lot of women who fit in that category. Who knows," Beulah said with a wink, "perhaps we'll get to talking about what we can do about that oppression."

"Sign us up," Lily said without hesitation.

"You aren't afraid that it will cause problems with your store?" Daisy asked.

Beulah laughed. "I run the store to help people and because I like to visit with folks. I wouldn't get to do much of that if I just holed up back here. Besides, I have a monopoly on supplies in this town and enough money not to work for the rest of my life, so I'm not worried. But I do want to help women to understand that if they want any rights—however small they might be—they are going to have to unite and fight for them."

"It'll most likely only be baby steps at first," Lily said.

"That's better than standing still," Beulah declared. "I'll put the word out. All I'll have to do is tell a couple of women and it'll spread. We can have our first meeting right here in my store a week from tomorrow. That'll give folks a week to tell others. Maybe by then you'll find a building and be almost ready to set up your seamstress shop, and we can announce that."

Lily chewed slowly and then washed her food down with a sip of iced tea. "Why did you wait so long to do this?" she asked. "You have evidently wanted to start something to help women for a long time."

Beulah looked up to the rough wooden ceiling rafters. "I was waiting for the Lord to give me a sign. That came when y'all walked into my store—two independent women who traveled alone and didn't seem to be interested in getting married real soon. And then when you mentioned your friend was helping with women's rights, that was like an angel sat down on my shoulder and whispered that the time was right. I came up with the women's auxiliary thing as I watched all the women in church this morning. When a boy is twelve years old, he knows to behave during services, but it would be real nice if families could sit together and the menfolk could help with the smaller children."

Lily had thought the same thing that morning. Maybe it wasn't an angel on Beulah's shoulder, but simply the spirit of liberated women joining forces.

Daisy spread butter on a thick slice of homemade bread. "Families sitting together would be a good starting point."

"I agree that sitting together on Sundays might be the first of the baby steps," Lily said. "But be aware, even that little bit won't come without a war."

Chapter Four

Of all the days for the skies to open up and let loose with hard rain, it had to be the morning that Lily and Daisy were supposed to meet with the judge at the courthouse. Lily stared out the bedroom window at the muddy mess of a street they would have to cross. She dreaded getting the hem of her best skirt dirty or stepping in a mud puddle in her good shoes.

"Too bad we don't have a chivalrous gentleman to throw his coat down on the street so that we can get to the courthouse without tracking mud into the judge's quarters," Lily said.

"That don't happen in real life." Daisy's tone had an edge to it.

"Are you all right?"

"Why would you ask that?" Daisy fired back.

"Tell me what has got you so riled up. Did I do something to upset you?" Lily asked.

Daisy threw her hairbrush across the room, and it bounced off the far wall. "It's not you. I get a ball of anger in my belly when I even think about Judge Wesley Martin. He could visit me at the brothel and whisper sweet things to me, but I'm still just a prostitute, even though I've left that life behind me. I can see it in his eyes every time I've been around him."

"The first step in getting over the past is not letting it control us," Lily told her as she picked up the brush and handed it back to Daisy.

"And we both need to remember to say that we are from Spanish Fort and not mention that we lived at the Paradise."

"You are right about the control, but it's easier said than done," Daisy snapped. "I want to do something to wipe that better-than-you sneer off his face."

"There's more than one way to kill a snake," Lily said.

Daisy sat down in the rocking chair and closed her eyes. "Shoot it or chop its head off with a garden hoe. I could easily do both to him without blinking an eye."

"Why are you closing your eyes?" Lily asked.

"I'm imagining how good it would feel to put a bullet right between his pretty eyes," she answered. "I still carry my little pistol with me."

Lily pulled the ladder-back chair from the corner and sat down in front of Daisy. "So do I, but there's not a man alive on the face of this earth worth hanging for, and that's what will happen if you kill him. You've already stretched your luck pretty thin with the blackmailing. Remember what Miz Raven taught us?"

"Never get attached to a customer," Daisy answered, but she did not open her eyes.

"That's right."

"I used to pretend that other men were Wesley."

"I can't speak for the others, but I used to do the same. Not Wesley, but another repeat customer who was always very nice to me. It was a way we got through the guilt. If we imagined that the customers were our husbands, then we didn't feel like our kinfolks were sending us to hell for what we did."

"I never did pretend that a customer was John Andrew, but I do still feel guilty," Daisy admitted.

"Me, too, but we're going to put all that behind us," Lily assured her with a sideways hug.

"Baby steps, right?"

"Yes, one at a time until the past is nothing but a blur in a dense fog behind us," Lily said.

Daisy began to brush her hair. "Thank you."

"You are welcome. When I get mad and throw something, you can talk *me* out of committing murder."

"It's a deal," Daisy said. "Let's get this business over with, and then I don't ever intend to deal with the almighty judge again."

"His loss," Lily said as they finished dressing. "If he was truly honest about taking you home with him, he must have loved you at one time."

Daisy stood up and donned her hat. "Or he was just spouting off words that didn't come from his heart."

"What if he wasn't able to buy the property?" Lily asked. "Or if he calls your bluff and slaps cuffs on your tiny little wrists?"

"Then it will be time for you to get a big dose of bravery, pull your pistol out of your purse, and shoot our way out of the courthouse," Daisy told her.

Lily opened the door and stepped out in the hallway. "I'm willing to run from the law if it comes to that, but the first bullet might have to go toward Preacher Jones."

"From 'soiled doves' to respectable women to outlaws. That would be quite a story," Daisy giggled. "I just hope that he doesn't get so mad that he takes his wrath out on Alma and the girls."

"If they do, she and her daughters could move in with us, and Alma can help us in the shop," Daisy suggested. "That could be her salvation. And any man who acts like Joshua Jones is not a good preacher. He's a wolf hiding in sheep's clothing."

"It could be the death of Alma if he gets really angry," Lily fretted. "But we can't worry about what might happen because . . ."

"What will be will be—and what won't be, might be anyway," Daisy said.

"More words of wisdom from Miz Raven." Lily smiled. "I needed that today. Just think, if we get this building, we won't have to live in this hotel much longer. I'm so ready to cook our own meals and get our business started."

"Then it seems like we better brave the weather and go see Judge Martin." Daisy growled his name.

"We'll do that right after breakfast," Lily said. "I've appreciated having our meals here, but I'm tired of the heavy food three times a day. Ready for pancakes?"

Daisy held her head high and led the way down to the dining room. "Definitely, and I'm also ready for our own place like the Paradise, where we don't have to get dressed in the mornings."

"Where is Paradise?" Frank asked.

His voice startled Lily so badly that she whipped around. Finding him at the top of the staircase, she lost her balance and had to hang on to the rail to keep from falling down the last two steps. "Where did you come from?"

"I had to run a pitcher of hot water up to a guest," he answered. "I didn't mean to eavesdrop."

"We were thinking about our home in Paradise, when we arrive there," Daisy said and bowed her head for a moment as if in prayer.

"Well, then, what are you ladies having this morning?"

"Pancakes and coffee," Daisy answered.

"People are already talking about y'all," Frank whispered. "Are you sure you want coffee? And maybe you shouldn't sit by the window."

Lily nodded. "Yes, we are sure, and we like to watch the people, so the window is a fine place for us."

He set the empty pitcher on a nearby table and frowned. "Suit yourselves, but you aren't making friends in town by acting the way you are."

"What does that mean, Mr. Calvin?" Daisy asked.

Frank set his mouth in a firm line and drew his brows down. "You shouldn't be keeping company with Beulah. And it's never a good idea to make one of the preachers angry, especially Preacher Jones. Both he and Beulah can sully a woman's reputation."

"Is that all?" Lily asked.

He squared his shoulders and glared at them. "You should not be ordering coffee. Women drink tea. In some places, women even have private rooms to eat in public. We didn't think to have one here, as the ladies *we* host travel with their husbands."

"Well, we're not traveling with any, so we'll have to make do," Lily informed him.

"And we don't really care what Preacher Jones thinks of us," Daisy added.

"And one last thing—Beulah is our friend, so don't besmirch her to us," Lily said. "But answer me this: Did us attending church with Beulah and then visiting with her for lunch generate all this gossip you are talking about?"

"That didn't help," Frank answered in an icy tone. "She's a troublemaker. Poor old Orville was a good man and just wanted to manage her money for her. Womenfolk aren't made to take care of such things."

Daisy's brows shot up toward the ceiling. "Oh, really? So men are the only human beings blessed with brains in their heads? Women just have empty space between their ears?"

Frank tilted his chin up and looked down his nose at Daisy. "I'll get your breakfast, but if your business doesn't do well, don't come crying back to the hotel."

"I believe we can manage not coming back here just fine, Mr. Calvin," Lily told him. She didn't have a big *S* embroidered on the back of her jacket for *Shady Lady*—not yet, anyway—but she didn't intend to do business at the Crockett Hotel again after they'd both left the place.

"Can you believe this?" Daisy whispered. "Just because we have a meal with Beulah and drink coffee—"

Lily shot a dirty look toward Frank's back. "And don't have a man to submit to . . ."

"—we aren't a bit better accepted here than we were in Spanish Fort. It doesn't matter what a woman does, saint or sinner. She has practically no rights," Daisy finished.

"Seems that way," Lily said with a nod. "But that doesn't mean we have to run away. We can fight and teach any other women who are sick of the way things are done these days to join us."

Daisy unfolded her napkin and laid it on her lap. "We might still get run out of town. But like you said before, we can always join the others in Jacksonville or Nechesville if we do."

Frank set a plate and a full cup of coffee in front of each of them. "Enjoy your breakfast. I believe this is your third day here. You will want to start looking for another place soon."

"We plan on seeing what we can do about that right after breakfast," Lily answered with a sarcastic smile.

"That would be good," Frank said, then stopped at several tables full of people to whisper, no doubt about the new women in town who didn't know how to hold their tongues.

He had barely cleared the room when the judge came into the hotel and sat down at a table next to Lily and Daisy.

"Ladies," he said and tipped his hat toward them.

"Good morning," Daisy said in an icy tone.

"I understand that you are looking for a place to set up a seamstress shop," he said.

"Yes, sir, we are," Lily answered.

The judge didn't crack a smile or show any emotion. "I have recently come into possession of the old hardware store. I do not want to sell it, but I would be willing to lease it to you on a month-to-month basis. Are you interested, or do I offer it to someone else?"

"We are interested." Lily wasn't happy with the deal, but she and Daisy were backed into a corner. "But only if after six months, we can apply the rent money toward the price of buying the property."

"I think we can work with that," the judge said.

"Will we need to sign a contract?" Lily asked.

Miz Raven's voice popped into Lily's head. *Don't be disappointed. This gives you the ability to leave the area if you decide you can't make a good living in this town.*

"Not since this is just a monthly lease. If I decide to sell the property, we will draw up a formal contract and deed," the judge said. "I have the keys here if you are agreeable to a thirty-day lease, after which time I will have the right to renew or not."

Daisy reached up and took the keys once he handed them over.

Lily stood up with her hand out for a shake. "How much do you want for a month's rent?" She was concerned he might not renew after a month but hoped that her fears were just anxiety.

The judge shook her hand and then dropped it. "The fair market price is ten dollars a month. I will need the first month's rent now."

"Why can't you sell it to us?" Daisy asked.

"I still want to hold some cards in this blackmail business," he hissed at Daisy, then raised his voice back to a normal volume. "Like I said, I might want to sell the place at a later point."

Lily opened her purse and handed him some crispy bills. "Then we can begin to move in today?"

"And we won't need to come to the courthouse?" Daisy asked.

"Yes, you can and"—he lowered his voice again and shifted his gaze over to Daisy—"no, you won't, not until next month when your rent is due. If I'm not in the office, you can leave it with my secretary, Benjamin."

Frank didn't waste a moment hurrying over to the judge's table. "What can I get for you this morning, sir?"

"Pancakes and a cup of coffee," he answered.

"Do you know these ladies?" Frank asked.

"No, but I just rented the old hardware store to them. I bought it this weekend from Preacher Jones. Just between me and you, I don't expect them to last more than a month." The judge slid a sly glance over at the women and chuckled.

Lily's Irish temper didn't flare up too often, but at that moment, she wanted to slap the judge, even if it landed her in jail.

Frank turned around, shot them a dirty look, and then rushed back over to talk in low tones to the people at a table on the other side of the room.

"Looks like the cards are stacked up against us," Daisy said. "How is it possible to adore a man for months and then hate him so much after only a few days?"

"Hate and love are two strong emotions. I'm not feeling much of the latter right now, but I've got a whole wagonload of the former in my heart," Lily said.

"From the look on your face, I'd say that you are the stick of lit dynamite today," Daisy teased.

"Probably a whole box full of explosives," Lily told her. "But to answer your question, when you can be indifferent to him is when you are truly over the image you had of him being a wonderful man."

"Then I'll work on that and realign those cards that I said were stacked against us," she declared.

"If we can buy enough furniture and get it delivered, we can be out of here by tomorrow morning," Lily said. "So let's go see Mr. Maguire about buying what we need so we can get out of this place. That might put me in a better frame of mind."

Frank came back to their table. "If you leave the hotel before Friday, I will apply what you have already paid toward your food bill and the extra it will take to have your trunks delivered to the old hardware store," he said.

Lily clasped her hands in her lap to keep from standing up, looking down on the man, and knocking him flat on his skinny ass. "Thank you, Mr. Calvin."

"But . . ." Daisy flashed a fake smile. "It's not a hardware store anymore. It is now a seamstress shop."

"Not for long," Frank replied with a smug look on his face.

Lily picked up her mug and took a sip of the coffee. "Someday women all over Texas will figure out how much better this is than a cup of weak tea."

"That day will never come," Frank snapped before he headed across the room to wait on two more men who had sat down at the judge's table.

Lily held the cup tightly in her hand to keep from hurling it across the room. Maybe if she did, the coffee would stain Frank's mustache and make it more visible.

Daisy broke the rage in Lily's heart when she threw up her hand and waved. Lily jerked her head around and saw Beulah peeking in the window with a big smile on her face. She motioned for the woman to come on in, but she shook her head and pointed down the street. "Got to get back to the store."

Lily nodded and forced a smile.

"How much willpower did it take for you to grin like that?" Daisy asked.

"More than a week's worth," Lily answered. "I hope the women's auxiliary takes off like a cannon shot and we show men like Frank, Preacher Jones, and even the judge that women can do whatever they damn well please."

Daisy giggled. "Including swearing in public."

"Even that," Lily hissed. "We might not live long enough to vote, but we'll do our best to take steps toward letting other women go to the polls."

"Amen, sister," Daisy agreed and then chuckled. "I mean, *cousin*."

When Daisy and Lily opened the squeaky wooden door into the wagon yard, an elderly man swept his hat off with a flourish.

"Good mornin', ladies. I'm Elijah Maguire. What can I do for you today?" A rim of snow-white hair circled around an otherwise bald head, and his brown eyes sparkled. "Do you need to rent a wagon or a couple of horses? I have sidesaddles."

"Thank you. We have rented the old hardware store and plan to start a seamstress shop," Lily answered.

Daisy inhaled the musty scent of horses and dirt blended together with the smell of coffee and bacon, and was reminded of the stables behind the brothel. After she'd learned to enjoy the freedom of riding without a sidesaddle, she had often saddled up her favorite horse and ridden the path around the acreage that went with the Paradise.

"I heard something about that," Elijah said. "What I've got for sale is in the barn out back. Go on out there and make a list of what you want. I can't make a delivery today, but I can rustle up enough men to deliver it tomorrow."

Daisy pulled a small piece of paper and a stubby pencil out from her beaded purse. "How do we know how much each item will cost?"

Elijah settled his hat back onto his head and motioned for them to follow him. "There's a tag hanging on each one. I don't gouge the folks I do business with, so I keep my prices fair." He slid back the barn door to reveal a space filled with everything from the coveted sewing machine to crates full of bedding, pots and pans, and even fabric. "Y'all write down the name of whatever it is that takes your fancy and the number on the tag. That way I'll know what to deliver tomorrow."

Daisy headed straight for the sewing machine and wrote down the number and price on her paper. "This, for sure."

"I'll leave you ladies to it," Elijah said and disappeared through the open door.

In thirty minutes, Daisy's paper was full on both sides. She added up the total cost and whistled through her teeth. "We better start making money the first few weeks."

Lily looked at the final number and nodded. "That's more than half of our funds, and we need to save back enough to live on for at least two months. We will have to cross out some of the items."

"We have to buy the sewing machine and the crates of fabric, but we could do without the icebox. We'll need the stove, but we could use our chests to keep our clothing in and do without the two dressers." She ran a pencil line through three items.

"We need the crate with the bedding in it—and that comes with the doilies, which will dress up the shop," Lily said.

Daisy ran her finger down the list and said, "How badly do we need the kitchen table?"

Lily frowned and cocked her head to one side. "We could put it in the shop to use as a cutting table by day and a place to eat by evening after we close up."

"The sofa could also go in the shop for the ladies to sit down and have tea—or coffee—while they pick out the fabric they want us to use for their dresses or undergarments," Daisy suggested.

"That sounds good," Lily agreed. "All I need in my room is a chair and a bed. Later, when we are shipping our creations to the big cities, we can buy fancy furniture."

"Or build a huge house like the Paradise," Daisy dreamed out loud. "And show Mr. Perfect Judge Wesley that we've come up in the world."

Lily giggled. "Even if we did, we'd be too busy to ever spend much time there. And if we're truly independent, we won't give a damn what he thinks."

"I'm afraid that I'll have to work on that because I still want to make him pay for treating me—*us*—like trash." Daisy tucked a long, blond strand of hair back up into the bun at the nape of her neck and refigured the amount on her notebook. "We can afford the rest because we won't have to order fabric to work with."

"Why don't we use the shelving on the west side of the store to show off our stock," Lily said.

"When we do need more, maybe Beulah can help us with that. I saw a few bolts of calico in her store."

"We can ask her, for sure." Lily found another crate stacked full of fancy fabric—brocade and silk. "We need to look around a little more.

If there's more like this, we definitely won't have to order anything for a long while."

"I'm amazed anyone would give away these gorgeous bolts of material." Daisy sneezed as she prowled through several more areas.

"Gorgeous, but dusty." Lily brought a hankie from her purse and handed it to Daisy. "All this dust, plus what's waiting for us in the store, is going to have us sneezing all day tomorrow."

Daisy wiped her nose and handed the hankie back to Lily. She'd left hers by the washstand in their room.

"Keep it. I have an extra if I need it. We'll also be washing out bedsheets and hanging them up to dry, so we can make up the beds. Can you believe that we've been lucky enough not only to find a place but also all this good stuff?"

Daisy tucked the handkerchief into the sleeve of her jacket. "Got to admit that it does put me in a little better mood."

"Once we get the store cleaned, we could run a clothesline from one end of the kitchen area to the other and hang the sheets in there," Lily suggested.

"Great idea!" Daisy was now glad that they were only renting the building. Buying the place would have severely limited their resources. They might have had to sleep on the floor and eat mush three times a day until their business took off.

"Are we ready?" Lily asked, then pointed to another crate of fabric. "We've got to have that one, too. I see batiste for undergarments and some spools of ribbon."

"Okay." Daisy wrote down the numbers and descriptions. "But unless we want to starve, this is it."

Elijah poked his head inside the sliding door and asked, "Y'all about done? It's gettin' close to my lunchtime."

Daisy turned around and headed across the floor. "We have our list, but we would be very interested in any more bolts of fabric that you might come by."

"I'll keep that in mind," Elijah said. "Let's go settle this up. From what all is written here, I reckon that it'll take more than one wagonload to get it all delivered. I can understand the preacher wanting to clear out the store, but sometimes it breaks my heart when folks have to unload precious stuff off their wagons before they head west. I happened upon the pianos in both of the town's churches that way. At the beginning of a trip, people don't realize that they'll be lucky to get to the West Coast with the clothes on their backs and maybe an intact wagon. When they have to unload their prized possessions . . ." Elijah's chin quivered. "It's downright sad."

Daisy just nodded, but the memory flashed through her mind about how close she had come to loading her meager things into a covered wagon and going west with her distant cousin. Before she could make up her mind, Miz Raven had come along. Later, Daisy got word that all the folks in that caravan had been wiped out long before they even reached their destination—first by cholera, and then the rest were killed in a raid carried out by bandits.

"What are you thinking about?" Lily asked as they followed Elijah to the tiny room he called his office.

"Choices and the difference they can make in our lives," she answered.

"That's the gospel truth," Lily said.

Elijah sat down in a chair on the other side of a desk that took up most of the room. "If you'd have come in here tomorrow, we couldn't have gotten your stuff delivered before Friday. Day after tomorrow is July Fourth, and that's a big deal here in Autrie. Folks come from all parts of the area."

"What happens?" Daisy asked.

"People set up stands to sell baked goods and all kinds of food, and the ladies sell eggs, embroidered pieces, and other things. The little boys run around poppin' firecrackers or playing cops and robbers with toy guns. It's quite a day, and there's usually at least one duel before the day is out. The town doctor stays busy from daylight to dark," he explained between figuring the price of all the items. "And that comes to . . . Wait a minute . . . if you spend this amount, you get a ten percent discount, so the total is . . ." He rattled off the sum.

Lily opened her purse and counted out the money. "Thank you for the discount, and we were serious about any more bolts of fabric."

Elijah shoved the money in a drawer and nodded. "Pleasure doing business with you. If things don't work out for you, then come see me and I'll buy all this back from you."

"It's going to work," Lily assured him.

We are not going to fail, Daisy thought as she and Lily headed back outside. She pulled a fan from her purse and tried to create a little air. It didn't help, so she folded it and put it back. "We sure aren't getting much encouragement from the menfolk in town."

"No, we are not, but we can prove them wrong," Lily declared.

Chapter Five

"My entire body aches," Lily groaned when she awoke. "Who would have ever thought an empty store could get so dirty?"

Daisy threw back the thin sheet and sat up in the hotel bed. "Or that cleaning it up would use every muscle in our bodies. Twenty buckets of water carried from the pump behind Beulah's place is a testimony to how hard we worked, and we still have to do the windows today. But with any luck, we will be moved in by tonight, and we won't have to endure that awful hotel manager's self-righteous remarks anymore."

Lily sat up with another groan. "I wonder if he sneaks off and spends some time at the saloons with the women who work there."

"I doubt it. He thinks that he's too important to be seen with one of the saloon girls, but I'll bet that he dreams about them." Daisy stood up and crossed the room. She picked up her brush from off the vanity and ran it through her hair.

Lily got out of bed and went to the washstand. The water was cold, but as hot as the day already was, she didn't mind it being less than warm. "I agree—but then again, if he visited those women, he wouldn't be so sour and judgmental. He might even crack a smile or stop twirling that thin mustache he's got."

Daisy twisted her hair up into the usual thick bun at the base of her neck and handed off Lily's brush to her. "Absolutely."

Lily usually braided her red hair before she went to bed, but she'd been too tired the night before. Now she had to suffer through brushing the tangles out before she could style it. "Do you think women will ever be able to wear short hair and perhaps discard all the underwear that we have to wear?"

"I hope so," Daisy said. "I would gladly cut mine off up to my shoulders and wear it down every day."

Lily thought of Alma and what she had to endure at the hands of her husband, and shivered at the thought of what Preacher Jones would do if his wife went to church without a hat and wearing her hair flowing freely.

Daisy slipped a petticoat over her pantaloons and tied it at her slim waist. "You can't be cold in this heat."

Lily told her what notion had crossed her mind, and Daisy nodded. "That would send a chill dancing down any woman's spine. Poor Alma. Seems like she's doomed to be miserable."

"Unless she takes a stand," Lily said. "Breakfast here, or should we go by Beulah's and buy a pie to split between us?"

"I've had about all of that insufferable Frank Calvin that I can stand," Daisy answered. "Let's get our things packed and tell him to deliver our trunks to the store this morning."

"Yes!" Lily exclaimed. "And we never have to come back here again."

"We won't have a choice about returning to this place. We won't be welcome back here, remember?" Daisy said.

"I'd guess that holds true for Preacher Jones's church, too, but I'm fine with either or both of those." She finished dressing and then arranged all her things in her rolltop steamer trunk. When she had closed the lid, she opened the door out into the hallway. "Goodbye to this hotel."

"One leg of the journey is over, and another one begins today." Daisy stepped out and started down the stairs. The dining room was full, and Frank was hustling about between tables. He looked up, and any semblance of a greeting like they'd had the first couple of days had completely disappeared.

"Pancakes and coffee?" he almost growled.

"Not this morning," Lily said. "We need to settle up our bill—we wouldn't want it said that we didn't pay what we owe."

"You are leaving early, so we'll just call it even," he said, and then lowered his voice. "But I was serious about you not coming back in the hotel. This is a respectable place, and you've already caused trouble."

"Does that cover taking our trunks to our new store, or do we owe for that?" Lily asked.

"We are even," Frank grumbled. "Your trunks will be delivered between breakfast and lunch today."

"Well, then, I suppose you have our word that we will stay away," Lily said and marched outside.

Beulah was in front of her store sweeping the wooden sidewalk, and she waved when they were still several feet away. "I heard y'all were moving into your own place today. Need some help?"

"I think we've got it covered, but we could use a pie for breakfast," Lily answered.

"Come on in," Beulah said. "I've got a pot of coffee that's still hot. I'll share a cup while y'all eat. I don't know why I feel the need to come out here and sweep my part of the sidewalk every morning. By noon, the dust and dirt from the street has it covered again."

"It looks nice for a little while," Lily said.

Beulah stepped back to let them go in first. "That's what my dad always said. I also heard that Frank was being a real horse's ass about y'all drinking coffee instead of tea. That pompous little fool is going to reap what he's sown one of these days. He tried to court Alma when we were young, but her folks didn't like him. Of course, they didn't have the sense God gave a gnat or they wouldn't have forced her to marry Joshua Jones, either. But that's enough of my ranting. We should be celebrating your move."

"How did you hear that we were leaving the hotel today?" Lily asked.

"A couple of women—the kind that drink tea—were just leaving when you came down this morning. They heard it all, though most were shocked that that little Frank Calvin was so rude," she explained. "What kind of pie do y'all want?"

"Blackberry," Daisy said.

"Lemon," Lily added. "And we'll take what we don't eat to the store for a snack in the middle of the day."

"I'll bring over some sandwiches at noon to go with whatever is left of the pie," Beulah said. "And some of my sweet tea with a little kick, to give you enough energy to get through the rest of the day."

"You've done so much already . . . ," Lily started.

Beulah held up both palms. "That's what friends are for, and I've been lonely these past few months. Folks come in to buy supplies, but if there was another general store, the men wouldn't let their women do business with me. 'Course not, since I couldn't hang on to a good man like Orville. 'Good man'?" Beulah laughed. "With y'all, I can visit without fear of whoever you are married to throwing a fit. Look . . ." She pointed out the window. "There's the first load of your stuff coming down the street. I'll get those pies ready to go and bring them and the coffee in a little while."

Dark clouds shifted back and forth over the sun as Daisy and Lily passed the saloon, a saddle-making shop, and a bakery that smelled like fresh bread. Lily had just opened the door to their new shop when the two men driving the wagon hopped down from the buckboard and hurried around to the back side.

"Looks like it could rain, so we brought anything that shouldn't get wet first," Matt said. "Miz Lily and Miz Daisy, this is my helper and cousin, Claude Maguire. Claude, these are the ladies I told you about."

"Pleased to meet you," Lily and Daisy said at the same time.

Heat that had nothing to do with the weather shot through Lily's whole body. She wasn't sure how to even think about feelings like these—she had never had them before. Her fiancé had been horrible to her, and the men she'd entertained at the Paradise were just customers. Was this what women talked about when they said they were attracted to a man?

"Same here," Claude said and hoisted a huge box of fabric onto his broad shoulders. His thick, blond hair curled around the collar of his chambray work shirt, and his light blue eyes seemed to take in everything at once. He was built a lot like Matt—all muscle and very little extra weight. But that was as far as the resemblance went. Matt had dark hair and brown eyes and was a good bit taller than his cousin.

"I wasn't expecting you to make the delivery." Lily focused on Matt as he picked up another crate.

"Uncle Elijah knew we were coming into town for the big day tomorrow and asked us to take care of this delivery," Matt explained.

"Who's minding the sheep?" she asked in a teasing tone.

"The hired hands will do fine for two days and one night," Matt answered as he headed inside the store. "Some of my family will be here tomorrow morning. I imagine my sister Abigail is chomping at the bit to get everyone to promise to leave the ranch before the crack of dawn."

"Just how big is your ranch?" Lily asked.

"A couple thousand acres," Claude answered, but his eyes were on Daisy. "You should come out next spring in shearing time and see how it all goes. We have a big feast afterwards. You could ride out with Uncle Elijah."

"Does Elijah have sons working at the ranch?" Daisy asked.

Claude shook his head and carried the crate inside the store. "There's several family members who work at the ranch. Uncle Elijah didn't have young'uns of his own, but he came from a big family with lots of brothers. He and our fathers are the only ones left of that generation, so we're stepping up to fill in where we can. Okay if I just sit this on the floor? We've got another wagonload, and we hope to get it all inside before it rains."

"Thank you, just put everything wherever you can find a place," Daisy answered. "Lily and I will figure out where we want it later."

"Yes, ma'am," Claude said and set the crate against a far wall.

Matt did the same, and they hurried back outside to carry in a sofa, two chairs, and two bed frames, along with springs and mattresses. "Sure you don't want us to set these up for you?"

"We can manage," Lily said, but it was hard to get the words out when her heart was doing double time.

"Okay, then, we'll go get the rest of the order and be back soon." Matt tipped his hat toward her as he left.

Before Matt even got the wagon turned around and the horses headed back down the street, Beulah arrived with a basket in her hands. "I brought coffee with some heavy cream and sugar in it, and the two pies y'all asked for. Looks like y'all just about bought out Elijah's stock."

Lily sat down in one of the chairs and looked around at the crates. "We would have bought more, but we figured we'd better save a little back to tide us over until business picks up."

"Looking for one of these?" Beulah brought two forks out of the pocket of her apron.

Daisy reached for one and dug into the blackberry pie. "Thank you. We've got some dishes and kitchen stuff coming on the next load."

Beulah parked herself on the end of the blue velvet sofa. "Matt and Claude must be in town for the celebration tomorrow. They're both a rare breed."

"I would suppose that's high praise, right?" Daisy asked.

Lily used the edge of her fork to cut a slice out of the lemon pie. "What does 'rare breed' mean?"

"It means that they are both good men—but then, Elijah and his brothers were all good people. Though there's only him and the other two still living," Beulah answered and pulled a third fork from her pocket. "We can share the coffee from the quart jar, too, since I don't see any glasses."

"That works for me," Daisy said. "Help yourself. Now, tell us more about that family. Claude made it sound like there are a whole bunch out on the ranch."

"Oh, there are—the younger generation. It speaks volumes to their character that they don't fuss when their women come to town and visit with me. Their husbands are a friendly sort, and they treat their women with respect. I've never heard any of them talk down to their wives," Beulah said, and then lowered her voice. "The cattlemen in this area don't like them because they are sheep herders."

"What does that have to do with anything?" Lily asked.

Beulah shrugged. "Back when Texas had open range, the cattlemen said that the sheep grazed too much land, leaving the cattle with too little. And according to them, the sheep polluted the water sources. It's only been a couple of years since the barbed wire fences went up around here. The Maguires have fences, but they've always kept their sheep out away from the cattle ranches close to Autrie. But folks still tend to look down on them—even though they're probably richer than any of the ranchers in these parts. Elijah is tolerated because he has the wagon yard, but most folks kind of shun Matt and his cousins."

"That's as bad in its own way as us women having to fight for our rights," Lily declared.

Beulah took another bite of the blackberry pie and then stood up. "That's the way I see it, too. See y'all at noon for lunch." She crossed the floor and waved over her shoulder before she went outside.

"Thanks for everything, Beulah," Daisy called out before the door closed behind her.

"I do believe that Claude was flirting with you," Lily teased when they were alone.

"Maybe so, but he'd turn tail and run if he knew what I'd done for a living the past five years. But while we are talking about flirting, seems to me that Matt is showing up around you pretty often," Daisy said.

A couple of big, burly men with full beards and round faces came through the door, each carrying a chest on their shoulder. "Are you Daisy and Lily?"

"We are," Lily answered.

They set the chests on the floor with a thump, and the one doing the talking said, "Frank said this concludes your business."

"Thank you, and we are glad that it does," Lily told them.

Lightning flashed in long streaks, and within seconds thunder rolled as the men left without another word and didn't even look back.

"That's an anticlimactic end to our stay at the hotel. I hope we're not in for a storm in our lives beyond the actual one that's coming on fast," Daisy said.

"We are about to start fighting an uphill battle," Lily told her. "As women, we have been treated like possessions for so long—and in some cases, worse than cattle or even hogs—that change won't come easy for menfolk."

"I'll fire the first cannon shot, so to speak," Daisy said and glanced out the window. "I hope Matt and Claude get the rest of our things delivered before it starts raining."

"Matt had said they'd wanted to, but it's definitely too late. Look at what it's doing to our clean windows." Lily pointed across the room. The wind had picked up dust from the street, added it to huge raindrops, and blew mud balls against the windows.

"Maybe it will pass while they are getting the rest of our things loaded down at the wagon yard. Right now, we've got plenty to get organized while we wait," Daisy said. "Like we talked about yesterday, those shelves will be great for stacking fabric on. If we throw a tablecloth over a couple of empty crates, they could be used for tables at the end of the sofa."

"And a doily on top of the tablecloths to make it fancy." Lily had to raise her voice to be heard over the raging storm.

"Yes," Daisy agreed. "We can get started by unloading all the fabric and then turning over the empty crates for tables."

Lily stood back and studied the shelving. "Let's arrange things by what we will use for undergarments—calico on the bottom shelves and then the fancy stuff like brocades and silk toward the top."

Daisy picked up a bolt of brocade and handed it to Lily. "You are tall enough to reach without having to crawl up on a chair."

Like most storms in Texas, this one lasted just long enough to muddy up the street out front again and to make a mess out of the windows and the wooden walk. In less than half an hour, the clouds had parted and sunshine appeared. By that time, Lily and Daisy had unloaded four crates, set one on each end of the sofa, and put two of the same height and width together to make a longer table in front of it.

They were busy draping tablecloths over their handiwork when Matt and Claude arrived to bring in more stuff.

"Sorry about the mud," Matt said. "The roads are a mess when it rains, even when all we get is short showers."

"No complaints from either of us," Lily said with a smile. "We're just glad that our things aren't soaked."

"Hopefully, the roads will be dried out tomorrow and folks won't track too much more mud into your store. Maybe we'll even get to see you ladies sometime during the day?" Claude asked.

"We will look forward to it," Daisy answered. "As of yet, we don't know many people in town. Just Frank Calvin and the judge, both of whom we would as soon not know—and Beulah, who has become our good friend."

"Understandable on all counts." Matt nodded and went back out to help Claude bring in the sewing machine and then the stove for the kitchen. "Beulah can put you in touch with whoever she buys her wood from. You'll only need enough to cook with during these hot months, but in the winter, you'll need more to keep the store and your living quarters warm."

"Thanks for that," Lily told him.

"Of course, I didn't mean to say that you didn't know how to order wood," Matt blurted out.

"I didn't think so, and I appreciate your kindness," Lily said with a smile. "But Daisy and I have been taking care of ourselves for quite a while."

Matt stared into Lily's eyes. "An independent, strong woman is . . ." He blushed and looked away.

"A good thing," Claude finished for him.

"Yes, it is," Matt said. "Hope to see you tomorrow sometime in town."

I cannot encourage whatever this is between us, Lily thought.

"We'll be right here," Daisy said with what Lily could swear was a genuine flutter of her lashes.

You shouldn't be flirting, either, Lily silently scolded.

"Anything else we can help you with before we leave?" Claude asked.

"Not a thing, but thank you for all that you have done," Daisy answered.

"Then we'll get on back down to the wagon yard. Uncle Elijah has another delivery for us to make after we have a bite of dinner at the little café on the other end of town. They have good home cookin', if you ever want to try it," Claude said and headed for the door.

When they were gone, Daisy shook her finger at Lily. "Not a word."

"What did I say?" Lily said in a fake whiny voice.

Chapter Six

Daisy tossed and turned, stared out the window at the moon and stars for what seemed like hours, beat her feather pillow into shape several times, and even tried counting fluffy little sheep. But the little white critters reminded her of Claude being a sheep herder, and that caused even more insomnia. Could Lily be right about him flirting with her?

She had just dozed off when gunshots woke her up. She sat up in bed and wished she was back at the Paradise, which was located so far out of town that she never heard all the hullabaloo that went on in Spanish Fort. Lily peeked in the door and then opened it wide.

"Good morning. Did the firecrackers wake you?"

Daisy covered a yawn with her hand. "Good morning to you. I thought it was gunshots. Is that coffee I smell?"

Lily sat down on the edge of the bed. "I found a few sticks of wood out back and started a small blaze in the stove so we could have coffee with the rest of our pies for breakfast. Evidently, from all the noise I hear out on the street, the holiday has already started. Let's eat and then get dressed. Maybe we should walk down to Beulah's place for some staples and see if a crowd is already gathering. We can't live on pie and coffee forever."

Daisy slung her legs over the side of the bed. "But we can this morning. Did you sleep well?"

"No, I did not," Lily answered. "It'll take me a while to adjust to the sounds of city living. I grew up in a quiet little town, and then we more or less lived out in the country in Spanish Fort. But last night I could hear the piano music playing from the saloon down the street, and my mind went around and around like a wagon wheel. How about you?"

"Same as you." Daisy slipped her nightgown over her head and dressed in a royal blue skirt and red-and-white-striped shirtwaist. She wasn't about to admit that Claude Maguire was the primary reason she couldn't sleep. "Are you going to dress for the holiday?"

"Oh, yes, I am," Lily answered with a grin. "I'm wearing my red skirt and blue calico shirtwaist."

"Red?" Daisy laid her hand over her heart in mock horror. "Coffee for breakfast, swearing in public, and now a red skirt?"

"If the folks in town knew what I did to make the money to put in this shop, a red skirt would be at the bottom of the list of all my many sins."

"You got that right," Daisy agreed with a slight nod. "We are both stirring up trouble. My shirtwaist has red stripes, so neither of us are setting a good example for the ladies in Autrie."

"It could get worse if Beulah's plans work out concerning women's rights." Lily led the way into the store, where she had already set the table. "Thank goodness we found some curtains in those crates and got them hung last evening."

"Not quite ready to let the whole world look in the windows at you in your nightdress?" Daisy teased and sat down in one of the mismatched chairs.

"Not today. Maybe not ever. I've had enough of men seeing me dressed in thin cotton," Lily declared, and brought two cups of coffee from the kitchen.

"Should we get some cookies from Beulah to put out for anyone who might come into the store today?" Daisy asked. "This is a lot like a grand opening, so we should put on the fancy for any prospective customers, right?"

Lily took a sip of her coffee and then a bite out of the lemon pie. "I was thinking the same thing. Maybe we should make some each morning to have over there on the counter every day when we are really open for business."

"We'll have the fanciest store in town," Daisy said.

"At least for a month," Lily agreed.

Lily hadn't been totally honest with Daisy about her sleepless night. She had gone right to sleep but dreamed about Matt Maguire and woke up weeping into her pillow. When and if he ever found out the truth, he would wish he'd taken them to the hotel where the saloon ladies worked instead of the Crockett.

"Why do I have to be attracted to the wrong men?" she asked her reflection in the tiny handheld mirror that matched her hairbrush. Circumstances almost beyond any of her personal control had put her in the brothel business, and because of that, Matt, a decent man, would never look sideways at her again if he knew the truth.

"Life is not fair," she said and laid the mirror to the side.

When she finished dressing and had twisted her hair into a topknot, she left her bedroom and went back into the store. Daisy had opened the curtains, and light flowed into the large room. Several little kids had their noses pushed up against the new shop's windows, and the whole town looked to be alive with people milling about everywhere.

"If you'll mind the store, I'll go down to Beulah's and try to rustle up refreshments. If we don't get any folks in here today, we can enjoy them ourselves," Daisy offered.

Lily nodded in agreement. "I will gladly let you fight that crowd. I don't think I've ever seen so many people in one spot."

Daisy donned her straw hat with the red and blue streamers hanging down her back. "Me, either, but you got to admit, it's very exciting."

She unlocked the door and stepped out onto the board sidewalk and waved at Lily through the window as the kids scattered in front of her.

The crates, some empty and others half-full of bedding and other items that weren't in use, had been shoved into the kitchen. Lily was heading that way when the little bell above the door sounded. Figuring that Daisy had forgotten her purse, she whipped around to find Beulah coming inside with two other women.

"Oh my!" Beulah gasped. "You've got things arranged and fabrics on the shelves. This is beautiful. And you bought the sewing machine. I'm sorry, where are my manners? This is Edith Monroe, wife of the bank president, Wallace Monroe . . ." She pointed to a tiny woman with salt-and-pepper-colored hair and a face so full of wrinkles that she looked like a dried-apple doll. "And this is Maudie Lawson, her sister. Maudie always comes to town for a visit on festival day. I brought them in to meet you, but I wasn't expecting to see things all put away."

Maudie was taller than Edith, but her hair was totally white, and she didn't have nearly as many wrinkles.

Lily chuckled. "I'm glad to meet you ladies, but please don't look in the kitchen."

"Looks like you are going to have a very nice store here," Edith said. "I will definitely be interested in doing business with you. I already know that I'll need a new dress for my niece's wedding, which is set for September. She's marrying Judge Martin. She hasn't found a seamstress to make her wedding dress yet, either, and that white brocade might be the very thing. Could you set the bolt back for me? I can bring her in next week."

"I would be glad to do that," Lily said and removed the bolt from the shelf. "I'll just take it to the back room and hold it for you."

"Thank you," Edith said and sat down on the sofa. "This would be a good place for the new women's auxiliary to meet. Plenty of room, but we would need more chairs. Elijah has a couple of old church pews at the wagon yard. When we put new ones in at the church, we sold them to him. I would be glad to donate them to the cause. They would fit fine under those shelves."

"That's very kind of you," Lily said.

"Consider it done," Edith said.

"We could barter," Lily suggested. "I could make *your* dress for the wedding in exchange for the pews." She had trouble keeping her laughter at bay at the thought of church pews in a shop run by two reformed brothel workers.

"That sounds like a wonderful idea," Edith said. "Is that coffee I smell?"

"Yes, ma'am, it is," Lily answered.

"If it's not too presumptuous of me, I would love a cup," Edith whispered.

Lily smiled. "Not at all. Give me a moment to get some clean mugs."

"Make that two," Maudie added. "We don't dare order such in the hotel—and truth be told, I hate hot tea. I do like Beulah's sweet tea." She shot a broad wink across the room toward Beulah.

Lily made a mental note to pry more information out of Beulah about these two women, who by all appearances were quite well-to-do. Apparently, they came into her store pretty often and visited if she shared her special sweet tea, but she had told Lily and Daisy that most women's husbands didn't want them to have anything to do with her.

"I'd say to pour me up a cup, also, but I'd best get back to my store," Beulah said. "Y'all have a good visit, and I'll tell all the women I see about the meeting next Monday afternoon at two o'clock."

"Daisy is on her way to your place to buy cookies," Lily said.

"I ran out of baked goods an hour after I opened the store, but I steered her down the street to a vendor. Claude's mother from the sheep farm is selling fresh strawberry muffins. She should be . . ." Beulah pointed toward the window. "There she is now. See you later this evening when they set off the fireworks." She opened the door and stood back to let Daisy in, then closed it behind her.

Lily made introductions. "This is Edith and Maudie, and this is my partner, Daisy. Put those muffins on the table, please. I'm going to get the ladies some mugs for coffee. Do you take sugar? We are still trying to get things organized and I can't offer cream, but we do have sugar cubes."

"Sugar is good," Maudie said. "We'd ask for a little dollop of bourbon if you had it."

"I'm sorry, but I'll try to have it ready the next time you come in," Lily said and hoped that she masked her surprise. Proper women asking for coffee was a shock, but bourbon? Maybe she'd had the wrong idea about how the other half lived.

Edith stood up and took a seat at the table. "This is going to be a wonderful place for us to have our meetings."

Maudie followed suit and sat down in one of the other four chairs. "Yes, it is. I'm only sorry that I can't be here for every meeting. Ten miles is just too far to come all the way from Nechesville every week."

Lily stopped halfway to the door leading to the living quarters. "We have three friends who are going to open a seamstress shop in Nechesville."

"Oh!" Maudie's voice raised an octave. "That's wonderful. Maybe I can have them fit me for a dress for the wedding. It's going to be the event of the whole year, right here in Autrie."

"Wedding?" Daisy asked.

"These ladies can tell you while I get some coffee cups."

When she returned, Edith and Maudie were both having a muffin, and evidently they hadn't said anything about their niece or about the judge, because Daisy had a smile on her face.

"Did you hear that Edith is officially our first customer?" Lily asked. "She had me set back that bolt of white brocade for her niece's wedding dress."

"That's wonderful," Daisy said. "They were telling me that you have done some bartering for two old church pews to give us more room for the ladies' auxiliary meetings."

Lily set a full sugar bowl on the table, then poured coffee for each of them. Daisy raised an eyebrow, and Lily slid a sly wink her way. "They said that they couldn't get coffee this morning at the Crockett."

"Sometimes I have it as a little midmorning pick-me-up at home," Maudie said with a shrug. "But I don't tell my husband. He thinks he's been married to a lady for the past thirty years."

Edith laughed. "What they don't know won't hurt them, will it?"

"Amen to that," Maudie answered.

"Their niece is getting married to Judge Wesley Martin in the fall," Lily said. "Remember that he mentioned his fiancée Sally Anne when he stopped and talked to us after church services?"

Daisy's eyes widened, but as Lily had hoped, she kept her composure. "Yes, I do recollect that he said something about her not being able to attend services that day. Do I understand that we'll be designing and making her wedding dress?"

"We hope we will, if she likes the brocade," Lily said, but thought, *Of course Miss Princess Sally Anne will like the brocade.*

"I really think she will," Edith said.

"She has several pictures of dresses that are all the rage in Paris that she wants to work with." Maudie finished off her muffin and drank down the rest of her coffee. "We should be going, Edith. Our husbands will think we are conspiring against them."

"We are," Edith said with a short chuckle. "Not really, but it doesn't hurt them to think that. Makes them nice to us for a few days. We'll walk down to the wagon yard and get Elijah to deliver those pews before the first meeting."

"And you can come in for a dress measurement whenever you have time." Lily smiled, walked them to the door, and opened it for them. "It was so nice to meet you both. Have a wonderful day."

She closed the door and turned around and hurried over to hug Daisy. "Hearing that we will most likely be making the wedding dress had to be a shock. I'm sorry that's our first customer."

The Paradise Petition

"Thank you, but it's not like I ever expected him to ask me to marry him—and I've had some time to let it settle that he is marrying a very wealthy young woman from right here in town," Daisy told her. "After the way he's looked down at me, if he did drop to one knee, I would laugh in his face."

Lily took a step back. "That's the spirit. The past should not define us. What we do in the future should be the story of our lives."

Preach on, sister. Miz Raven was back in Lily's head. *But be sure you totally trust what you are saying, because if you don't, you won't be able to help others believe.*

Daisy sank down into the sofa, dabbed at the sweat on her forehead with a hankie, and stared at the ceiling. "That doesn't mean that I'm not aggravated at him."

"Throw your hairbrush at the wall when you think of him and the fact that he won't sell us the building." Lily eased down onto a kitchen chair.

Daisy giggled and then laughed out loud. "Or maybe when either of us start looking back more than forward, we should beat up a pillow."

"Or maybe have more than one shot of good liquor." Lily laughed with her. "Which reminds me, I promised Edith that we would have some liquor for the coffee we serve the next time she comes in the store. How do we buy that stuff here in Autrie?"

"We could get Elijah or Matt to go to the saloon and get us a bottle," Daisy answered. "No!" She sat up straight. "That's not right. If we want to be a voice for women's rights, we should go in the saloon ourselves and buy a bottle of their best whiskey."

"With the seal intact, so that we know it hasn't been watered down," Lily suggested.

Daisy stood up and narrowed her eyes into little more than slits. "We might as well go right now and strike our first blow for women's rights."

"Are you sure?" Lily asked her. "The fireworks will be starting soon, so folks who frequent those places are going to want one more shot before their families drag them home. We could wait and go tomorrow morning when things are quieter."

"No, ma'am. This is an excellent opportunity to show the town we aren't afraid of anything. The more people who see us, the better. I hope the very engaged, pompous Wesley is in there." Daisy slammed her hat down on her head, picked up her purse, and marched across the floor. "You don't have to come with me if you don't want to."

Lily followed her outside. "I'm going with you, for sure, but making a scene could affect the amount of business we have. Are you sure about this?"

"We are the only seamstress shop in town. Like Beulah said, folks come in her store because there isn't another general store, and if the only reason you are going is to protect me in a fight, then you can stay here," Daisy told her in a daring tone.

"Honey, I'm not going to protect you, but rather whoever gets in your way," Lily informed her. "When you are this angry, even *I* wouldn't cross you."

Daisy stopped at the door. "I shouldn't be this mad."

"Men!" Lily picked up her own purse and headed for the door. "Can't live with them, and we get hanged if we shoot them."

"I already said the same thing—but yep, when they take up residence in your heart . . ." Daisy let the rest of the sentence drop and followed Lily outside.

The sidewalks were packed with people, so they had to make their way through the crowd. Music blared from the piano in the saloon, filling the air with a lively tune that Daisy had played all too often at the Paradise. When she reached the open door, she marched in like a woman on a mission.

Cigar smoke hovered around the ceiling like gray winter clouds. The stench of sweat, blended with chewing tobacco and cheap whiskey, filled Daisy's nostrils, but she held her head high and headed for the crowded bar.

"You ladies are in the wrong place," the man from the middle of the room called out. "The café is on the other end of town, and the Crockett Hotel is on down the street."

"Neither of those sell whiskey, do they?" Lily snapped.

"I'll buy you a shot." A man got to his feet and slung an arm around Daisy. "For a dance, I might even buy your big old friend one, too."

She took a step forward, picked up his arm, and dropped it like trash. "I'm not interested in a shot or a dance. I came in here to buy a bottle of whiskey, so stand back and leave me alone."

That's when she saw the judge sitting at a nearby table with a scantily dressed woman whispering in his ear. It took all her willpower not to storm over to where he was sitting and knock the smirk off his face.

The dark-haired woman, whose clothing wouldn't have sagged a clothesline, glared at Daisy with big brown eyes. She popped her hands on her hips in a defensive gesture, crossed the room, and went nose to nose with Daisy. "Your kind isn't welcome here."

Four other women, dressed just as scantily, appeared out of nowhere to stand beside her. "Meet Ruby, Lula, Betsy, and Molly."

"And we agree with Frannie," Molly growled. "Your kind ain't any more welcome here than we are in your church."

Daisy folded her arms across her chest and tapped her foot on the wooden floor. In some ways she felt sorry for the women. She might have worked in an upscale bordello, but the job was the same, no matter where. Not sorry enough to walk out the door or let them talk down to her, though.

Frannie glared at her and then shifted her eyes over to Lily. "If *you've* got a mind to dance, I can probably rustle up a man who don't mind sinking his head into your bosom."

Laughter rang out in the room so loudly that it drowned out the piano music.

"I'll leave that job to you and *your kind*," Lily whispered in an icy-cold tone that put a damper on all the laughter.

Had Lily really just voiced aloud what Daisy was thinking? And how had they both gotten so far from their past so quickly?

A few men—the judge included—threw money in the middle of the table. No doubt about it, they were betting on which woman would win if Frannie pushed it any further. The piano music stopped, and an almost eerie silence filled the room. Daisy focused on Frannie, and neither of them blinked for a long, pregnant moment.

Finally, Frannie gave Daisy a solid shove. Daisy's fist was a blur as it made contact with the woman's eye. It didn't matter who the woman was or what she did to make a living, no one had the right to put her hands on Daisy. Frannie dropped to the floor, grabbed Daisy by the ankles, and brought her down with her. Lily reached down, grabbed Frannie by the arms, and pulled her up to her feet.

"I'm protecting you, woman!" Lily hissed. "Daisy has been trained to fight, and she's already mad. So take a moment to think about the beating you are about to get."

"Buy your whiskey and get out," Frannie snapped as she went back over to the judge and sat down in his lap. "I didn't want her to ruin my hair," she announced loudly. "Sweet little churchified ladies like y'all should run along now."

Lily extended a hand to help Daisy up from the floor, but she ignored it and rose to her feet with the grace of a boxer. She marched over to Frannie, drew back her fist, and was about to land her another black eye when Frannie ducked, and Daisy hit Wesley square on the chin.

Wesley shoved Frannie off his lap so hard she landed on the floor with a thud. Then he pushed back his chair so fast that it tumbled backward with a second hard thump. "You . . . you . . . ," he stammered as he knotted his own hands into fists.

"Do you have something you would like to say to me?" Daisy lifted her skirt and stepped over Frannie so she could get right in his face. "Or

The Paradise Petition

maybe you would like to tell Sally Anne that Frannie has been sitting on your lap. I could do that for you if you are too ashamed to do so."

"You might do well to remember who owns your shop," he answered as he stood up and headed for the door. The bartender grabbed a bottle of whiskey from under the counter, hurried over to Daisy, and shoved it into her hand. "You've got your whiskey. Now get out."

Lily threw a silver dollar at him and looped her arm through Daisy's. "That should cover the cost of it, plus some. We'll be going now. Next time a woman comes in here, just sell her the whiskey and don't make a big scene."

"Or try to make a laughingstock out of her." Daisy made a sweeping motion to take in all the room. "We have as much of a right to drink as all you men."

"Ladies don't drink," Wesley said as he brushed past Lily. "Not coffee, and definitely not whiskey."

Daisy's hands knotted into fists again. Her breath caught in her chest, and she grabbed him by the arm. She pointed her finger so close to his nose that he jerked his head back. "And engaged men don't visit women like Frannie."

She didn't even realize that Lily was beside her until she heard her voice. "We've done what we came to do. It's time to go."

Daisy put on her best fake smile and turned around to face a quiet bar. "Y'all have a nice day, now."

As soon as they had cleared the saloon's front porch, Lily heaved a sigh of relief. Frannie would have a black eye, and Wesley would sport a bruise, but neither one would need the doctor's attention. Or worse, the sheriff's.

"Do you feel better now?" she scolded Daisy.

"No, I do not. And for that matter, can you leave me alone? There's still some mad left in my heart," Daisy barked.

"You've at least let some of it out," Lily said. "And that was a fantastic little smart remark at the end there."

"I thought so, but mad that's left over is still boiling," Daisy told her and then smiled brightly when she saw Edith, Sally Anne, and Beulah coming toward them.

Edith gasped when she saw Lily with a bottle of whiskey in her hands, but Sally Anne ran over to the judge, who was a few feet from them.

"My sweet darlin'," she crooned and touched Wesley's face.

"It's nothing to worry about, dear," Wesley said. "Someone pushed me into the doorjamb as I was leaving the saloon. Don't you worry your little mind about me, Sally Anne."

"I'll get some ice from Miz Beulah," she said.

"Don't bother. It probably won't even bruise," he said and took the short, blond woman's hand in his. "Let's cross the street. We can get a much better view of the show from the front steps of the courthouse."

"Chicken," Daisy whispered. "He just doesn't want to be anywhere near me or the other folks filing out of the saloon. His precious Sally Anne might hear something that would burn her innocent little ears."

"Did you really walk right in the saloon and buy that?" Edith asked. "And what's that about my sweet niece?"

"Daisy was just saying how crossing the street like Sally Anne might give us a better view," Lily covered, hoping that their impulsive act wouldn't hurt the women in town.

"And yes, ma'am, we certainly did buy it," crowed Daisy, taking the bottle from Lily.

A broad smile covered Edith's face. "Your bold purchase is a definite strike in our favor and will bring even more ladies to our auxiliary meeting next week."

"Do you think so?" Lily was glad for the support, but even more so that Edith hadn't gone on to talk more about Sally Anne.

"Absolutely," Edith whispered. "If you are willing to do that, then they'll all see that you are committed to the cause. And besides, you've got whiskey now."

"Hello!" Beulah waved. "Y'all about ready for the fireworks? We could drag some of your chairs out onto the sidewalk, and I brought sandwiches for us to have while we watch the show."

"And some sweet tea?" Daisy held up the bottle.

Beulah's eyes widened. "Sweet Jesus in heaven! Did you actually go into the saloon and buy that?"

"We did," Lily answered.

"That was not a baby step," Beulah said as she followed them inside the seamstress shop. "That could be considered a giant step for womanhood."

"Especially not when Daisy and Frannie, a saloon girl, got into a fight," Lily told her, taking back the whiskey from her shorter friend and putting it on the shelf in plain sight. "Since so many people have already seen me carrying this down the street, I don't imagine that we need to hide it."

Beulah picked up a ladder-back chair with her free hand and started across the room. "As women, we shouldn't have to sneak around like Alma and I do with our letters. We should have as much freedom as . . ." She stopped at the door.

"As everyone else, no matter what kind of plumbing is in their undergarments?" Daisy asked.

Beulah giggled. "Well said, my friend. We can discuss that more later, but right now let's go outside and have some food. I brought ham sandwiches."

They lined chairs up right under the window, and Beulah passed out sandwiches made with fresh bread and thick slabs of cured ham. Then she took a jar of sweet tea from the bag and set it on the wooden sidewalk between her and Lily. "It's simply plain tea for tonight. Be best if no one smells it on your breath."

"We have a bottle sitting out for all to see," Daisy reminded her.

"Yep, you do, and lots of womenfolk keep a bottle for medicinal purposes on their shelves or in their cupboards. The difference is that they send a male relative to buy it for them," Beulah said between bites. "If y'all save that bottle for the meeting, it might loosen some tongues."

Lily's heart threw in an extra beat and her hands trembled slightly when Matt stepped out of the crowd and stood beside her. "Good evening," she said, her voice echoing in her own ears, like it came up from the bottom of a well.

"Good evening to you, Miz Lily," he said in a deep voice.

"Have you enjoyed the day?" Lily wished she could ask him more personal questions, but she didn't know him that well—not yet.

You defied society by walking into a saloon, creating a disturbance, and buying a bottle of whiskey. If you can do that, you can ask him if he has a woman waiting back at the ranch or maybe taking care of a vending place at the festival, Miz Raven's voice fussed at her.

"Yes, ma'am, I truly have. Claude and I hauled a few things for Uncle Elijah. I was sorry I missed getting to bring those pews to your store. But I've got to admit, I'm more than ready to go back to the ranch. I've had enough excitement to last until the fall," he answered. "How about you? Have you had a good day?"

"A very busy day to have only opened our doors this morning," she said.

"Evenin', ladies," Claude said as he joined them. He focused on Daisy. "I hear you had an eventful evening already."

"News and gossip both seem to travel fast," Daisy said.

Matt caught Lily's eye and smiled. "So, you like a little nip of whiskey?"

"Yes, sir," Lily answered without even a hint of a grin. "Do you have a problem with that?"

"No, ma'am, my mama still likes a shot before she retires. She says that it helps her to sleep and keeps her heart beating," Matt answered. "How about you, Miz Beulah?"

"Your mama has got that right, but I think you were asking about my day, not if I take a little whiskey at night—for purely medicinal purposes," Beulah answered. "Seems like everyone needed to buy supplies of all kinds since they were already in town. Are you and Matt staying the night with Elijah?"

"No, ma'am," Matt answered from the other end of the row of women. "We'll be late getting back, but we need to be there to relieve the shepherds that stayed back to work while we came to town. We'll be back for supplies soon, though."

"That will give me time to restock my shelves," Beulah said as an array of colors burst through the air. "Oh, look! There's the first one of the fireworks, and it's so pretty."

"I heard today that the judge is planning an even bigger display than this at his and Sally Anne's wedding," Matt said. "They'll go off right after the sun sets while he and his new bride board the train to go on their honeymoon. They won't be back for a month, but the judge from over at Nechesville will be taking care of things in his absence."

"A man with his wealth can do things like that," Beulah said.

"Sounds like an adventure, not a honeymoon, to me," Lily said, and wished that she could be thinking about a lasting relationship with a good man—but she might as well fancy a trip to the moon.

"I agree," Matt said with a nod. "I'm going to be a bit brazen and say that you look beautiful today in your red-white-and-blue outfit, Miz Lily."

"Thank you, Mr. Maguire," she said.

"That's just Matt, please. Mr. Maguire is my father."

After all the excitement of the whole day, the evening was a bit anticlimactic when the fireworks ended, and people began to load their families up in wagons and buggies. Clouds had begun to move in from the southwest, and the distant roll of thunder said that another unusual July storm was on the way.

"You fellers be careful and dodge any lightning strikes on the way home," Beulah said as she stood up.

"We're probably going to get wet, but as hot as it's been all day, the cool rain might feel good," Matt said.

Claude chuckled. "Mama says that neither of us are sugar, so we won't melt. Besides, rain in July is a rare thing, and it will green up the pastures for the sheep. Good night, Miz Daisy," he said with a tip of his hat. "Maybe I'll see you the next time I come to town."

"That would be nice," she replied as she stood, and after a few more pleasantries, the men left.

"What was that?" Beulah whispered when all three were in the shop and had closed the door.

"What was what?" Lily asked.

"Have y'all never been courted?" Beulah asked. "Matt and Claude were staking their claims by watching the fireworks with you. The only thing more definite is if you were seen taking a buggy ride with them."

Daisy giggled. "We already did that."

"Matt gave us a ride from the train station to the hotel the day we arrived," Lily explained.

"Just be careful. Those are two good men, but . . ." Beulah plopped down on the sofa.

"But what?" Lily asked.

"But I'm being selfish. You just got here, and it's only natural that the bachelors in this area will flock around you, but I don't want you to get serious about any of them just yet," Beulah said. "And on that note, I'm going back home."

Lily draped an arm around Beulah as she rose and walked her to the door. "You don't have to worry about a thing, my friend. There's not a man in the whole state that would want to marry independent women like us."

"Thank God!" Beulah said with a laugh and a sideways hug before she left.

Daisy and Lily watched her walk away, and giggled at her reply.

"You really believe that about no one wanting to marry us?" Daisy asked.

"What do you think?" Lily answered with another question. "No one should go into a relationship with secrets. What would Matt and Claude do if they knew ours?"

"Run for the hills," Daisy replied as she locked the door and headed across the room.

"Absolutely," Lily said.

"But it's kind of nice to be courted," Daisy said with a sigh.

Lily covered a yawn with her hand and admitted to herself for the very first time in her life that she wanted a real relationship—maybe not with Matt Maguire, but with a good man who treated women right.

Chapter Seven

Daisy had made apple-spice muffins that morning, but so far no one had come into the store, and here it was nearly noon. The window of the shop was open, letting the aroma of cinnamon waft out onto the sidewalk. Lily took a bolt of calico from the shelf, got her patterns from the bottom of her trunk, and chose a simple one that wouldn't take long to make.

"I'm not sitting on my thumbs waiting for women to come in and special order," she declared. "I am going to make a day dress to go in Beulah's store."

"You are itching to get at that sewing machine, aren't you?" Daisy teased.

"Yes, I am," Lily answered. "I need something to keep me busy."

"So that you won't spend the whole day thinking about Matt Maguire, right?" Daisy asked.

"Is that why you were up at the crack of dawn making muffins and putting bread on to rise? Did that work to keep your mind off Claude?" Lily unrolled fabric across the table and then laid out pattern pieces with strategically placed knives, forks, and spoons to keep them flat for cutting.

"Absolutely," Daisy admitted. "I dreamed about him last night. We were on a wagon train going west. That would never happen. He's too devoted to the ranch, and we both know that *we* are going to be old maids with a cause."

"I would call us 'independent women,' not 'old maids,'" Lily argued. Daisy handed Lily a pair of scissors. "What's the difference?"

"The latter have probably never shared a bed with a man," Lily informed her.

"Poor little darlin's," Daisy chuckled.

The bell above the door jingled, and both women whipped around to see Edith coming into the store with Sally Anne right behind her. Edith sniffed the air and smiled. "Cinnamon and coffee, right?"

"Yes, ma'am," Daisy answered, hiding a wince at seeing her blond double. "Would you like a cup and an apple-spice muffin?"

"Indeed, I would!" Edith sat down on the sofa and pulled out a sheaf of papers from her purse.

Sally Anne said, in a husky voice that was nothing like Daisy's, "I'm very anxious to see the brocade that Aunt Edith has been telling me about. I brought pages from magazines and newspapers to show you what I have in mind."

Lily began to clear her things from off the table so that the two ladies could lay out their ideas while they had refreshments.

"Don't mess up your job there," Sally Anne said. "We can put everything on this nice table right here in front of the sofa."

"Why don't I get the brocade now?" Lily nodded toward the shelf where the whiskey sat on full display. "Then we can have coffee, and if you would like, we can add a little shot."

"I would like that very much," Edith said. "But Sally Anne likes wine, not whiskey."

Of course she does. One of the wealthiest ladies in Autrie would sip wine, for sure, not throw back shots of whiskey or rum, thought Daisy.

Lily returned with the bolt of brocade and set it up on a kitchen chair. "Well, what do you think of this? Daisy and I are of the opinion that we can turn it into a lovely wedding dress."

Sally Anne clapped her hands and beamed. "This is absolutely gorgeous, Aunt Edith. I simply love it, and it will be perfect with the design I have in mind. Wes is going to think an angel is floating down the aisle toward him."

Daisy felt a stab of pain for having to design a wedding dress for the bride of the man who had stolen her heart. Especially a bride who looked so much like her. But the sting of the pure aggravation of not telling Sally Anne that her groom was a two-timing son of a bitch was even more bitter than the former ache.

"I hear this is going to be the wedding of the year—maybe the whole century," Daisy said, but she was thinking that Sally Anne, in all her innocence, must have a brain the size of a hummingbird if she believed that Wesley was only in the saloon for the card playing.

"I suppose," Sally Anne said. "I would have rather just got married quietly, but Wesley wants the big to-do, and there is a lot of planning involved. Thank goodness I have Aunt Edith to help me or I'd pull out all my hair."

Probably to show off and put his name out there for a higher political position, Daisy thought, but she didn't say the words out loud.

"Why did you choose September?" Lily asked.

"It's a little cooler then, and just the thought of wearing a big, heavy wedding gown in this kind of heat gives me the vapors." Sally Anne fanned her face with her hand. "I hear y'all are having your first women's auxiliary meeting right here in this shop. I've been spreading the word to all the ladies I know. Aunt Edith tells me that it's going to be a legitimate organization to raise money for the school but that it's also going to be a place to talk about women's rights."

"Hopefully," Lily said.

"You never know what might happen if women stand together," Edith said.

"I'll get the coffee and muffins," Daisy offered—anything to get away long enough to collect her thoughts and catch her breath.

The Paradise Petition

Lily dragged two chairs over to the other side of the table in front of the sofa. Even though she was sure Daisy had been swearing under her breath in the kitchen, when she returned she had plastered a smile on her face as she carried a large silver tray with four cups of coffee, four lovely lace-edged linen napkins, and half a dozen muffins arranged beautifully. Miz Raven would be so proud of her.

"These muffins are delicious," Sally Anne gushed when she had taken the first bite. "Maybe we can exchange recipes at the women's meetings?"

"Great idea," Edith agreed. "And I'm so glad you like the brocade. When I saw it, I just knew that it would make the perfect wedding dress."

Daisy took a seat and laid her sketch pad on her lap. "I can work up a couple of designs from the pictures you have here, and then you can come back in to get measured in a few days. I'd say you could see them when we have our first auxiliary meeting, but I'm sure you don't want anyone to even see a picture of the dress until you walk down the aisle."

Sally Anne took a sip of her coffee. "You are right about the dress, and about the coffee. It's so much better than tea. My housekeeper and I have a cup every now and then. Maybe that will be something we talk about at the meetings. We can ask for the right to drink what we want, wherever we want."

"Or buy a bottle of whiskey or wine without repercussions," Daisy added.

Had it been any other woman, Lily would have been very excited to be working on a wedding dress, but visualizing the expression on Wesley's face when he'd flirted with Frannie sure took the fun out of the job. Poor Sally Anne had no idea what kind of future she was in for, but it wasn't Lily's or Daisy's place to burst her little bubble. Besides, she probably wouldn't believe anything they would say against the judge, anyway, and telling her could cause their shop to lose their first paying customer.

Daisy talked as she completed a very rough sketch. "So, from what I'm seeing, you want a fitted bodice with covered buttons up the front, mutton sleeves extending to a fitted wrist, and the skirt should be straight in the front and billow out into a cascade of lace ruffles in the back that will extend into a long train."

"Exactly," Sally Anne said. "If I leave these ideas with you, can you have something for me to look at next week and take my measurements then?"

"I'll sketch three different styles, and we will talk about what you want different and maybe what kind of lace you want. We've got two bolts on the shelf right now. If you want us to put both back until you return, we'll be glad to do that." Daisy drew the whole time she was talking, then turned the sketch pad around for Sally Anne to see. "This is rough, but maybe like this?"

"Yes!" Sally Anne exclaimed. "But I would like to see a couple more just so I have options. And can I see the lace?"

Lily stood up, crossed the room, and brought down two bolts from a top shelf. She stood both of them up beside the brocade. "We could use a combination of both, and if you are interested, we could use the same for your dressing gown and robe."

"Yes, yes, yes," Sally Anne said. "And that purple silk would be wonderful for my bridesmaid's dress."

Edith laid a hand on her niece's shoulder. "Don't forget, honey, you have to invite your cousins on your mother's side. Your mama would turn over in her grave if you slighted them, and the five girls will be hurt if you don't ask them."

"Do you have time to make six?" Sally Anne's voice turned into a semi-whine.

"We can devote the next two months to nothing but your wedding," Lily answered.

"But only if we have the material in the store," Daisy added. "If we have to order it, there's no guarantee that it could get here in time."

She pointed at bolts of taffeta. "Those five fall colors will do fine—but don't use the orange for Essie Sue. She'll look like a big pumpkin."

"Sally Anne!" Edith scolded.

"It's the gospel truth," Sally Anne argued. "But even though she's a big girl, she's got a huge heart, and of all my cousins, she's the one I like best. She speaks her mind and doesn't care what anyone thinks of her—but orange would be a horrible color on her."

"We could use the mossy green for her dress," Daisy suggested.

"Good idea," Edith said. "But never worry, darlin', all eyes will be on the gorgeous bride. We should be going." She pulled a velvet bag of money from her purse and laid it on the table. "This will be the down payment for whatever all this costs. Just tally up anything over and above it, and I'll take care of that later. Oh, and I'll want my dress made from the light green taffeta up there on the shelf—maybe a skirt and shirtwaist, with a nice little dark green jacket. That way I can wear it to other events that might come up, or even to church after the wedding is over."

"Yes, ma'am," Daisy said. "We will take down what y'all have picked out and set it aside."

"Thank you, and we'll both see you at the meeting on Monday," Edith said as she stood up at the same time Sally Anne did, and the two of them looked at the work Lily had laid out on the table.

"Who ordered a calico dress?" Sally Anne asked.

"No one yet," Lily answered. "I'm just going to make a couple of day dresses for Beulah to sell in her store."

"Good idea," Edith said, and with that, the ladies departed.

Daisy was about to lock the door that evening when a man poked his head inside. "Hello. I have mail for Lily Boyle. Do I have the right place?"

"Yes!" Lily hurried across the room.

"And a letter for Daisy Lindberg. Miz Beulah from down the street said that you were the newcomers in town. These came today, and I'm on my way home for dinner, so I figured I'd just bring them to y'all. I'm Stanley Harris," he said, bobbing his head in almost a bow. "I take care of the post office. It's located over by the courthouse, if you want to check in every few days to see if you have mail or maybe send letters out."

"Thank you so much." Lily took the two letters from his hand. "We'll be writing letters back to our friends and bringing them to you real soon."

Stanley acted as if he was afraid to take a step inside the shop. "Okay, then." He quickly closed the door behind him.

Lily locked it and held the letters to her chest for a moment before handing Daisy's off to her. "I can't believe we've already got mail. It's only been a week tomorrow since we arrived."

Daisy sat down on the sofa, carefully opened her letter, and read it out loud:

> Dear Daisy,
> We have been very busy since landing here in Nechesville. Holly has landed a job as a schoolteacher and will begin teaching on Monday of next week. The former teacher is getting married over the weekend, and rumor has it that there's a shotgun involved. I'm sure that, if our secrets were known, Holly wouldn't have been hired.
> We've found a nice little house on the edge of town and have hung out our shingle to do seamstress work. We already have a few women who want things custom made, and we have fabric on order. I have to admit, we are a little bored while we wait on customers and on product to work with, but we are doing the best we can to make friends and settle in.
> We are waiting to hear from Poppy and Rose as well as from you two. An acquaintance of a woman

named Maudie said that she was coming over your way to celebrate Independence Day with her sister. I almost sent this letter by her, but I don't know her well enough to trust her with mail.

All three of us are well, but this heat is worse than it was in North Texas. It's like a blast from a stove most days, and when it rains, it just brings steam. I miss the cool breezes and the mint juleps in the middle of the morning when we all sat out on the porch.

Let us hear from you soon. We miss you both. Please let Lily read this also. We didn't have much news but wanted to share what we did have with you both.

Love,

Holly, Iris, and Jasmine

She folded it and carefully put it back into the envelope. "I will keep this forever. It's the first mail I have ever gotten in my life."

"Me too. I expect mine is from Poppy or Rose . . . but I'm wrong," she said once she had opened the envelope.

"Who is it from? Please tell me that your fiancé hasn't tracked you down," Daisy said.

"It's from Miz Raven," Lily whispered.

Daisy grabbed her chest. "I can't believe that a letter has already made it here. I wish she hadn't moved so far."

Lily took a deep breath and read:

Dear Ladies,

I trust that you have arrived at your destination and are adjusting to a very different lifestyle. Jems and I will board a ship tomorrow morning for England. By the time this reaches you from New York, we should be well underway. I'm eager to arrive in my old environs and get to work, but I have to be patient and careful, as I suggest you be as well. I will be going back to my family home. My father is gone now, so he can't scold me on a daily basis for my choices in life. My sister has been quite active in the movement, and so I will be helping her. Things seem to be moving faster for women in London than in the US.

I'm looking forward to the salt air for the next days, but I do miss you ladies so much. I'm sending a letter to the others also and will include my address so you can write back to me. Your letters will take a while to arrive, but I will be so glad to get them when they do.

Love,

Raven

"I can't believe that we got a letter from the queen herself, or that Holly and the others already have made acquaintances," Daisy whispered.

"We'll cherish this mail forever and ever." Lily wiped a tear from her eye. "Do you know how often I went into the post office in Spanish Fort and asked if there was mail for me?"

Daisy shook her head. "I never even checked. My folks left Texas going north not long after I married and moved again the next year, from the news I heard. I didn't figure they'd ever try to find me or even know that they needed to."

"I went once a week for more than a year before I finally gave up," Lily said in an icy tone. "When I told my mother that I was running away because my fiancé had forced himself on me, she told me that he wouldn't have done such a thing if I hadn't given him the wrong impression. And then she said that no man would want damaged goods, so I might as well marry him."

"Thank God once again for Miz Raven," Daisy said with a long sigh.

Chapter Eight

The seamstress shop was packed on Monday afternoon, and Lily could already tell that one pot of coffee and one of hot water for tea wasn't going to serve so many ladies. Besides that, they didn't have nearly enough cups and saucers to serve the group. She was trying to figure out a way to explain that she hadn't expected more than a dozen women when Beulah whistled—loud and shrill—and all the conversations stopped. The whole room was suddenly so quiet that Lily could hear the leaves rustling on the trees at the back of the store.

"Good afternoon, ladies," Beulah said. "We didn't know what to expect at this meeting, so we aren't prepared to offer refreshments, but next week we will be better equipped. Our primary purpose here today is to discuss making things to sell at next year's Independence Day event. The money we make will be divided three ways—one third to each church and one third to expand our school."

Edith raised a hand, and Beulah acknowledged her with a nod.

"I will see if Elijah has a crate of cups that I can buy, and next week I will volunteer to bring iced tea for everyone to enjoy while we visit," she said.

Sally Anne didn't wait to be given permission to speak. "I vote that we sign up, ten at a time, to bring a dozen cookies or cupcakes each week. That way we can all chip in. Lily and Daisy are doing enough by letting us meet here."

"All in agreement, raise your hands," Beulah said.

Lily raised her hand and glanced around the room to see that all hands were up except Alma's. Poor woman must have been so beaten down that she was afraid to even offer to bring a dozen cookies to a women's meeting without asking Joshua.

After the vote, the women began to gather in groups of four to six and visit, some talking loud enough to be heard, others whispering behind their fans. Beulah grabbed Lily's arm and pulled her across the room to where Alma stood back in the corner.

She draped an arm around Alma's thin shoulders. "Are you okay? I noticed you didn't raise your hand to help with cookies."

"I'm fine, but Joshua is angry with me for coming to the meeting. He says that such a thing is giving woman entirely too much power. I reminded him that we were gathering to talk about funds for his church, but . . ." Tears rolled down her cheeks.

"Did he hit you again?" Beulah asked.

"No—I'm afraid he's punishing the girls to get back at me, so I'm going to sneak out early," she answered, and headed for the door. "I don't know how much more of this I can take. I have dreams about killing him."

"I've got a lot of land behind my old house," Beulah said. "If that ever happens, they'll never find his body."

Alma almost smiled but stopped herself. "You are a good friend, and sometimes I would risk going to hell to have that happen—if not for me, then for my daughters. The way he treats them is not a good example. I'll write you a letter and see you later in the week."

"I'll be looking forward to it, and if you need help between now and then, you know that you and the girls will always have a safe place with me," Beulah assured her, then turned back to Lily. "I don't expect you to understand where Alma is coming from, but I do. Orville didn't ever lay a hand on me. If he had, my father would have carried his cold dead body out to the end of our land and fed him to the coyotes. But he was abusive in other ways. Constantly putting me down for not being able to have children, or not staying as slim as I was when he married me. I often dreamed of him being dead, too, and always awoke with a smile on my face."

"I really do understand." A shiver danced down Lily's spine. "But that's a story for another day."

Edith knocked on the table to get everyone's attention. "Daisy and Lily took a big step on Independence Day—come to think of it, that was a good time to show that women could buy whiskey, and we need to support them and each other in our fight for real freedom. I vote that next Sunday, all of us women march into church and sit down with our husbands. It will take some courage, but it's a step in the right direction if we are ever to have any rights at all. I love my husband. We've been married for forty years. But as women, we have about as many privileges as a cow out in the pasture."

A lady in the middle of the room spoke up. "I don't feel like I even have that many benefits. My husband would be looking out over the crowd for a new wife at my funeral, but if one of his cows died, he would be a wreck for a month."

"You got it, sister! Preach on," another one piped up.

"My husband is a good man. He treats me well." The third woman to speak took a step toward the door. "When I had our last baby, he even cooked and did laundry, so I won't be taking part in all this fuss about women having rights."

"Keep him," the first one said. "There's not many who are brave."

"I've got a good one, too, but I'm willing to stand up with all y'all for some rights. I would love to sit with my husband in church, and maybe have a cup of good black coffee without sneaking it," another woman agreed. "But I probably wouldn't vote if we were given the right. I don't know anything about politics. I leave that to the menfolk."

"I've heard enough of this balderdash," said the dissenting woman. "The good Lord made woman to be a help for menfolk, and I'm a God-fearing woman. I'm leaving right now, and I won't be back." She stormed out of the building.

Edith took control again. "Well, glad you-all met Gertrude Abernathy. We are not forcing anyone to stay. You are welcome to leave if you don't want to have any more say-so about your lives. But until we start to stand up for ourselves, even in small ways, we will never reach the point where we are counted as equals with men. I hope you were as pleased as I was when the bill passed that said married women could own their own property, but that isn't enough. We have to take this to a new level here at home. I, too, am tired of not being able to sit with my husband in church. God made families for a reason, and I can't find a single place where Jesus said that men should treat women like property. Are we together on this, even if it will cause problems?"

The majority of the hands went up, including Sally Anne's, which surprised Lily. But a few women focused on anything in the room other than Edith. A handful even started to leave.

Beulah nudged Lily on the upper arm. "Looks like most of the women are with us."

"I see fear in some of their eyes, though, even if only a few have left," Lily told her.

"I didn't expect a unanimous vote," Beulah said. "I'm just glad for those who are willing to join us here at the first. When the others see that we're making progress, they might come over to our side, too."

"Okay, then, we will take our first step next Sunday, but until that time, we will be diligent little wives and do our handiwork to sell for the school and missionaries," Edith said. "And now let's end this part of the meeting and just visit for the rest of the hour." She made her way through several of the small groups and laid a hand on Beulah's shoulder. "I realize that you got this whole thing started, and I apologize if I overstepped by taking over."

"Nothing to apologize about," Beulah said. "Thank you for taking a role in this. I wasn't sure how many to expect or who might attend today. I'm just glad to see that some of the women are willing to stand together and make some noise."

Edith chuckled. "Not noise, my friend. I intend for us to roar."

Lily took a deep breath, let it out slowly, and walked across the room to stand behind the table. She knocked on the table three times and everyone got quiet. "For those of you that don't know me, my name is Lily Boyle. I don't know how many of you are comfortable sharing your stories, or even any private things about your life. But it might help us all if a few of us tell about how we came to battle for women's rights. I'll go first for this week. I came from the far west side of the Texas Panhandle. I was engaged to a fine upstanding man in town. My parents were happy I was making such a good marriage, and out in public he treated me well—most of the time, anyway."

A few women nodded, and that gave Lily courage to go on.

"But," she said with a long sigh, "he abused me in the worst kind of way by forcing himself on me more than once, and he justified what he did by quoting that Bible verse that said women were to be submissive to their husbands. When I cried and told him that he wasn't my husband, he left bruises on me. They weren't where anyone could see them, and I was too ashamed to even show them to my mother. When I told her about what he had done to me, she asked me what I had said or done to give him the impression that he could do that, making it my fault."

Several women dabbed at tears.

Lily went on. "Then she said I was damaged goods now, and I had to marry the man because he was the only one who would ever have me. I took what little money I had and ran as far as I could. A kind woman took me in, and I worked for her for the next five years. That's my story and why I want to help other women—so they don't ever have to suffer like I did."

Beulah and Edith started a round of applause, and the other women joined in. A robust woman with brown hair streaked with gray came up to the table and stood beside Lily.

"I am Hattie Wilson. Most of you know me from the café down the street. I want to thank Miz Boyle for sharing her story. Mine isn't that bad, but until my husband died a couple of months ago, there were nights when I wished he would drink one more shot of whiskey and never wake up. Like Miz Edith said, most men treat us like we are property, and that's because for the most part, that's the way it's been in the past. And it's what we've been taught to believe since we were little girls. Learn to cook and take care of babies so that we will be good wives. Obey your husband. Even the wedding vows say to honor and obey. I appreciate the women in the bigger cities who marched and fought for our right to hold property and hold on to our own money *after* we are married. But that's not enough. Even in small towns and communities, we need to remember to do our part. I don't attend church, but I'll be praying that none of you lose your courage on Sunday morning. And those of you who aren't married or don't have fiancés, please do what you can in supporting those who do."

The next round of applause came close to bringing down the roof, and then several women came up to the table to give Lily a hug and write their names on the refreshment list. Her hands trembled and her chest felt tight, but saying her piece publicly—even if she did skirt the whole truth a little about the Paradise—was more liberating than she'd ever thought it might be. Until that very day, only Lily's mother, Miz Raven, and the six women she had befriended at the brothel knew what she just told the whole crowd.

When the store was finally empty, she backed up and eased down onto the sofa. Daisy sat beside her and patted her on the shoulder. "That took courage. I'll try to work up enough to tell my story another week, but I'm proud of you for opening the door for others to talk about whatever is buried down deep in their hearts."

Lily held her hands tightly in her lap. "A big, tall woman like me shouldn't be shaking in her shoes. I should be fearless and able to lead the troops into battle without any sign of weakness."

"How tall or short, how thin or heavy, or even what color a woman's hair or skin is doesn't matter," Daisy assured her. "We all have basically the same size heart, and that was where your speech came from today.

The Paradise Petition

We need to hear from our sisters in this war. It gives us what we need to face the battles and not turn tail and run."

"Thanks for that," Lily muttered.

"Let's walk down to Beulah's and buy a pie to celebrate our first meeting going so well," Daisy suggested.

"I could go for that," Lily said as she stood up.

Daisy looped her arm through Lily's and led her outside. She stopped long enough to lock the door. "There. Now we don't have to come back at any certain time."

"And besides, we are booked solid for the next couple of months with Sally Anne's wedding and whatever dresses we can make to go in Beulah's store," Lily said. "Did Sally Anne surprise you—even a little?"

"Oh, hell no!" Daisy said. "She didn't just surprise me. She blew me away. That woman is no shrinking little wallflower like the judge probably thinks she is."

"What makes you say such a thing?" Lily asked.

"She's too independent to have stuck to the rules. I can just feel it in my bones," Daisy answered.

They reached the general store at the same time Elijah did. "Hello, ladies," he said and held the door open for them. "I heard y'all had quite the ladies' meeting at your shop today and"—he lowered his voice—"that you put Frannie in her place on Independence Day."

"Gossip travels fast," Lily said. "It's only been half an hour since the meeting broke up."

"Yes, ma'am, rumors do get through the air in a flash—kind of like lightning. But y'all all need to remember that the thunder that follows can be loud. I hear there's some menfolk who are not happy with your meeting—and some of the women, like Gertrude Abernathy, who is on a soapbox about you two coming into town and causing trouble." Elijah's expression left no doubt that he was serious.

"We didn't expect all the women to stand by us," Lily said. The euphoria she had felt earlier seemed to dissipate.

"Well, a lot of them are willing to follow y'all and Beulah. One of the men came by the wagon yard and told me that a few women went home from the meeting and told their husbands what's coming next Sunday. Looks like the first shot has been fired for the upcoming war."

"Afternoon," Beulah said from behind the counter. "What can I do for all y'all?"

"We need a pie," Lily said. "I can actually feel the tension in the air."

"I need a couple of pounds of sugar-cured ham," Elijah answered. "There is a strange feeling in town. Like the whole place is sitting on a powder keg and somebody lit the fuse. Y'all ladies have plumb stirred up a hornet's nest."

"I agree, and somebody might get stung, but it's got to be done," Beulah said with a nod. "I feel it, too, but back to business. I've got the ham, but Hattie bought my last four pies on her way back to the café. You could probably buy a slice down at her place if they haven't all been sold already."

Lily was suddenly starving, even though she had eaten two bowls of potato soup for lunch. "Got any cookies or muffins?" she asked.

"Got plenty of those," Beulah answered and headed toward the back of the store. "I'll get that ham wrapped up for you, Elijah. Why are you buying so much?"

"Got a hankering for it." He laid a loaf of bread and several tomatoes on the counter. "I figure I'll have it for breakfast, dinner, and supper until it runs completely out. Then I'll be tired of it and get me some beef."

"I'm a habitual eater, too," Beulah said as she wrapped up the ham. "Want some butter while you are here? One of the ladies in town brought in half a dozen pounds of sweet butter last week to trade for flour and sugar. I've kept it in the icebox, so it's still fresh tasting."

"Matt brought me a couple of pounds, so I'm good there. Got mine in the icebox, too," Elijah answered. "Whoever invented them things was a very smart man, but I wish the deliveryman would come more often than once every two weeks."

For a moment Lily wondered about the butter. The Maguires were sheep herders, not cattlemen, weren't they? But then she remembered hearing that they were almost self-sufficient out there on their ranch. That must mean they kept a few heads of cattle for milk and beef.

Beulah nodded. "At least in the winter, we can freeze it ourselves by setting a panful out in the backyard each evening."

Elijah stood by and raised his voice. "I don't even bother with that. I just clean off a shelf in the storage barn and keep everything in there. I tried freezing in pans, but I got tired of dealing with the bugs that got in it."

"Smart idea," Beulah agreed, "if you've got a place like that that stays cold. Want me to put this on your bill?"

"Yep, and I'll be in the first of next month to settle up like I always do," he said with a nod. "I reckon you and these two newcomers are going to take a lot of the blame for all this hoorah that's going on in town already. Preacher Tobias is furious, and I heard that Joshua Jones got wind of what went on, too. He says that he will refuse to preach if that happens in his church, but I reckon that would be a blessing." He laughed so hard that tears rolled down his round cheeks.

Daisy giggled, and Lily laughed out loud. Soon they were all guffawing along with Elijah.

"How did they find out so quick?" Beulah asked, just as lightning flashed outside and thunder rolled in the distance.

"News travels fast in this town, no matter if it's bad or good. I've never seen so many storms around here at this time of year, both the kind that come out of the sky and the ones that fly out of homes," Elijah said. "Most usually in July, you ain't able to beg, borrow, or steal a breeze until fall comes around. But now you womenfolk have stirred up a pure old gale that is going to put the War Between the States to shame. Why, I wouldn't be surprised to find out that the end days are just around the corner."

Beulah sat down in her chair behind the counter. "Seems more like the good Lord is sending a message to all the men in town, trying to tell them that the storm that's coming will bring big changes. And the only end they're going to see is the one that makes them treat women more fairly."

Elijah picked up his purchase and took a step toward the door. "I'm glad I ain't got a woman, and that my kinfolks out on the sheep ranch ain't got the problems that these town men have got"—he lowered his voice to a whisper—"y'all need to know if the going gets tough, I'll do what I can for you ladies." He stepped back and let Edith enter the store before he went on outside.

"Thank you," Beulah said and waited until he was outside before she focused on Lily, Daisy, and Edith. "Y'all come on back here behind the counter and sit down a spell."

"Do you really think there will be a violent reaction?" Daisy asked as she rounded the end of the counter and took a seat.

"Honey, men have the notion that they are big, mean, and smart. They will fight back in some way if the women stand together in church," Beulah replied.

"You don't think the husbands and fiancés will abuse the ladies, do you?" Daisy asked with worry in her voice.

"They had better not!" Edith declared.

Lily could almost feel Jimmy's hands around her throat and his fists pounding into her thighs to force her to spread her legs. Her chest tightened, and her breath came out in short gasps.

Beulah touched her on the arm. "Are you all right? You went pale. Would a shot of whiskey help?"

Lily took a hankie from her purse and wiped the sweat from her face. "I didn't think things would progress this fast—but yes, it would help."

Beulah stood up and started across the room. "With or without iced tea?"

"Maybe just ice water, please," Lily muttered.

"I'll have a glass of cold water, too," Edith said. "After the empowering speeches we heard, I'm not a bit surprised that some of the women had enough courage to go home and tell their men what was coming, and I'm glad the news is spreading around town. That will give the women time to set their heels and the men a chance to realize that they mean what they say."

Daisy scooted over closer to Lily. "Would a cold cloth help?"

Lily shook her head. "I'll be fine. I'm just being a big baby. I guess standing up in front of those women and saying my piece brought back a flood of horrible memories."

"I dropped by the bank and told my husband. Rumors are already spreading over town like wildfire—but then, when a bunch of women get together, what can anyone expect?" Edith said.

"What did your husband say?" Daisy asked.

"He's not a bit happy, but after forty years, he knows not to cross me when my mind is made up. And Gertrude Abernathy was in the bank and told me that she is forming a group made up of women who aren't interested in what we're trying to do."

"I wasn't expecting backlash until tomorrow or maybe even later." Beulah handed a glass of cold water to Lily, but before she could even lower herself into the one empty chair, the door flew open and Sally Anne rushed inside.

"Aunt Edith, have you heard the news? I was at Hattie's when the doctor came in and told us that Preacher Jones is dead. He dropped with a heart attack right after our meeting. Is it wrong of me to be happy for Alma?" Sally Anne gasped.

Edith wrapped her arms around her niece. "No, it's not wrong."

"Well, how about that?" Beulah chuckled. "Sometimes I guess the good Lord answers prayers after all."

"Beulah!" Edith scolded. "It's ugly to speak ill of the dead."

"Then write *ugly* in big red letters on a sign and hang it around my neck. Alma and those little girls have suffered too much already. Maybe now they can have a decent life," she declared. "Sally Anne, can I get you something to drink?"

"Ice water would be wonderful. Thank you."

Lily held her glass against her forehead before she took a sip.

"Sally Anne, you drag up a chair," Beulah said. "You might as well sit a spell with the rest of us—and besides, those black clouds are most likely going to dump rain on us."

Lily wondered if she had somehow had a premonition that Alma's abusive husband was going to be struck down dead. Could it be why she'd gone pale and felt like the world shifted beneath her?

Edith settled in her chair, but Sally Anne was pacing the floor when Alma came through the door. Both little girls were with her, and she was weeping uncontrollably. Beulah jumped to her feet and handed her the glass she had been drinking from. She led her back to the chair and gave Abbie and Elsie each a lollipop.

"You girls go on to the kitchen and . . ."

"I'll go with them," Daisy offered.

"Thank you," Alma managed to get out before more sobs racked her body. Finally, she took a deep breath and dried her eyes. "I knew he would be angry when I got back home, but he was beyond that. He jerked his belt off and began whipping all three of us, yelling and screaming that he would teach me and the girls that women did not get out of their place. He said that he would see me dead rather than let me go back to another meeting. Then he just fell over on the floor in front of the stove. His eyes rolled back in his head, and I told the girls to go to their room and not come out. I ran out of the house and found the doctor in the saloon. He said that Joshua died from a heart attack. I think he died because of what I told y'all just before I left the meeting."

"About dreaming that you killed him?" Beulah asked.

Alma nodded. "Did I do this?"

"No, darlin'," Edith said. "You did not. If dreams come true, we would all be in trouble."

Lily nodded in agreement and wondered if her former fiancé was still alive. If so, she hoped that he was somewhere far away and married to a woman who gave him hell at every turn.

Chapter Nine

Daisy and Beulah flanked Alma at the cemetery, and Lily took care of the two little girls right behind them. Both were ready to catch Alma if she fainted or needed help. Several members of Joshua's church were there, the men standing stoically beside their wives, who wept silently into their handkerchiefs.

Alma's frame felt rigid by Daisy's side, and her gaze stayed locked on Tobias Adams, the preacher for the other church in Autrie, as he read Psalm 23 and then said a quick prayer. Flashes of the day that Daisy's husband had been buried went through her mind. The preacher had read the same Psalm then, and although she couldn't remember the words of the prayer that had been said, the somber tone was the same. She had shed a few tears, but they had been out of fear for the future, not for love of the past.

Several of Joshua's deacons lowered the wooden coffin into the ground, and the hollow sound of the first shovelful of dirt brought Daisy back to the present. She felt a movement to her side and turned to see that Alma was ushering her girls slowly out of the cemetery.

Daisy fell into step with Beulah and Lily, and followed all the way around the church to the small parsonage behind it. Alma sat down on the porch and told the girls they should change out of their good clothing and get ready to leave.

"I wish you would stay and work for me," Beulah said. "Folks say that you shouldn't make a hasty decision so soon after a loved one dies."

"I didn't love him," Alma said. "And I need a brand-new start away from this place. I could stay right here until the new preacher's family arrives next month, but I want to wash all the bad memories from the past years out of my mind and heart."

"You have to do what your heart tells you, I suppose," Beulah said with a long sigh.

"Yes," Alma answered. "I feel guilty that I don't feel guilty. Does that make sense? I robbed my girls of a father by going to that meeting. But Elijah came to my rescue the very day that Joshua died and offered me a job at the sheep farm. My girls can be free to run and play without fear and can go to school out there. This is a fresh start for them as well as for me."

Daisy had had the same feelings of guilt because after the first blush of being a wife was over, she'd figured out that she really didn't love—or even like—her husband. Her parents had said if she married a scalawag like him, she wasn't welcome in their home any longer. That had just made him more desirable—at least for a week or two. He gambled away most of what he made each week, and she had scrimped and scraped by on what she could grow in a garden most days. The main difference had been that she didn't have an Elijah to come to her rescue.

I came to your rescue. Miz Raven's words came to her mind.

I thank God for you every day, Daisy replied silently.

Beulah sat down beside Alma and draped an arm around her shoulders. "Did you really rob those girls from having a father, or did you save them from abuse?"

"To be honest, it was the latter," Alma admitted.

Beulah swiped a tear from her eye. "I'm being selfish because I already know that I will miss you horribly, but you are right about leaving. I know that you will have a chance at a better life, both for you and for the girls, out on the sheep ranch. The girls will make new friends with the folks out there, and they won't have to be fearful that they'll be punished for every little thing. If all those folks have good hearts like Elijah, Matt, and Claude, just think of it like—"

Alma butted in before Beulah could finish. "The Lord is my shepherd."

"Absolutely," Lily said.

Daisy's mind returned to the day that she'd walked into town with nothing but a pillowcase full of her personal clothing. Miz Raven had found her sitting outside the general store. She might not have been a shepherd, but she had been a saving grace when Daisy was about to ask the cattle-drive boss if she could join them as a cook.

"I'll miss you, Beulah," Alma said, "but you can always come out to the ranch, and we don't have to sneak letters anymore. I'll send one in by Matt when he comes for supplies, and you can send one back with him."

Beulah drew Alma closer to her for a tighter sideways hug. "I'll get the buggy out once a month and come out there, or else, if I'm feeling like a good fast ride, I'll get on one of my horses and come to see you. I want you to be happy."

Alma finally smiled. "Come on Saturday evening and stay over until Sunday. I'll be living in a small house that one of the hired hands vacated when he went west on a wagon train."

"What's your job?" Daisy asked.

"I'll be cooking breakfast and supper in the bunkhouse," Alma answered. "Elijah says that sometimes the ladies come out in the evenings, and oftentimes they pitch in and help. Cooking for fifty will be different than fixing for four, but I think I can figure it out—and the bunkhouse is only about a hundred yards from my new place."

Daisy was still thinking about her first impression of the brothel and Miz Raven when the rattle of wagons approaching cleared her mind.

"Sounds like your golden chariots are on the way, Alma," Daisy said. "This day is not about me, but I have been where you are, and . . ." She took a deep breath before she went on. "I had to bury a husband I thought I loved—*tried* to love—and then felt like you do when it comes to the guilt. I can tell you from experience that the feeling will fade quickly and happiness will replace it."

"Thank you," Alma said with a sad nod. "I hope you are right."

Abbie and Elsie ran out of the house with their rag dolls hugged closely to their chests. "Mama, are we really going to live in the country with lambs and go to a different school?"

"Yes, we are," Alma said. "And it's going to be a great adventure for all of us."

Abbie tucked her head down to her chest. "Do we have to dust the church and get a whuppin' if we miss a spot?"

Alma hugged both girls tightly. "No, my darlings. No one is ever going to whip you again."

"Is anyone going to hit you?" Elsie asked.

"No, sweetie. There will never be any more hitting," Alma promised. "We are going to be happy. I promise."

"Miz Alma." Claude tipped his hat as he hopped down from the buckboard of the first wagon. "I'm sorry for your loss, but I'm glad you are coming to the ranch. Ben has been cooking for us this past month, and what he puts on the table is edible but it leaves a lot to be desired."

Matt pulled the second wagon up beside the first one. "Mornin', ladies," he said and smiled at Lily. "I'm also glad Uncle Elijah found us a cook. Miz Alma, are you ready for us to load these wagons and get going?"

"Yes, I definitely am," Alma declared. "Everything is in the living room. Beulah and these ladies helped me pack. The stove is still in the kitchen. The deacons told me I couldn't take it."

"You don't need it anyway. The house you will be living in has a stove in both the kitchen and the living room. One for cooking, one for heat in the winter," Claude said.

"Thank you." She took two keys from her pocket and held them out toward Beulah. "Since you technically own this building and the parsonage, I want you to keep these and give them to the new preacher when he arrives. Until then, if you need to use the church for the women's meetings, feel free to do so. Or if you need a safe place for a woman who . . ." She paused. "Well, you know, then feel free to use the parsonage. I'm sorry I can't be here to help with things, but I'll be thinking of y'all."

Elsie stood beside Lily and looked up at her. "Someday I'm going to be as tall as you, and I'm going to wear a pretty white dress like you did at the hotel."

"When you get as tall as me, I will make you a pretty white dress."

"Promise?" Elsie's eyes widened.

"Yes, I will. Now, why don't you come over here and sit with me on this end of the porch so we won't be in the way of these good men while they load the wagon?"

"Where are me and Abbie going to ride?" she asked.

"I imagine they'll make a pallet for you in the back. You and your dolly there can take a nap on the way out to where the little lambs are waiting to see you," Lily answered. "If you sleep long enough, when you wake up, you'll be there."

Matt came out of the house with a crate on both shoulders. "You are really good with children."

"These girls need good in their lives," Lily answered.

"Amen to that," he said and shifted his load onto the first wagon.

When the house was empty, Abbie wrapped her arms around Daisy's waist and hugged her tightly. "I'm glad we are leaving," she whispered. "Maybe Mama won't cry so much."

"She's going to be so happy that she will forget all about being sad," Daisy told her.

The final moment had arrived. Claude picked up Abbie and set her down in the space right behind the buckboard, then did the same with Elsie. "Your baby dolls are probably tired, so why don't you sing them to sleep? I'll try to be quiet so I don't wake them."

"Dotty—that's my dolly—wants to see everything," Abbie told him and then waved at the parsonage. "Goodbye, house. Goodbye, church. We are leaving now."

Daisy noticed that she didn't tell her father goodbye. Then she remembered that when she'd met Miz Raven, she didn't even think of her dead husband, who had only been in the ground a few days.

"Miz Alma?" Claude asked.

"Just one more minute." Alma wrapped her arms around Beulah. "Thank you, my everything. No one will ever tell me what to do again, I promise."

"That's the girl I knew when we were growing up," Beulah said. "Now, get in the wagon and go before I start bawlin' like a newborn calf. I'm supposed to be stronger and meaner than a two-headed rattlesnake, not a whimpering little kitten."

"Don't you dare cry or I will. I am going to be happy. I can feel it in my bones," Alma declared.

"If you see a tear sneak out of the corner of my eye, then it's a happy tear. I'll look for a letter the next time Matt comes to town."

"He'll have a nice long one for you, and I'll expect you to let me know what's happening with the women's meetings," Alma said and then turned to Claude. "I'm ready."

Claude helped her up onto the buckboard.

For a split second, Daisy wished his hands were on her waist, and that she was going to the ranch.

"It's been good to see you again," Matt told Lily just before he took his place on the buckboard.

"Likewise," Lily said. "We still owe you a shirt, so next time you are in town, come by the shop so we can measure you." She had thought nothing could ever make her blush again, but the vision that popped in her head of her hands on his broad chest made her face burn. When his brown eyes locked with hers, the heat in her body jacked up several more degrees.

"I will look forward to it," he said in a deep drawl.

"I hope she gets a good reception," Lily said as all three women waved at the two wagons until they were nothing but dots out there in the distance.

"Alma deserves some good in her life after what she's been through." Lily brushed the dust from her skirt.

Beulah nodded and took a step back toward town. "We all do. Let's go back to my store and have a glass of something cold—maybe iced coffee today, with a little heavy cream and sugar. I've decided on the spur of this moment that we will have our meeting in the church until the new preacher arrives. I'll put the word out tomorrow. Maybe the menfolk won't be so against us when we are gathering in a place of worship."

"You own this building?" Lily fell into step with the two other women.

"How?" Daisy asked.

"It's just one of my many properties in town," Beulah answered. "Orville's daddy built the church and parsonage and leased it to a group who were dissatisfied with Tobias. Orville's parents raised him in that place, and my folks raised me in the other one."

"So you own one church and attend the other?" Daisy asked.

"That's right," Beulah answered. "It created quite a stir when we married and didn't go to the same place on Sunday, and might have even been when folks started thinking that I wasn't being a submissive wife. I never got the whole story, but evidently the church was in financial trouble a long time ago, so my father bought the property and now it's mine."

"That's quite a story," Daisy said.

"Yes, but the truth is stranger than fiction. Maybe God is showing us that He never intended for us to be used like a doormat."

Lily wasn't sure that God had anything to do with the way things had happened since Eve partook of that fruit, but she didn't say anything. She did, however, shorten her long stride to match theirs.

"I would love to change out of these dark clothes before we have our coffee. I'm sweating so bad that my undergarments are getting damp."

"Me, too, so let's stop by the shop before we go on down to Beulah's place," Daisy suggested.

"I'll wait until you get there to add the ice to the coffee," Beulah said. "That way it won't all melt before you arrive."

Lily tried not to think about all the moisture that had poured down her neck into the stiff collar of her black jacket. Instead, she visualized Alma's little girls running and giggling across green pastures full of sheep and baby lambs. Someday, if luck was with her, Alma might even find a new love out there in the country. She deserved to have a companion that would love her and treat her right.

All women do. Miz Raven's voice was clear.

Lily agreed with a slight nod, but no matter what Miz Raven said, she didn't believe that the day would ever come when she could honestly feel like she deserved a man like Matt Maguire.

A strange air seemed to fill the whole town of Autrie on Sunday morning, even though the sun was out. Just the way Lily remembered the moments right before a tornado dropped out of the sky.

"Do you feel kind of eerie, too?" she asked Daisy when they left the store and headed through town to the church.

"No music out of the saloon. Few people on the street. Even the day that Preacher Jones was buried did not create such a ghostly feeling," Daisy answered with a shiver. "I feel like we should be wearing black again instead of our white outfits."

"Me too," Lily replied.

Beulah came out of her store, locked the door behind her, and fell into step with them. "If the ladies can all muster up the courage, we fire the first shot in Autrie for women's rights this very morning."

"Do you feel something strange?" Lily asked.

"Yep, it's like when there's about to be a gunfight on the street. Everyone scampers to a safe place, and even the saloon is silent," Beulah answered. "But it all passes. One man usually lays bleeding on the street and the other is buying everyone a drink in the bar."

"Seems like the wind is afraid to make the leaves on the trees wiggle a little this morning," Daisy said.

"I don't think it's even this quiet before a gunfight at high noon," Lily added.

"To tell the God's honest truth, I've lived here my whole life, and I've never seen anything like this outside of a tornado," Beulah said. "Maybe this is the calm before the storm, and all hell is about to break loose."

Lily wondered if anyone had thought far enough ahead to form an idea about what the women would do if all their menfolk refused to even attend services that morning, and perhaps even demanded that their women didn't go, either. Would it turn out that the three of them—and maybe the preacher's wife—would be the only ones who showed up?

When they got closer and she could see that the yard was full of wagons, buggies, and horses, she realized that the building would be packed full. "Oh my!" she gasped. "Do you think they'll have room for three more?"

"If we have to, we'll sit down front on the altar," Beulah answered as they carefully wove their way through the horses and wagons. "Be careful where you step or we'll be scraping and cleaning our good shoes when we get home."

When they entered the church, the women were on one side and the men on the other, just like always. Daisy figured there would be celebrations that afternoon at the saloons. Men would be patting each other on the backs and buying drinks for one another because they had all put their women in their proper places.

She was still visualizing that when she, Daisy, and Beulah found enough room on the back pew to sit, but they were shoulder to shoulder. Beulah, bless her heart, glared at the backs of the women in front of her. Daisy patted her on the knee and whispered, "We won't give up."

"Damn right, we won't," she hissed.

"Good morning, everyone." The preacher, Tobias, took his place behind the big oak lectern. "We welcome all the newcomers and invite you to keep attending our place of worship until your new preacher arrives. This morning, I am going to speak to you from Colossians where it says that wives should submit unto their husbands. This does not mean that a man should be abusive to his wife, but that there should be mutual respect in a marriage."

Edith stood up, crossed the aisle, and sat down beside her husband, Jasper. Sally Anne, who had been sitting beside her, followed her example and wiggled into the space between the judge and his assistant, Benjamin. That created an exodus—one by one, the women began to move across the aisle. When there was no room left in the pews, they stood behind their husbands with their babies in their arms and other children lined up beside them. Gertrude remained on the other side of the sanctuary with six in her group. Their noses were held high, and an air of self-righteousness surrounded them.

Beulah stood up and went to the other side to stand behind the last pew. Daisy and Lily joined her without hesitation. Tobias ignored the bunch of them and kept right on talking about how God made man first and woman second to be a helper to the man. That's when all the men got to their feet and walked out of the building. Tobias glared at the women on the right side of the church. His jaw worked so hard that his beard seemed to dance, and his breath came in short bursts.

"What do we do now?" Lily whispered to Beulah. "He looks like he might drop dead with apoplexy."

"We stand right here to support the women," Beulah told her.

The noise of wagons leaving the yard was the only sound that was heard for several minutes. The ladies who had been standing sat down in the vacated seats.

"This is unacceptable in the eyes of the Lord," Tobias finally said. "I will not tolerate such insolence in my church."

His wife, Maggie, who had been sitting with Gertrude, got to her feet and moved to the other side. Gertrude and her four followers sat right where they were. The preacher closed his Bible, stared at his wife with angry eyes, and said, "Don't come home tonight. One of these women can take you in until you come to your senses."

"You can stay with me," Beulah called out.

When he reached the back of the church, his glare toward Beulah was so full of fire that she should have melted into nothing but a pile of ash right there at the back of the sanctuary. But she met his stare with her own, and for a full minute it looked like he might raise a hand to her. Then he walked out without even looking back, with Gertrude and her four minions waddling behind him like ducklings.

Edith got to her feet and walked up to the lectern. "If our sweet Maggie has to move out, then I'm going with her. I will go home and pack a bag. I'll sleep on the sidewalk before I back down, now that the line has been drawn."

"I've got permission to use the other church and parsonage," Beulah said, raising her voice. "And I own the property next to the church. My old home and barn are also available for anyone to use, to anyone who wants to join us. I will be closing the general store until the men come to their senses."

"What about food?" Sally Anne asked.

"We can use what I have, and I'll make arrangements with Elijah to bring us supplies. He's not against our cause," Beulah answered.

"Are we going to need to close our shop?" Daisy asked Lily.

She nodded and said loud enough for everyone to hear, "If Elijah will move my sewing machine into the church, we'll close up our place, too. Daisy and I have to work on Sally Anne's wedding dress."

Sally Anne held up a hand. "No, ma'am, you do not. If Wes can't accept this small thing, then there won't *be* a wedding."

Daisy could almost hear the men telling one another that if they gave the women an inch, they would take a mile. *Well, guess what?* she thought. *We just took a whole mile today.*

Chapter Ten

Lily carried two stuffed pillowcases and a satchel from her bedroom into their shop, where Daisy was already waiting. Her thoughts ran in circles, from worrying that some of the women who had offered to join the campaign might just be doing so to fit in, to wondering whether only a handful would show up that evening. Maybe others would trickle in one by one but then go back to their husbands after a couple of days.

She felt as if she were missing something important, so she mentally checked off what she had packed in the pillowcases. Were other women doing the same thing? Were they nervous about leaving homes that they might not go back to for weeks, or maybe even all summer? She was ready to make that commitment, and would try to encourage others, but she wasn't a wife who possibly loved her husband. Nor was she a mother who might not see her children for a while.

"Are we really doing this? How many do you think might join us?" Daisy asked.

"We are, and I have no idea if we'll have half a dozen or a hundred," Lily answered. "This is a much larger step than I ever thought we'd be doing in less than two weeks."

"I wonder what it will be called in fifty years," Daisy said. "When a couple of generations of women have passed, what will history refer to these days as?"

"We already are called 'suffragists,' but this battle will definitely have a name before it's all said and done." Lily dropped her pillowcases on the floor. "I knew I had forgotten something. I need to tuck in my writing tablet and a pencil."

"I put extra in my things. I'll share." Daisy took a few steps toward the door, then stopped. "You're not going to believe this."

Lily's heart stopped. Had Gertrude and her protestors already arrived to block their way? If things got violent, would two little pistols keep her and Daisy safe?

"Holy hell!" she gasped.

She was afraid to blink for fear that she was just imagining what was before her. Finally, she rubbed her eyes with her fists and then looked out the window again. The scene had not changed.

Daisy took a deep breath and let it out in a whoosh. "I don't think hell is holy, but I agree with you. I never expected such an outpouring. Beulah said we had given the women courage when we waltzed into the saloon and bought a bottle of whiskey and stood up for ourselves. To tell the truth, I felt kind of sorry for Frannie after that. If Miz Raven hadn't found me in Spanish Fort that day, I could have been just like her."

"If Joshua Jones was out there yelling at the women, it might really be holy hell," Lily whispered, still unable to believe that so many women were joining them. There had to be a hundred out there—maybe even more—and lots of children skipping along beside their mothers.

"Pinch me. I'm dreaming," Daisy said.

Lily blinked a few more times, but still nothing changed. Edith and Sally Anne led the parade of women down the street. All of them were looking straight ahead with their heads held high. Babies were in carriages. Smaller children seemed to think they were going on a trip. The ones who had no children helped others by carrying their satchels or pillowcases.

"It's time to lock the door and support the cause," Daisy said.

"I wish Miz Raven could see this."

Daisy opened the door and stepped outside. "She would be so proud."

"Hello!" Beulah called from the buckboard of a wagon. "Y'all throw your things in the back and crawl on up here with me. I've got room, and you might as well ride as walk."

"Why . . . ? What . . . ?" Lily stared at the wagon loaded high with supplies.

"I'm puttin' my money where my mouth is," Beulah declared. "These woman and children have to be fed—and besides, all that meat in my store will go bad if we don't get it used up. Now, hitch up them skirts and get on up here. We'll . . ." She stopped and pointed.

The women from the saloon had lined up behind the other women, bringing up the rear of the parade. Some of them marched with their heads held high. Others looked more than a little sheepish. Lily understood both. Every time she had gone into Spanish Fort after she'd started working at the brothel, she felt inferior to the women on the street, but she bluffed her way through the experience.

Beulah finally found her voice and yelled, "Welcome! No woman will be turned away."

Several of those women, who had been staring at the street, seemed to take courage in Beulah's words and lifted their heads. Daisy hiked her skirt and hopped up onto the buckboard, and Lily followed right behind her. Lily remembered the last time she'd ridden in a wagon, and the emotions that had rushed through her body when Matt put his hands on her waist. Even through several layers of clothing, she had felt a rush of heat.

"You are flushed," Beulah said. "You aren't having second thoughts, are you?"

"No, ma'am, I am not!" Lily declared, and almost blurted out that she could have been in the same shoes they were wearing a few years before.

"Are you mad because I'm not turning the women from the saloons away?" Beulah asked, as if hearing Lily's thoughts. "They have the right to fight for better circumstances, just like we do."

"Of course they do," Daisy said. "I can be aggravated at Frannie, but it's not because of her job. It's more that she made me mad in the saloon."

"And even then," Lily said, "it was more that you were letting off steam because you were mad at . . ." She stopped before she said too much.

"At that damned judge," Daisy went on, "because he wouldn't sell us the store."

"He is probably the most pompous man in the entire male population in Autrie," Beulah said.

"To get back to this wagonload of food . . ." Lily waved a hand toward all the women. "I didn't even think about feeding this crowd—but then, I had no idea there would be so many. Do you think there's any left who aren't brave enough to join us?"

Beulah snapped the reins, and the horses began to move. "From the looks of this parade, I'd say only a handful stayed behind to support Gertrude and her merry little band of followers."

"Where did you get this rig?" Daisy asked.

"The wagon and the horses are mine," she answered. "Elijah takes care of them for me. Sometimes I still like to go saddle up one of them and ride out into the country. I've even gone all the way to the sheep farm when they're having a celebration like sheep-shearing week. And I do not ride sidesaddle."

"You are a brave woman," Lily said. "Are we going to keep the horses and wagon at the church?"

"I'll put the horses in the corral behind the barn and stake them out through the day to eat whatever green grass is in the pasture. I'd thought I would keep the wagon in the barn, but from the looks of this group, we're going to need all the space we can rustle up for sleeping quarters. My rig will be fine in the churchyard," she answered.

"How do we decide who sleeps where?" Lily asked.

"I have no idea, but we're women on a mission," Beulah said. "It won't be hard to work all that out when we get there."

Long before Beulah parked the wagon, the buzz of conversation inside the building filtered all the way out into the yard. Lily slid off the buckboard and then helped both the other women down. "From the sound that's coming from inside the building, it looks like we've got a full congregation."

Beulah parked the wagon and headed for the door. "Yep, women all over Texas are tired of being treated like property. I'm hoping that the news travels far and wide, and that we're setting a precedent for others to follow. Today is the first time I've been in this place. My folks never did like the loud preaching—but hey, after Tobias said what he did to Maggie, I'm not sure his heart is right, either."

Even though Lily was anxious to get inside the building, she walked slowly so that Daisy and Beulah could keep up with her. "This is going to sound silly, but I just thought of something. You've brought food enough to feed these women for a few days, but what about plates and spoons?"

"All in the wagon," Beulah answered. "Elijah helped me load up everything he thought we might need from the wagon yard right after we all left the church, and then he helped me with all the food and supplies I'm donating from my store. I wouldn't have been ready to join the parade if I'd have had to do all this myself. And he'll be bringing us whatever else we might need a couple of times a week. I don't care if we completely wipe out my stock—I want this to accomplish something good."

Daisy swung the door open. "That's amazing."

Beulah shaded her eyes with her hand and looked up at the sky. "No clouds in sight."

"What's that got to do with anything?" Lily asked.

"I don't want to get struck by lightning for instigating all this," Beulah chuckled and stepped inside the sanctuary.

Lily followed her down the aisle and up to the front pew, where Edith and Sally Anne were sitting. Fussy babies and children who didn't want to be in church for the second time on a Sunday filled the rows, and some of the single ladies and pregnant women were lined up against the back.

Lily figured that Joshua Jones was flipping back and forth in his grave so fast that he was too dizzy to even preach his way into heaven. After all, the women's group that had put him into a fatal stew were all in his church and were planning to strike a blow for the very rights he was so against.

Edith whispered something to Sally Anne, and she stood up, walked down the center aisle, and closed the door. Edith got to her feet and made her way forward, past the altar to the lectern. "If I could have your attention, please, just for a few minutes so that we can get organized. We have this church, two houses, and a barn to stay in. I'm not sure how to divide the sleeping space. Does anyone have a suggestion?"

"Before you go any further, I will not stay here if those women from the saloon are welcome," one woman with a small baby in her arms said.

"Anyone else feel the same way?" Edith asked.

A few hands went up.

Lily stood up, walked to the front, and turned around to face the packed church. "Frannie, I'm calling on you because I know your name. Why are you here?"

Frannie got to her feet and said, "We brought decent-women clothes with us, but we didn't have time to change into them before we decided to join. We are here for the same reason all y'all are. We know you look down on us for what we do, but we want better rights, too. The saloon owner only gives us ten percent of what we make; we get slapped around if we don't entertain enough men in an evening; and if we're sick, we have to work anyway or else we get knocked around again."

"So other than what you do to support yourselves, you are no different than the rest of us?" Daisy asked.

One woman jumped to her feet. "Don't you dare say something like that! We are moral women who—"

"Who are being judgmental," Lily butted in. "Do they judge *you* for not pleasing your husbands in bed? They are just doing their jobs. Maybe you can all learn something from them about keeping your men home at night instead of seeking pleasure outside your homes."

"Whose side are you on?" the first woman asked with defiance in her tone.

"The side that gets us all more rights," Lily answered. "If we're going to throw stones at each other, then we've lost the battle already."

Daisy stood and turned to face the whole group. "Either we all stand together, or we go home and fail. Once we do that, there will be no more meetings. When we lose the war, we can only go home to lick our wounds and put up with lack of power."

Lily nodded. "*Now* how many of you want to throw these women out of the church?"

Not a single hand went up.

"Okay, now that's settled. Tomorrow Frannie and her friends will look more like the rest of us, and they will work right beside us," Lily said.

"Thank you, Lily," Edith said. "On to the next question about organizing our group. We hadn't expected so many of you, but we can't even begin to express how much your support means to us."

Lily started to sit down, but she changed her mind and turned to face the group again. "To argue about who stays in which place would be against what we are united to do. Rather than dealing out portions of food each day for us to cook individually, I vote that we cook big pots of food and have community meals. All in favor, raise your hand," Lily said.

All hands shot up in the air.

"Thank you," Lily said with a smile. "Now, with that in mind, I vote that, unless more join us and we need the space, we keep the church free as a central place to eat and have our community meetings. It would create confusion to have to take up bedding every morning and put it down at night after supper. All in favor—"

She didn't even finish the sentence before everyone raised their hands.

"Thank you," she said again, then sat down.

"The barn does not have a stove," Beulah said. "The other three places do, so they should serve as cooking areas. Whichever group is willing to make breakfast could perhaps stay in the parsonage. Those who are able and willing to take care of the noon meal could live in my old house. And the ones that want to make supper will stay in the church—that good stove right here has been used in the winter to heat this place. That should narrow down the list considerably.

"I'll take my old house as well for breakfast," Beulah added. "I know the stove in there, and there's still an icebox where I can store as much meat as possible. I'll get Elijah to bring us a block whenever the iceman comes around."

"Sally Anne and I will supervise the parsonage," Edith said. "We would love to have any of y'all who are engaged or newly married join us. I've been teaching Sally Anne some of my cooking tricks, and I'll be glad to pass them on to all y'all."

Maggie raised her hand. "I'll take the church and serve supper right here."

"Does anyone else have anything to add?" Edith asked.

Beulah stood up. "There's plenty of straw in the barn for those willing to stay out there. Throw a quilt over a pile and it makes a good bed."

Frannie spoke up. "We'll be glad to take the barn, and to pitch in and help with anything y'all need. I'm a fair cook, so I can rotate between all three places—and thank you for letting us stay."

"Daisy and I will also take the barn," Lily offered. "And like Frannie, we can pitch in wherever you need us. We can also offer shooting lessons to anyone that wants to learn to load and shoot a pistol. We both brought two guns and ammunition, but if any of the rest of you have any, we would appreciate the use of them."

"I can offer to help any of you learn to ride astride a horse. I have two horses but no sidesaddles—but then, why are we using those things anyway? If we're liberated, we can use a man's saddle just as well as he does," Beulah said. "Since we might be here a while, we can make it a learning experience. We'll get those things organized soon—and remember, we are here to . . . What was that word again, Lily?"

"*Empower,*" she answered. "We are here to empower each other with confidence, not tear each other down with gossip and arguing."

The clapping was so loud that Lily wondered if the folks half a mile away heard it. Finally, Beulah held up a palm to quiet the bunch.

"There are two wells for our water," she said. "One is at the back of my old house. The other is behind the parsonage. There's four outside toilets: one behind each of the houses and two—one for the men and one for the women—a few yards at the back of the church. I don't imagine any of us will go to hell if we use the one meant for the guys. Two-holers are all alike once the door is opened."

Someone giggled, and then another, and soon the whole church was rocking with laughter almost as loud as the previous ovation. Lily figured it was because they were all a little nervous about leaving their husbands high and dry, but it was still good to hear that sound.

"Now that we have settled all that," Edith said, "Edith, Beulah, and Maggie will take in as many as are willing to help with meals as they can, so come on up. Thank you for listening to me and for being so agreeable. And a particular thank-you to the saloon ladies for joining us. That alone should help our menfolk to see that they've been left in more ways than just having a clean house and laundry and fresh meals on the table."

A woman with black hair in a single braid down her back raised a fist in the air. "I vote that our motto should simply be the word *together.*"

Another woman yelled the word, and soon the whole group was chanting, "Together, together, together . . ."

Edith allowed it to go on for a full minute before she pounded on the lectern to get their attention again. When quiet had been restored, she said, "Let's all keep the motto in mind every day that we are here. This is day one. We should get mentally prepared for many days—maybe even weeks—so keep up your enthusiasm. But for now, let's get ourselves settled into our sleeping quarters. Then whoever is on supper duty can report here to Maggie. This meeting is finished. The next one will be after supper tomorrow, and each evening after that. We'll already be here to eat, so that seems like a good time. Any questions or comments?"

"Just one more thing." Lily stood to her feet. "When we've all found out where our new sleeping place is, Beulah will need some help unloading the wagon and putting things where they belong. If I don't see some of you again, good night, and thanks for being here."

"That seems like a prayer in and of itself, so I'll just say *amen*!" Maggie said.

Chapter Eleven

When a semi-cool breeze swept through on Monday night, Daisy sighed right along with the two dozen other women stretched out on pallets in the barn. She closed her eyes and pretended that she was sitting out on the balcony at the Paradise in nothing but her thin nightgown. The night sounds hadn't changed from several hundred miles north of Autrie in Spanish Fort. Coyotes still howled in the distance. Locusts and crickets vied for attention, with an occasional tree frog or cat adding their song to the mix.

"What are you all thinking about?" Lily asked from a few feet away.

"The fact that I'd kind of gotten used to hearing piano music half the night. Now we just get the sounds of nature, like we had in the place that we were last summer at this time," Daisy answered, choosing her words carefully.

"I was married and living with my husband and son," Frannie said.

"What happened?" Daisy asked.

"He went to town like he always did on Saturday night—probably to spend what money he had earned from working that week on the railroad on whiskey and women," Frannie told her. "He ran the wagon off a cliff on the way home and died. We barely had him buried when my son took a fever and passed away a week later."

"I'm so sorry," Lily said.

"Last summer I was working in the same saloon I am now," Molly said. "More than anything, I want to get out of the business, but I have no place to go or money to get there. I've tried to save money, but . . ." She paused a moment before she went on. "Frannie was being honest when she told all y'all that the rotten saloon owner takes all but ten percent of what we earn. He says we owe him the rest for our room and board."

"And since he never tells us for sure what the men pay him for our favors, we don't know that he's not taking more than that," Frannie added. "We ain't wantin' y'all's sympathy. We just want a better life like y'all do."

"No wonder you joined us," Lily said. "When we draw up our letter for negotiations, what are you asking for?"

"A fifty-fifty split," Frannie answered. "And no more slapping us around if we don't bring in enough every night. What about all you *proper* ladies?"

A voice came from the other side of the barn. "To sit with our husbands at church, to be respected, and for them to not visit y'all. And if we're all going to be equal, you can't be prejudiced, either, by calling us 'proper ladies.'"

"That's fair enough," Molly agreed.

"If you want your husbands to stay home," Frannie said, "you best learn how to please a man. What I hear from most men is that they want more from their wives than for them to just do their duty."

"Will you teach us what you know?" another woman asked.

"Yes, we will," Frannie answered. "We'll have a class on that very thing—but first, I understand that we are going to learn to shoot the eyes out of a rattlesnake, which I can already do. But I can't ride a horse using a regular saddle, so I'd like to learn that."

"Until we are all totally independent, we'll always be the weaker sex, even in the jobs that we have in the saloon," Molly added.

"Ain't that the truth," a thin, high-pitched voice said from the far corner.

Daisy remembered Miz Raven teaching her seven girls all those things and how to be a lady at the same time. When the day arrived for them all to leave, they wore pants, sat in a saddle as well as any cowboy, and had pistols strapped on their hips. When they reached the town where their trunks had been shipped, they sold the horses and gear and had shown up as ladies when they boarded the southbound train.

Tomorrow, she and Lily would be passing along the shooting skill they had been taught. Before they finished, every woman in the group would know how to load and handle one of the pistols that had been gathered up from the group that evening after supper.

"Worried about tomorrow?" Lily whispered.

"Not really," Daisy answered. "We had a good teacher—and besides, only about half of the women don't know how to shoot. The rest are already trained."

Lily was only mildly surprised when at least three dozen—Sally Anne included—showed up the next morning after breakfast for shooting lessons. Women had been left alone for months and years during the war, and they had had to defend their families against varmints, both the four- and two-legged kinds. The smart ones had passed that skill down to their daughters, along with how to mount a horse with a leg on each side. However, from the size of the group, not all wives, mothers, and sisters had been so wise, just like she and Daisy had experienced.

"When their men came home, they stayed true to the old traditions and stepped back into the roles they had been given before the war," Lily said in a low voice.

"What was that?" Daisy asked.

"Just talking to myself," Lily answered, then turned to face the women. All sizes, all ages, and all builds. "Okay, ladies, it's really quite simple. We'll take six at a time because that's how many guns we could rustle up. Who wants to go first?"

Sally Anne stepped up to the makeshift table and picked up a pistol. "It's heavier than I thought it would be. I've only practiced with a one-shot derringer. Now what do I do?"

So, the princess of Autrie has at least held a gun in her hands, Lily thought.

"A six-gun is a little different than the small one you carry, Sally Anne. I'll demonstrate how to break the barrel to the side, put the bullets in, and snap it back into place." She showed them each step as she talked. "Now you are ready to aim and fire. You don't have to do a quick draw. Most men will instinctively back up if a woman has a gun in her hands. Hold it like this"—she used both hands—"and then use the sight to get a bead on one of the targets we've set up on stakes. Have you ever even shot that little gun you have?"

"A few times, but not often. Daddy always hired a bodyguard for me when we traveled. He didn't even know I had the little gun," she answered.

Frannie picked up a gun, expertly loaded it, and asked, "Can I picture the target as the saloon owner?"

"Yes, you can." Daisy focused on the rest of the women. "Have all of y'all really never shot a gun?"

"I didn't say that I hadn't shot a gun before, but it's been a long time, and I need to practice. Otis, the saloon owner, wouldn't dare let me get near one." Frannie smiled with a wink.

"We are supposed to be simpering little women who run at the sight of a mouse," Sally Anne said as she loaded the gun, took aim, and fired. "Whoa! That's got some kick to it. I missed the target, but I'll be ready next time. This is fun. Even if—or maybe I should say *when*—we go back to our homes, can we have a day every now and then to practice?"

"Of course! We could do that after a women's meeting," Daisy answered.

When several more blasts went off at the same time, one of the women dropped her pistol on the table and covered both ears with her hands.

Frannie picked up the gun and handed it back to her. "Get over that fear of noise, and don't ever drop your gun in a fight or you'll be the one who is dead. Also, if you run out of ammunition, then just use the pistol or rifle like a weapon and beat whoever is coming at you with it. But for now, take aim like this and fire."

"You'll get the hang of it, Amanda," Sally Anne said.

Amanda held the weapon with both hands and hit the center of the target on her first try. "I bet all that noise makes all the menfolk in town wonder what in the hell we're doing out here."

"Looks like you are a natural," Lily said. "Maybe they'll even figure out that we mean business."

"It will take a lot longer than just two days." Amanda laid the gun down after she had shot one last time. "They haven't had time to get tired of burned suppers and a messy house. Which reminds me, I need to draw up some water and do a washing when we finish here."

"Not today, unless you're going to hang it in the barn loft to dry." Frannie pointed to the southwest. "I'd say we're going to get a storm in about an hour, so you had better all learn a little more about shooting before it hits."

"Storms in July," Daisy said. "Seems like an omen. I hope it's not a sign of bad luck."

Frannie just shrugged and laid down the pistol she had been using. "I won't waste more bullets. I just wanted to be sure I still had it."

"Evidently you do," Daisy growled.

Frannie stepped forward until she was practically nose to nose with Daisy. "I can probably outshoot and outfight you, but this isn't the place to test that, is it? What was that big speech that y'all all pitched in to deliver? *Empowering*—whatever the hell that means—and together? Were you just preaching at the proper women or all of us?"

"No, it is not the time, and we can keep our personal feelings aside for a later date, but you can be sure that we are trying to better *all* women's lives, no matter what path they come from," Daisy shot back in a hateful tone.

"What's the matter with you?" Lily whispered, thinking about where she and Daisy had come from.

"I don't like that woman," Daisy said out the corner of her mouth.

"Don't let her know that, or she has power over you," Lily continued, keeping her voice low enough for just Daisy to hear.

"That sounded like Miz Raven."

"I meant for it to," Lily told her.

Sally Anne emptied the three remaining bullets from her gun and laid it on the table. "Ladies, I'm going to head to the parsonage before the storm hits. Aunt Edith and I are making cookies this morning for an afternoon snack. The children play so hard that they are hungry between dinner and supper."

"So am I," Frannie said. "I saw lightning streaking through the sky, and I don't test the powers that be by standing out here under these trees."

"Talk about the lamb laying down with the lion," Daisy said as she and Lily watched the saloon worker and the princess of Autrie walking together. "I wonder what Sally Anne would have to say if she knew that Frannie was probably taking her fiancé upstairs at the saloon for a little romp in the sheets?"

"Maybe Frannie will give her some lessons that will help her keep the judge so happy he won't ever want to go back to the saloon again," Lily said.

"I don't think she needs them."

"What makes you say that?" Lily asked.

"There's something not so innocent in her eyes," Daisy answered. "You remember how a man's eyes looked like a scared bunny rabbit the first time he came to the Paradise and cheated on his wife?"

Lily nodded.

"Now, think about those who were pretty regular and the expression they had."

Lily clamped a hand over her mouth for a moment. "You are so right," she said. "I always kind of felt sorry for those who were cheating on their wives."

"I did not," Daisy declared. "And I will wager that the judge is *not* getting a blushing bride."

"If what you are saying is right, then . . ."

"Then he gets a socialite in the day and a Frannie at night," Daisy said through gritted teeth. "He wins."

Lily gave her a quick hug and slipped several of the guns and ammunition into a pillowcase. "There's a lot of time between now and September."

"Like I said before," Daisy said, "all women need lessons in how to please a man before they get married—not only that, but she might even have to teach him how to please her. Then it wouldn't just be their duty, but an enjoyment for both the husband and wife. If we weren't living on the straight-and-narrow pathway, we might be able to teach those lessons."

"One more shot to see if I've still *got it*." Lily loaded the final pistol and fired once at each target. She imagined that the black spot in the center was her ex-fiancé's eye, and hit dead center every single time.

Chapter Twelve

Daisy tiptoed across the barn floor and went outside to get a breath of fresh morning air, watch the sun rise, and listen to the birds singing. Early morning—before the day began with all its troubles or worries—was her favorite time of the day.

"What are you doing out here?" Frannie asked from the shadows.

"I might ask you the same thing," Daisy answered.

"I like this time of day. You know that I really don't like you, right?"

"The feeling is mutual," Daisy said. "Do you have a reason?"

"Do you?" Frannie snapped.

Daisy nodded. "You have a nasty attitude."

"Well, you think you are better than me, and you have a hot temper, too," Frannie said.

"And you don't?" Daisy chuckled.

"Do you know why I like some quiet time in the morning?" Frannie's voice cracked, but she went on. "It's when I can spend a little time thinking about my son. It's when I'm not dressed like a . . . a . . . ," she stammered. "Whatever you ladies call us. 'Soiled doves.' 'Prostitutes.' 'Shady ladies.' Take your pick. It's when I can put on a calico day dress and pretend that it's time to wake him up to go to school. You are not a mother, so you wouldn't understand."

"My grandmother used to say, 'Once a mother, always a mother.'" Daisy swallowed hard but the lump in her throat seemed to be stuck.

"So did mine," Frannie said. "She was so right about that."

"Think we'll ever be as smart as those who endured the war as grown women?" Daisy asked.

"You think that smartness just fell out of the sky and landed on them? No, it did not! They had to cut their own path, just like we're doing. They taught us that women are tough and we can do whatever men can do—and even better, because women had to do it and still be ladies. Hopefully, we will make it so much better for those coming behind us that none of them ever have to work in saloons or brothels because that's the only place left for them." Frannie's voice cracked again, but she seemed to get past it quickly. "I'm going to go help get things ready for breakfast. Don't think this talk means I like you."

"Like I said, the feeling is mutual—but maybe you should be standing up after supper some night and saying all that to everyone else," Daisy told her. "See you here tomorrow morning." A mixture of both sympathy and guilt washed over her. She could have so easily been in the same place as Frannie had it not been for a stroke of pure luck.

"Probably. But you don't have to talk to me. I'd rather you didn't. I get up early to enjoy the quiet," Frannie said before she disappeared into the barn.

"Me too," Daisy muttered, and watched two young squirrels come out of a nest high up in a tree. The rising sun lit them up as they chased each other around the limbs. She smiled at their antics and thought of Alma's little girls, who were probably helping their mama fix breakfast in the bunkhouse.

"Rising sun," she whispered. "We're all like this right now."

"We're like what?" Lily asked.

Daisy was so wrapped up in her own thoughts that the sound of Lily's voice startled her. "You shouldn't sneak up on a person like that."

"Good morning to you, too," Lily snapped.

Daisy looked down at the two buckets in Lily's hands. "Sorry for my tone. Looks like you are off to get some water?"

"Yep, after I visit the outhouse," Lily answered, then asked again, "We are like what?"

"The rising sun," Daisy answered.

Lily set the empty buckets on the ground. "How do you figure that?"

"I don't know if I can explain it. But think about how Alma's little girls are just finding out that they don't have to be scared of every move they make for fear of punishment. As a group of women, we are pretty much the same. Alone, we aren't strong enough to make a stand, but we're finding out that with the right circumstances, we can cut a path—not only for ourselves, but for those coming behind us. Abbie and Elsie, and all of us, are like the rising sun. I'm not explaining it very well, but that's what I felt this morning."

"That's deep thinking, almost like one of those parables in the Bible." Lily picked up the buckets, took a few steps, and looked back over her shoulder. "I like it, though. No matter what place we are in, we are merely waiting on the light to shine to show us the path."

"Exactly," Daisy said and went back into the barn.

After breakfast Lily carried the pistols and the ammunition down to the shooting targets and laid them out on the table for another lesson. Daisy had stayed behind to give a self-defense class. Lily was so wound up in her thoughts about what Daisy had said that morning about the rising sun that she didn't even notice the little girl sneaking along behind her.

She tried to figure out why she was jittery and jumped from one idea to another without figuring out anything. All alone in the wooded area a hundred yards from the church, she sniffed the air and got a whiff of something that smelled like a bushel of cucumbers.

"I bet there's some wild ones growing down in the rocky bottom of that old, dried-up creek that Beulah told us about, or else the birds spread the seeds from the last garden that Beulah made up at her old place and they've produced. I might go hunt them down and pick some for supper after the shooting lesson this morning." She shaded her eyes with her hand and looked up at the sun, now a nice big ball right over the tops of the trees. "The sun is still heating up the day. Daisy is right: the sun only goes up a little each hour. Kind of like us women as we take steps toward the end result of being equal with men. I wonder how far we are today?"

She'd barely gotten the words out when she heard a gasp right behind her. She turned and saw a little girl with long, blond braids hanging down her back. The child opened her mouth to scream, but nothing came out. She pointed in the direction of Lily's feet and shivered all over as if she were having a high-fever seizure.

Lily followed the little girl's finger all the way to the ground . . . right to the biggest rattlesnake she had ever seen. Apparently, the tail of her skirt had gotten caught in the rough wood of the table leg and had been held back as she walked. And worse yet, her naked ankle was now only inches from the snake's slithering tongue, darting in and out of a mouth that looked like a deep black hole from Lily's viewpoint.

She was afraid to blink for fear that even that motion would cause the snake to strike. If that happened, would the little girl come out of shock enough to go for help, or would this be Lily's last day on earth? Wasn't her entire life supposed to flash before her eyes? Maybe after all the men who had passed through her doors, whoever was keeping track of Abigail Carolina Boyle's heavenly record had given up on her years ago.

The snake began to shake his tail, sending off its warning rattling sound. The feeling of fight or flight rushed over Lily, but she really had no choice. She couldn't go two steps without being bitten. A bunch of doves flew up into the sky when something spooked them in the tall grass not far from the table, but Lily didn't have wings and God wasn't going to miraculously give her a pair—not with her background.

Using as few motions as she could, she eased her hands to the table, picked up a pistol, and carefully loaded it. Then she very gently turned back around, aimed, fired, and prayed that she didn't shoot herself in the foot. She didn't realize she was holding her breath until her chest began to ache. After a moment, she got the courage to look down to see that the varmint's head had been blasted away, but the long body was still wiggling and trying to slither away.

The child gasped again, and Lily's gaze left the snake and focused on the little girl. Her big blue eyes were wide and full of fear, and her little chin quivered. She raised a hand and pointed not three feet behind Lily and whispered, "More."

Lily had five bullets left and there were four more huge snakes gliding along the ground, coming toward her. She took a few steps forward, grabbed the little girl around the waist, and set her on the table. "Cover your ears," she said, then aimed and fired at the nearest one.

Where were they all coming from? And what if one made it through the line and got up on the table with the kid? She remembered her father talking about a nest of the vile critters that had holed up under a neighbor's barn. He had said that the whole place smelled like cucumbers. She sniffed the air and the scent got stronger with each breath she took.

Stop thinking and fire! Miz Raven yelled loudly in her head.

She popped off four more rounds, hit a snake every time, and then turned to the little girl, who had her hands over her ears and her eyes closed.

"It's all right. They're all dead." She motioned with a sweep of her hand to take in the snakes.

"No they ain't," she sobbed.

Lily looked back to where the dead snakes were having trouble giving up the ghost and saw the grass waving back and forth—but there was no wind, not even a breeze. She checked the path back toward the church and barn. Nothing was making waves in that area.

"Run! Run as fast as you can toward the barn and find your mama!" she yelled at the child.

The little girl shook her head and appeared to be frozen to the table.

"Did your mama ever teach you how to shoot?"

"Daddy wouldn't let her. He said that boys shoot guns. Girls cook," she answered.

"Okay, then. You cover your ears and don't move." Lily hitched up her skirt and hopped up on the table beside the child. "What's your name?"

"Beatrice, but Mama calls me Bea," she said.

"I'm Lily, and we're about to kill a lot of snakes."

"Make them all dead. I want to see my mama again," Bea whimpered.

Lily loaded every gun on the table. She had no idea how many snakes had been in the nest, but she got ready to make them all dead like Bea had asked. Pretty soon, three crawled out of the grass, and she took them all out. She swore under her breath because she missed one and wasted a bullet.

"You said a bad word, but that's okay." Bea inhaled the sulfuric smell floating in the air and coughed several times.

"Here comes the next round," Lily said and fired twice more, then grabbed another pistol to kill two others. "The creek bed must have been a haven for them, and the storm that's on the way is going to flood it . . ." She talked to herself as she waited for more to come into the clearing.

When there were a dozen that were either completely dead or still wiggling, the grass finally stopped moving. Smoke still hung around the table while Lily reloaded the empty guns and then hugged Bea next to her. "You were a brave girl. Thank you for having a sharp eye and saving our lives."

"You killed them," Bea said. "I didn't."

Lily hugged her tighter. "But you're the one who saw the first one and pointed out the others."

"Mama is going to be mad," Bea said. "She told us not to come down here around the guns."

"I'll talk to her," Lily promised and then saw a movement to her right. She raised the pistol lying in her lap and took aim before she realized that it was Daisy leading a group of women down the path.

Daisy raised her hands and then sniffed the air. "We heard a lot of shots and came to see what was happening. What are you doing on the table? And what is that smell?"

Bea raised a finger and swung it around to take in the first snake and then all the others. "She made them all dead."

"Made who dead? And, Beatrice Eleanor Grant, what are you doing down here?" Amanda snapped. "I told you to stay away from this area and play in the churchyard."

"Saving my life, and most likely a bunch of y'all's as well. You might want to stay back for a few more minutes," Lily shouted. "Just to make sure there are no more of those demons coming this way."

Frannie watched her step, but she walked right up to the table and picked up a gun, checking whether it was loaded. "I got to shoot yesterday, so I'll help you keep watch for more snakes while the rest of them learn or practice."

"Thank you." Lily eased off the table, then lifted Bea down to the ground.

"Mama!" she yelled and ran into her mother's open arms. "I won't never sneak off again."

"I'm just glad that you are all right. Now, go on up to the safe places, and watch out for snakes on the way. You were a brave girl today and I'm proud of you, but next time something like this happens, you will be punished." Amanda's tone said that she was both glad that her daughter was safe and angry that she had disobeyed her.

"Yes, ma'am." Bea lifted her skirt and ran so fast that she was barely a blur.

Frannie grabbed each snake by the tail and dragged them, one by one, over underneath a shade tree. "I'll skin these out and take them up to the church for our next meal." Then she stood up and focused on Lily. "Are y'all really going to make hats in your store?"

"We are," Lily answered.

"Then I'll keep the skins, take them back to the barn, and stretch them for you to use as hatbands," she said. "Folks go crazy for that kind of thing."

"Thank you," Lily said. "But how are you going to watch for snakes and do all that at the same time?"

Frannie raised the pistol and fired, killing two more snakes. "Just like that. I can take care of skinnin' and shootin' at the same time. If there's a lot of them out of the tall grass, maybe we will have enough to feed us all for supper. I bet there's a big nest of them nearby. Just be sure that you leave those severed heads alone. They can still produce venom for an hour or so after they've been killed."

"Beulah told us that there's a dry creek bed not far from here," Lily said. "I bet instinct has told them that the storm that's coming will put water in it, and they're all moving to higher ground."

"I'll watch out for more," Frannie said with a nod, "and maybe make a trip down there to kill the slow ones that are left before the rain starts. That'll for sure give us enough for supper."

"No, you will not hunt them!" Daisy yelled.

Frannie's eyes twinkled. "I thought you didn't like me."

"I don't, but I don't want to watch you die a horrible death, either," Daisy shot back at her. "So promise me you won't go down there."

"Okay, then, I'll just kill what slithers out of the grass—but it might be best if y'all call this off for today. I'll hang back and keep watch around this area while I skin these out."

Lily raised an eyebrow at Daisy.

"We cleared the air this morning," Daisy whispered. "I'll tell you about it later. And I'm going to hang back with Frannie and help her. One of those vicious things could sneak up on her while she's cleaning the dead ones."

"Are we really going to eat rattlesnake?" Lily asked.

"Best thing next to chicken that there is," Frannie said. "If anyone doesn't want it, then they can shove their share over to me."

Lily wasn't sure if she could put snake in her mouth after the rush of pure fear that she had experienced.

"Anyone home?" Elijah's voice came through the open church doors that evening. "Matt and I come bearing supplies."

"Come on in, and welcome," Beulah called out.

"Did you know they were coming today?" Lily snapped at Beulah.

"Nope, but it's a good thing they did. We are out of meat and used the last of our salt pork to make beans for tonight. Thank goodness Frannie brought in that tub of rattler steaks to fry up," Beulah said. "Besides, why are you fussin' at me? I can see that you have got a thing for Matt. It's either him or Elijah, and he's old enough to be your grandpa."

"No I do not!" Lily answered.

"Methinks the lady named Lily protests too much with that tone," Beulah teased as she walked past.

"Oh, hush!" Lily growled at her retreating back.

Matt was the first one to come inside, and he had a crate full of wrapped meat on one shoulder and another one of what looked like slabs of bacon on the other. "The mutton is from our sheep ranch. Elijah rounded up the bacon from one of the husbands, who sure wishes his wife would come home."

"Just sit it down on the front pew, and please tell your family and whoever sent the bacon that we are obliged to them," Beulah said.

"This is a bushel of potatoes from another husband who says he misses his wife and will sign anything to get her to come home," Elijah said as he hauled in more supplies.

Matt tipped his hat toward Lily. "You are looking very pretty today."

"Thank you." Lily blushed in spite of her efforts to keep the redness from her cheeks at bay. "Thank you so much for all this."

"We are glad to do what we can to help," Matt said and then went back out to the wagon to help his uncle bring in more. This time he brought in a twenty-pound bag of sugar on one shoulder and one of flour on the other. "Uncle Elijah tells me that the men are grumbling about not having supper on the table when they come in, and that they're really upset that there's no women in the saloon. Speaking of which"—he pointed toward the crate—"you'll find a couple of bottles of whiskey in the bottom of that crate over there. I know how Beulah likes a little shot in her coffee and tea."

"Did you think of that?" Lily wished she had been given enough notice to at least wipe the sweat from her face and put on something that fit better than a calico housedress.

"Yes, I did. You might need it for medicine," he whispered.

"Thank you, again." Her voice went all high and squeaky.

"Mr. Elijah!" Bea skipped down the center aisle and hugged the old man. "Lily killed a hundred snakes this morning, and Frannie skinned them, and then she cut them up in pieces and we are eating it for supper, and I ain't never et snake before . . ." She stopped long enough to take a deep breath and went on. "Mama and Miz Frannie says it tastes like chicken."

Elijah reached inside his pants pocket and brought out a small bag of hard candy. "I love rattler steaks, too. I thought you might like to give all the kids here a piece of this tonight."

"Mr. Elijah . . ." Bea's face lit up brighter than the Independence Day fireworks show. "You are my favorite person, next to my mama and Miz Frannie and Miz Lily. They saved my life today."

"I'm glad to hear that," Elijah said. "I'm going to the kitchen now to see if they've got enough rattlesnake to share with an old man like me. You want to go with me, Matt?"

"I'm good," he answered and sat down on the back pew. "I'll just rest here awhile and be ready to take you home before I start that long ride back to the ranch. Oh, I almost forgot . . ." He took an envelope

The Paradise Petition

from his pocket and handed it to his uncle. "Alma sent this to Beulah. Will you give it to her, please?"

"Sure will," Elijah agreed and headed toward the front of the building, where Beulah was frying snakes in bacon drippings with Maggie and her crew.

Matt looked up at Lily and asked, "So, how are things going? Did you really kill a hundred snakes today?"

She sat down on the pew but kept a respectable distance between them. "Not a hundred—but it seemed like it was when I was shooting them as they slithered out of the tall grass. Bea was terrified, so she exaggerated a little. Tomorrow it might be a thousand, but in reality it was more like a dozen. They must have been nesting down in the rocky creek bottom."

"You amaze me, Lily Boyle," Matt said.

"Because I can shoot a snake?" she asked.

"For that, and so many other reasons," Matt answered. "You help people—just look at all these women gathered. To me, that makes you one special lady."

Another blush started on her neck and shot around to her cheeks. "Well, thank you, Mr. Maguire."

He looked deeply into her eyes. "That's Matt to you, ma'am. I would like to invite you out to my family's ranch. I've told them all about you, and my mother would love to meet you."

For a few seconds, she was totally lost in his gaze. "I would like that very much," she said, and then wished she could put the words back into her mouth. She couldn't lead Matt on *or* meet his family. He was too good of a person for that kind of treatment.

Bea ran right up to them and grabbed Lily's hand. "Come quick, and bring your gun. One of them snakes has got into the outhouse."

Matt was on his feet in a split second and had his gun out of the holster as he ran ahead of Bea. "Show me where and I'll take care of it."

Lily wasn't used to running beside a person with legs as long as hers, but she found it to be exhilarating. She heard Bea say something, but it was lost in the heat of the moment and the hard thumping in her chest. Finally, Bea tugged at her skirt and screamed, "You're going to the wrong one! It's the outhouse behind the barn!"

Lily changed course and Matt followed her. The rattler had made its way out of the outhouse and was slithering to the open barn door when Matt shot it. The noise rang out through the whole area, and women ran out of every building to see what had happened.

"There's one more for the frying pan," Matt said as he holstered his pistol. "You ladies need to be very careful. This whole area is bad for rattlers this time of year."

Lily could have listened to him read Job or Exodus out of the Bible all evening just to hear his deep voice. "I promise we will be on the lookout. I'll even address the next community meeting about the need to be aware of snakes."

"That's good," Matt said. "I wouldn't want anything to happen to you . . ." He paused. "Or any of the ladies."

"You ready to go? Miz Beulah has fixed me up with a whole platter of snake meat to take home with me," Elijah called out from the back of the barn.

Matt held up the dead snake. "Look what I shot. This will replace whatever those sweet ladies gave you."

"Well, give it to Frannie. Seems like she's the one that can skin them out," Elijah said. "You need to get going toward the ranch. You don't want one of those varmints to spook your horse and then have a bite of you for their midnight snack."

Matt laid the six-foot snake on the porch and used his free hand to tip his hat toward Lily. "Good night, Miz Lily. I'll see you next time I'm in town, and maybe this will be over by then."

"I hope so," she said with longing in her heart for what could not be. "Safe travels back to your ranch."

Chapter Thirteen

Daisy and Lily hustled on Sunday morning, but they were still the last ones to make it inside the church. From behind the lectern, Maggie smiled at them when they came inside and took a seat in the back row.

"We might not live to see women at the voting polls, but we do get to see this," Lily whispered as she eased into a pew beside Beulah.

"And that is . . . ?" Daisy asked.

"A woman standing in the pulpit in a church," Lily answered as Daisy wedged into the small space left for her.

"We have a lot to be thankful for this morning," Maggie's clear voice rang out through the sanctuary. "So I thought maybe we could simply sing a few songs, have a moment of silence, and then go on about our business of survival in less-than-normal conditions. I don't reckon the day will come in my lifetime when a woman is allowed to really have this position, but these are unusual circumstances, so raise your voices to the heavens." She began singing a hymn that most of the women knew. Daisy eased out of the pew and went forward, sat down at the piano, and picked up the melody.

She was surprised to hear Frannie's sweet soprano voice right there on the front pew, only a few feet from her. Daisy remembered what Frannie had told her in the stillness of the early morning about her son and his death. She wondered if maybe singing the hymns brought back happy memories of sitting in church with the little boy beside her.

Elijah came through the doors with his hat in his hand. He sang right along with the group as he made his way to the front and stood beside Maggie until the song ended. "Could I have just a moment of you ladies' time?" he asked respectfully.

"Of course. And we want to thank you and your family once again for all the support you have given us in our mission," Maggie said and took a seat beside Beulah on the front pew.

"You are very welcome," Elijah said. He looked out over the crowd. "I'm here as a go-between for the men in town. There are several men who, like me, are not against whatever demands you have, but you have to write them down before they even know what to agree to. So I'm here today to ask you to do just that. If you can get them ready by the middle of the week, I will deliver them to Judge Wesley Martin, and negotiations can get started. You are missed, all of you"—he made a sweeping motion with his hand to include the whole crowd—"and your point has been made. Not only do your families need you, but so does the town. Many years ago, men who got the gold fever and rushed off to California found that that glittery stuff wasn't the be-all and end-all. Wagon trains full of mail-order brides were ordered so they could have wives and families. Women are the lifeblood of a town, and the men in Autrie have learned that the hard way. That's all I've got to say, so continue with your service here. Matt and I will bring more supplies on Wednesday, so maybe you will have something ready for me then."

"We will do our best," Beulah said.

"I'll see you then." Elijah walked back down the aisle and eased the door shut behind him.

"Well, ladies," Maggie said on her way back to the lectern, "it looks like we're making progress. Daisy, I am appointing you to be the person that each woman brings her list to. You can compile all of them, maybe with a number out to the side as to how many want that to be included in our petition."

"Why a number?" Frannie asked.

"That's so we can list them in order of priority," Maggie answered. "But rest assured that no matter what the request, we will add it into the list."

"Thank you for that," Frannie said. "There's only a few of us saloon girls, and what we ask for will be different than—"

"Than me, who is going to ask for the sheriff to not turn a blind eye when my husband knocks me around?" Amanda stood up and turned to face them. "Just because you work in a saloon and endure abuse does not mean that some of us don't get the same treatment. Maybe even more so. If the sheriff can arrest some drunk in the saloon for hitting another one, then he should be able to throw a man in jail for being ugly to his wife."

"I agree," Frannie said. "And that should be near the top of our list. Do we really want to do this as individuals or as a group? I vote that we start making the list right now. Daisy can find a pencil and some paper and start writing while we are all together."

"Is everyone in agreement with that?" Maggie asked. "It really would simplify things."

All hands went up, and then Daisy went to the front and sat down on the deacon's bench. "Is there a pencil and some paper on the shelf under that thing, Miz Maggie?"

She pulled out a tablet and a couple of stubby pencils and handed them to Daisy. "I'll go first: we want to sit as a family with our husbands in church."

Amanda stood up and said, "And like I already said, I want to be able to call the sheriff when me or my kids are being abused. If I wasn't married and a man hit me, he could hang for it. Why should it be any different just because I'm a wife?"

Daisy agreed with both issues and wrote them down on the paper. "Next?" she asked, looking up.

"I want to say something," Hattie said, "because I'm not sure the sheriff will do a thing about your situation. My husband was bad about hitting me until I stood up for myself. I waited until he went to sleep, then gently rolled the sheet over on him and sewed the edges shut. Then I took a broom and used the handle to beat on him until my arms got tired. He didn't go into Autrie for a month, not until the bruises healed. And he never raised a hand toward me again. Some things we have to handle on our own, ladies. I'm not saying to beat the hell out of anyone who is treating you like dirt. But you have to stand up for yourselves. We won't always be there as a group, and you'll be alone when you go home."

"Where is your husband now?" Frannie asked.

"Out there in the cemetery, not far from the preacher Joshua Jones. He died of the fever a couple of years back. I did not kill him—after that night, he might cuss at me, but he never raised a hand to hit me again," Hattie answered. "I'm not saying that we need to exclude having the law protect us. Maybe it will work, maybe not. One time seeing an abuser sit in jail might teach all of them a lesson. I'm just telling you that with or without it, you can fight a battle or two without the rest of us standing behind you. That said, if you need us, just yell and we will be there as soon as we can. This empowerment and togetherness does not end when we leave this camp."

"I'm offering this," Beulah said. "If the law don't do its job, you can always stay in my old house until the guilty party comes to their senses and comes around to apologize."

"A safe house?" Frannie asked.

"Exactly," Beulah replied. "And that goes for everyone in this room."

A woman with dark hair stood up at the back of the room and said, "I am Rachael Davies, and have been one of the two schoolteachers here in Autrie for the past five years. I'm supposed to get married soon, which means I can't keep my job, so I want to have it put in the demands that the rules be changed and married women can continue to work at the Autrie school."

Another lady from a few pews back stood up, tucked a strand of blond hair up under her bonnet, and said, "I'm the other teacher in the school, and rule number eight says that any teacher who smokes, uses liquor in any form, frequents public halls, or gets shaved in a barbershop will give good reason to suspect his worth, intention, integrity, and honesty. I do not intend to start smoking or get shaved in the local barbershop . . ." She waited for the giggles to die down and then went on. "But I would like to make a hot toddy when I get a fever or a head cold. If any busybody calls the male superintendent and tattles, I can lose my job. So I want it in writing that I can use liquor for medicinal purposes."

Amanda stood to her feet. "Speaking of that, I want it in writing that any woman can walk into the saloon and buy whiskey. What if something happens to our husbands and what we have at home to use to clean out wounds or help with whooping cough has all been used? We'd sully our reputations if we went into the saloon to buy another bottle."

"Send Daisy after it!" Frannie yelled from the back of the room.

"Don't test me, Frannie!" Daisy looked up from her writing. "I'll be glad to buy it for any woman in this room if you need it."

"I want to be able to get on the train and go over to Jackson to see my family without a male escort," a large woman named Eulalia said. "My husband can't leave the farm on a whim, and it's frowned on for me to travel even that far alone."

"Something I want for the future," said a woman from the second pew, "is for married women to have the right to have their own passport, and to file for divorce, and to wear pants in public."

"I agree, Lucy," Beulah said. "But today we're talking about what we can do to change things right here in Autrie."

"I understand that," Lucy continued. "But I want more than the right to vote—and put down that I want to come to town without a male escort, too. Do y'all even realize that in order for us to come to the meeting at the new seamstress shop, several of our husbands went to the saloon and waited for us?"

"And grumbled the whole way," Edith added.

After an hour, Daisy looked up from the demands and asked, "Anything else?"

"Yes, ma'am." Bea stood up and waved at Daisy. "I'm hungry. Can we eat now?"

"Beatrice!" her mother scolded.

"All of the ladies, young or old, can have a say-so in this meeting," Lily said. "This little girl is a hero—and quite frankly, I'm hungry, too. So let's adjourn and feed this crowd. I understand that Beulah has a cauldron of mutton stew ready to be dished up, and Frannie has made several loaves of sourdough bread to go with it."

"I agree with Lily," Daisy said. "I'll get this all written up in the next couple of days and ready to send to the judge on Wednesday."

A loud round of applause came from the crowd. When it died down, they all filed out of the church on their way to Beulah's old place for the noon meal.

"What are you smiling about?" Lily asked as she and Daisy brought up the rear of the group.

Daisy looped her arm through Lily's. "The way that the children have acted so freely this whole week. That first day, their eyes darted around like they were scared of their own shadows, but not anymore. I don't remember ever being so uninhibited as our little Bea when I was a young girl."

"Me either. 'Act like a lady. Don't run after butterflies. Don't cross your legs except at the ankle. Do not ever, ever, for fear of hellfire dancing up your skirt tails, wear your hair down after you are twelve years old,'" Lily said.

"'Grow up to be a good mother and wife,'" Daisy added and then frowned. "If you had a chance and circumstances were different, would you marry Matt Maguire and be a good mother and wife?"

"I'm not sure either of us can have children," Lily whispered. "Not after all the monthly tea we drank to keep us from having kids. And Matt deserves a wife who is as pure as an angel with white wings and a halo."

"He likes you," Daisy said.

"And Claude likes you," Lily snapped. "Are *you* going to marry him someday?"

"In my dreams, every night," Daisy answered. "But in reality, probably not. It's just one of those bad-timing things. Had I met him before I got married, I might have had a different life."

"Choices and consequences," Lily said.

"Exactly. Every choice—whether bad, good, or somewhere in between—has consequences, and if we're honest with ourselves, we are smart enough to know that we made the decisions that brought us to this day."

"So now we have to pay the fiddler, right?" Lily asked.

"Absolutely," Daisy agreed, and wished that her life had taken a different path.

You can't undo that part, Miz Raven whispered ever so softly in her ear. *But what if you told Claude and he didn't hold it against you?*

Chapter Fourteen

Lily heard a wagon approaching and peeked through rows of wet clothing on makeshift clotheslines running from the church to the parsonage. She held her breath and prayed it wouldn't be Matt and Elijah. She had been helping Amanda and several other women do laundry all morning. Her red hair hung in limp strands around her sweaty face, and truth be told, she didn't smell like a bouquet of roses. Even if nothing could ever happen between her and Matt, she didn't want him to see her in such an unkempt mess.

Elijah parked the wagon and eased down off the buckboard, and two other men followed him. Both were dressed in suits, so very different from Elijah's drab work pants and shirt. One carried a notebook and the other had some kind of equipment in his hands.

Lily slipped a pair of pantaloons to the side so she could see better. All three men went into the church. Could they be lawyers bringing divorce papers? Lord, she hoped not. Divorced women were looked down on as bad—or worse—than those who worked in saloons. "What is going on? Are those lawyers with Elijah? Daisy hasn't quite finished drafting our petition of demands, so why are these people here?"

"I've lived in this town my whole life, and I know both of the lawyers in town. That ain't either of them," Amanda replied.

The church bells rang one time, which on a normal day, meant it was mealtime. But breakfast had been served a while ago, and dinner was at least an hour away. No matter, the bell meant there was some kind of business that required all their attention. Sally Anne and another woman dismounted the horses they'd been riding astride instead of sidesaddle. Others, like Daisy and Lily, left their laundry in the pots, and still more came from the barn, where they'd been throwing old straw out to the horses and bringing new down from the loft for fresh bedding. Children dashed around in front of them, behind them, and even holding their mothers' hands as everyone in the camp made their way to the church.

"Do you think this is over?" Amanda asked. "I recognize Elijah's wagon—and I'm so ready to go back to my house."

"We haven't turned in our list, so it can't be over, but I guess we're about to find out," Lily answered.

The church was quiet when Lily and Daisy found a place to sit up close to the front. Maggie stood behind the lectern and looked to be every bit as sweaty and hot as the rest of the ragtag women who filed into the church and sat down. Elijah and the two men sat on the deacon's bench only a few feet away from Maggie.

"I'll be glad when someone tells us what this is all about," Daisy whispered as she tucked a strand of blond hair back into her bun.

"Me, too, but Elijah is smiling. That makes me think it's not anything bad," Lily said.

"I believe we are all here," Maggie said. "The men beside Elijah have gotten word about what we are doing for women's rights. They want to interview us for the newspaper in Waco, and then they want to include a photograph as well. All in favor of doing this, raise your hand."

The vote was unanimous.

"I am hoping that this will give more women the courage to make a stand," Maggie said. "I'll turn this over now to Wilbur Gibson, the reporter. This other gentleman is Alford Holt, and he's the photographer."

Mr. Gibson pushed up his wire-rimmed glasses as he stood and crossed the stage area to the lectern. For someone with such an interesting job, Lily couldn't see anything outstanding about him. If he'd been walking down the street in Autrie, or any other town, he would have blended in with his surroundings. Even his voice didn't have anything distinctive about it—just a normal man's voice, not too deep nor too high.

"Thank you, ladies, for doing this for us," he said.

Lily bristled at his words and rose to her feet. "Let's get something very clear, Mr. Gibson. We are not doing this *for* anyone but our fellow sisters. If you can spread the word, that is all good, but rest assured that all of us, no matter what station in life we are in, are united in our efforts."

Mr. Gibson wrote in his notebook the whole time Lily was talking and didn't look up until she finished. "May I quote you on that?"

"Yes, you may. My name is Lily."

"Lily what?" he asked.

"That doesn't matter. I vote that we all go by our first names only. Raise your hands if you agree with me," she said.

Again, every hand, including Bea's little one, went into the air.

"Okay, then . . . Miz Lily." The man raised his chin enough to look down on her. "I was about to ask for a spokesperson for the group. I think you will do fine."

"I'm willing to do that, but I would like to include the others in answering as well," she said.

"Agreed. We spent the last hour interviewing some of the men in town, including the owner of the saloon," Wilbur said. "I understand all of the women who work for him have joined this group. Is that right?"

"Yes, it is," she replied. "Like I told you, we are all equal women here, and we are in this battle together."

"That's amazing that you can do that," Wilbur said. "Most decent women would have gone back to their husbands rather than live with the likes of saloon workers."

Frannie stood up in the middle of the church. "I'll take any questions that you might have about the 'likes of saloon workers,'" she said with a sneer.

"Okay, then," Mr. Gibson said. "Why are you here, and how are the proper women of Autrie treating you?"

Beulah had been sitting right beside Frannie and was on her feet in a flash. "My name is Beulah, and I take offense to those words—*proper women*—and I do not want you to use them in your article. In this place, we are all equal, like Lily told you. There are no divisions."

Mr. Gibson adjusted his glasses again, apparently a sign of nervousness—or so Lily thought—and scribbled something in his book. "I will make a note of that. Are you a saloon worker?"

"I am not. I own the general store in Autrie. But we want all women everywhere in the world to know that we are working together for our rights and freedom," Beulah said. "And you may quote me on that, for sure."

"Okay, then . . ." His voice sounded a little bewildered.

"My answer," Frannie replied, "is that we are here to fight for our rights just like these 'proper women,' as you called them. We want a fair shake when it comes to our portion of the money that we make, and we don't want to be slapped around any more than all these other women do."

"I understand that you have made a list of what you want in order for you to go back to your homes. If those conditions are met, do you plan to go home soon?" Mr. Gibson asked.

"If the conditions are agreed upon, we will return to our homes and businesses," Lily said. "We will be sending our terms to Judge Martin today, whom I believe has agreed to negotiate for the menfolk. From there, it's up to the husbands, fiancés, and even the saloon owner whether we leave."

Daisy stood up right beside Lily. "Quite frankly, we've become very comfortable right here."

"And you are . . . ?" Wilbur asked.

"My name is Daisy," she told him.

He looked up from the paper he'd been writing on. "You've had no squabbles in the past ten days?"

"Of course we have," Daisy answered honestly. "Some of us don't have personalities that blend, but it doesn't mean that we can't live in reasonable harmony. We are working together, both for the cause and with each other. Those that didn't know how to ride astride a horse are learning. We've had shooting lessons, and I'm planning to teach some more defensive moves this week. If anyone thinks they can abuse one of us again, they'd better think twice."

Wilbur removed a hankie from his pocket and wiped sweat from his forehead. Lily wondered whether he had a wife at home in Waco, and how he might chastise her.

"There is strength in numbers out here, but what if someone is mean to one of you when they are alone?" Wilbur asked.

Daisy felt anger rising up from her toenails. "Then the next day that woman will call for a meeting, and we will decide the proper punishment for the offender. We will not be sweet little submissive women anymore. And you can quote me on that."

Wilbur wiped away more sweat, glancing quickly at the photographer. "That's very bold."

Daisy balled her hands up into fists. "It's fact, not just words blowing in the wind."

"Any more questions?" Lily asked.

"Yes, can we see the petition that you are presenting to the judge later today?" Wilbur asked.

"No, you may not. That is confidential," Lily said.

"Then if Miz Maggie, Lily, Daisy, and maybe Frannie will all step outside in front of this church, we would like to take a picture," Wilbur said.

"That's not acceptable," Daisy said. "Either all of us and the children will be in the picture, or none of us will be."

Wilbur set his thin mouth in a firm line and almost snorted when he released the air in his lungs. He closed his book and tucked the pencil into the inner pocket of his jacket. "Okay, then, line up on the porch from the shortest to the tallest. The children can sit on the grass in the front."

"What if a rattlesnake comes like it did when me and Miz Lily were at the shooting place?" Bea asked.

"*What?*" Wilbur asked.

Frannie raised her hand. "I'll take care of this one, Lily." She told the story, ending it with the fact that she had cleaned all the snakes and the women had them for supper that evening. "You can put that in your story if you would like. It's just one example of how we are taking care of each other and plan to do so in the future."

"I'll just add this," Daisy said. "While Frannie was skinning those varmints, she shot a few more slithering out of the tall grass. Which goes to show that we can kill and butcher our own food, cook supper, and defend ourselves at the same time. A cast-iron skillet isn't just for frying up bacon. It can be used as a very handy weapon."

"Can I get an *amen*?" Amanda said.

The whole group shouted out the word.

Five minutes later the women and children were lined up. The photographer took a picture and then nodded at Wilbur.

"Thank you for your time," Wilbur said as he crawled up into the wagon and sat down on the buckboard. The photographer loaded his equipment in the back and sat down beside it.

"I'll take these fellers back to the train station and then come back with supplies and get your petition," Elijah told Daisy as he passed by her. "Claude should have everything loaded up in another wagon by then. Miz Beulah's store is lookin' pretty pitiful. I hope y'all can get things settled soon or it will be plumb empty. We've been writing down the tallies for what we have taken out of the store so Miz Beulah will have an accounting, and I've seen to it that the menfolk have written down what they needed as well."

"I hope it ends soon, too." Daisy was tired of sleeping on a pallet in a barn packed elbow to elbow with other women. She missed her own bed and the privacy that having a room all to herself afforded.

"Are you thinking about Claude?" Lily joked as the two of them watched the wagon disappear down the road back to town.

"I wasn't, but I am now," Daisy groaned. "I can't do too much to freshen up or everyone will tease me worse than you do. But I look a fright."

"Go redo your hair at least and grab a clean apron from the clothesline. This heat probably dried everything while we were in the church. Beulah made cookies today, so you can offer Claude and Elijah some refreshments," Lily said.

Daisy's pulse jacked up several notches. "I shouldn't do any of that. What I should do is go on down to the shooting place and get rid of some of my frustrations by firing off a few rounds."

"What aggravated you the most, that man's smug looks or the twist he could put on his article?" Lily asked. "I bet he thought he would come here and find a bunch of whiny women griping because they had to sleep on straw beds and help cook meals for more than a hundred women. Can't you see the headline?" She waved her hand across the air. "'Unhappy Women Learn Lesson.'"

"Now he'll have to write 'Women Take a Stand,'" Daisy said. "I'd bet silver dollars to the rattlers Frannie cut off those snakes' tails that he is married and doesn't agree with what we are doing. Which . . ." Daisy frowned. "What did she do with those things, anyway?"

"I have no idea, but you can bet she'll do something with them," Lily answered. "Do you think Wilbur visits the upstairs rooms in a saloon in Waco?"

Daisy shrugged. "If he does, I feel sorry for the women who have to put up with him." She headed back to the barn to help finish up the rest of the barn ladies' laundry. If Claude singled her out, she made a vow that she would discourage him from flirting.

Miz Raven was back. *You've had these same thoughts more than a dozen times.*

"I know, but I have to keep reminding myself or else a good man could get hurt. If I admit to him that I'm really like Frannie, the story could get out all over town and ruin what we are doing," she said.

"What story?" Bea asked as she slipped her hand into Daisy's. "Are you going to tell us kids a story tonight?"

"Yes, I am, but for now, I've got some more laundry to do," Daisy said. "Do you want to help me fold some things so we can make room for more?"

Bea frowned and drew her eyebrows down. "Not really. I'd rather go play Kick the Can with the other kids."

Daisy gently squeezed her hand. "Then, darlin', you go play. Be a little kid while you can. When you grow up, you can't go back."

"What does that mean?" Bea asked.

"You'll find out soon enough."

Lily grinned and took a basket full of sheets to the clotheslines.

Amanda kept washing a tub full of bedsheets on a rubboard. When they were clean enough to suit her, she handed them off to Sally Anne, who dipped them up and down in a watering trough of rinse water. That done, they became Daisy's responsibility. She wrung them out and Lily hung them on the clothesline.

They had finished with the last two pillowcases when the noon bell rang out promptly at twelve o'clock. Daisy threw her shoulders back and rolled her neck to get the kinks out. "I'm starving," she said. "And I'm glad those newspaper men are gone. I didn't like them well enough to ask them to stay and eat with us."

"I didn't mind them so much," Amanda said. "If they'll get the word out that the women in Autrie are making a mark, maybe others will follow our example. It could be a good thing for all of us. I just hope he doesn't put a spin on the story that makes us look bad. Not a single one of us were cleaned up enough to have our photograph taken." She wiped her brow. "I'm famished, too, now that you mention it. Edith said we're having ham, beans, and corn bread for dinner today. She and Sally Anne made jam cakes for dessert." A wide smile spread across her face. "I wonder if Gertrude and her followers are standing over a hot stove all day for all those poor abandoned husbands?"

"I doubt it," Daisy said. "She seems like a lot of things, but generous isn't one of them. Though I have been wondering about what happens when that food Beulah has donated is all gone. Are y'all going to stick around if beans is the only thing on the menu for days on end?"

"I like beans," Lily said as she fell in step behind Amanda, Daisy, and Sally Anne, "but I figure if I can shoot a rattlesnake, I can sure hit a deer or a bunch of rabbits for our cooks to use. Maybe tomorrow morning you and I should go hunting."

"Y'all could take Frannie with you," Amanda suggested. "That woman is a good shot, and I bet she knows how to field dress a deer."

"Good idea, if Daisy is willing," Lily said.

"I might not want to be forever friends with Frannie, but I'm willing to go hunting with her," Daisy said.

She was glad she hadn't seen Claude getting down off the wagon before she spoke, because when she did see him coming at her with a big smile on his face, all the moisture was suddenly sucked out of her mouth and her pulse raced.

"Looks like we've got some company for dinner," Lily said. "I bet Elijah is here to get our list."

"I do, too, but look. That's Claude carrying supplies inside," Amanda said.

Claude threw a big burlap bag over his shoulder and headed inside the church without even looking around. Elijah set a wheelbarrow on the ground and loaded it as high as he could with more supplies, then rolled it inside the door.

Daisy was the last one in the church, and just as she stepped up on the porch, Claude came out the door—still smiling. "Good afternoon, Miz Daisy."

"Afternoon." She returned the smile.

"Matt tells me that you-all had some excitement out here when a bunch of snakes came calling," he said.

"We did, at that," she said. "Lily and Frannie shot enough to make our supper."

He leaned on the porch post. "Dipped in cornmeal and fried up crispy in bacon drippings?"

"Exactly," she answered.

"Ain't nothing better," Claude said. "I should let you get on inside. Your dinner is waiting."

"There's dozens of women and children ahead of us. I can wait a spell," she said and sat down on the top step. She was determined to let him know she wasn't interested—not just in him, but in any man. She had work to do for women's freedom.

"Are you tired of this life and ready to get back to your seamstress business?" he asked.

"A little, but it hasn't been so bad. Besides, all my customers are out here with me," she replied, but couldn't push forward with her intended statement. "How about you? Do you ever get tired of being a sheep herder?"

"Yes, I do," he admitted. "Though I wouldn't ever tell Matt that. He needs me to help run the ranch—but that's his dream, not mine."

Daisy's curiosity was piqued. Sure, she had been ready to leave Spanish Fort when Miz Raven closed down the Paradise. But she had never really wanted to just go farther south in Texas. She wanted to see more of the world. Maybe even go someplace where she could see a real snowstorm every year.

"What was—or should I say *is*—your dream?" she asked.

"To go north into the Idaho Territories and start my own sheep farm," he answered. "I'd like to be independent of my family, and live where it's not so blessed hot in the summers. I could take the snow and the high mountains better than this heat. Don't get me wrong, I love Matt and the whole bunch of my family. But I want to live somewhere—anywhere, really—where the sun doesn't try to bake a person to a crisp."

"I can agree with that." Daisy could hear the longing in her own voice. Maybe Claude just wanted a friend outside of his family whom he could talk to about his dreams. Perhaps he hadn't been flirting at all, so she didn't have to say anything to him about relationships. "If we want something bad enough, we might find that our dreams can come true."

Elijah came out of the church with a chunk of corn bread on top of a bowl of beans. "Lily asked me to bring this out to you," he said and handed it off to her. "It's hot out here, but it's scorchin' in that church. With no breezes at all, it's a good place for a preacher to remind his flock that hell is supposed to be seven times hotter than anyplace on earth. I reckon a lot of poor souls have been saved when they think about enduring that kind of heat."

"I imagine so." Daisy set the food on the porch. "I'll let that cool awhile before I dive into it."

"You about ready to go, Claude?" Elijah asked.

"Yes, sir," he said and tipped his hat toward Daisy. "Maybe I'll see you again?"

"Maybe so. Are y'all sure you don't want to have a bite of dinner with us?" she asked.

"We already ate," Elijah said. "Claude's mama sent along a couple of her chicken pies. She knows that's one of my favorite dishes. I want to get this list on over to the judge before he closes up shop today. I understand there's a town meetin' in the other church this evening to talk over the points you ladies have made. Who knows, you could be back home by the end of the week."

"That would be nice," Daisy said. "But there's a lot on the list for consideration, and we want all of it before we agree to leave our camp. Some of it will be a bitter pill for the guys to swallow."

"I imagine it will," Elijah said.

Claude shot another smile toward her, and then he and Elijah headed back toward town. Daisy watched them until they turned the curve in the road, then picked up her food and began to eat. Thoughts of deep snow and a big blaze in a fireplace flooded her mind. That would never come true, but she could enjoy thinking about it—especially in this blasted heat.

Chapter Fifteen

Apparently, the fear of snakes kept the women interested in shooting away from the area that Thursday morning. Lily fired off a couple of rounds and hit the target each time; then she hiked a hip on the table and sat down. Daisy did the same, and her short legs dangled in the air, but Lily pulled her long ones up and wrapped her arms around her knees. "Not very ladylike, but it looks like we are the only ones who are going to show up out here this morning."

"We were supposed to go hunting," Daisy reminded her, "but then Elijah and Claude brought in a whole deer last evening, already dressed out and ready to butcher. We don't need meat right now, but if this lingers on past when we eat all that up, we *will* go out to find food. If the flour and sugar from Beulah's runs out, we may have to eat venison or rabbit stew with no bread."

"'That which does not kill us makes us stronger,'" quoted Lily, and thought again of that first year she worked in the brothel. She had certainly come out of that experience a stronger, more determined woman.

Frannie approached them from behind a big oak tree with a wave. "If that's the truth, then my friends and I should be able to lift a good-sized longhorn bull. I'm not sure I'm ready to go back to the saloon. I've liked living out here and not dealing with . . ." She paused and hopped up to sit on the table with the other two.

"With what?" Sally Anne seemed to appear out of nowhere.

"With having to put up with several men every night and going to the doctor every month for him to be sure I'm not carrying a baby," Frannie answered bluntly. "What are you doing out here?"

Lily half expected Sally Anne to at least flinch at Frannie's curt answer, but instead she gave the saloon worker half a smile.

"I've been struggling with my wedding and future marriage—and I needed a place to think. I didn't know that shooting lessons were still going on today," she answered.

Frannie patted the table and extended a hand toward Sally Anne. "Scoot down far enough that she can sit with us," she said to Daisy and Lily.

Sally Anne took her hand and joined the three women. "I'm not sure I want to marry Wesley," she blurted out. "He wants a big wedding. I just wanted a small event with maybe a dozen members of the family there. I don't care a thing about a long honeymoon, and I'm not sure I want to have a houseful of children."

"That sure is a lot on your mind," Frannie said. "If you could do anything else with your life, what would it be?"

"I want to own and operate my own newspaper, to write articles for women's rights like Victoria Woodhull and others have done. I couldn't do it here in Autrie, of course, but maybe in a bigger town like Houston—or even farther away, where I could make the biggest impact," she answered. "Even if we get the things on our list and I marry Wesley, not a lot will change. I will still be expected to cook and rock the cradle and look beautiful when we are out in public together."

"You *are* beautiful," Frannie said.

"But in time that will fade," Sally Anne said. "Look at my aunts, Edith and Maudie. I've been told that they were beautiful when they were young. Age is catching up to them pretty fast. When I get old and die, I want to be remembered for more than being a judge's wife or hosting the tea for the church ladies once a month."

"Who is this Victoria that you mentioned?" Frannie asked.

"She is a free thinker. Especially about rights for women. She lives in England now, but I read everything I can get my hands on about her," Sally Anne told her.

"What do you mean 'free thinker'?" Frannie asked.

Lily knew very well what she meant. Miz Raven had preached the same thing to her girls more than once. Miz Raven had always kept up with everything that Victoria did, from her two failed marriages—the first one being forced on her when she was barely fifteen—to the day that she became a stockbroker and a newspaper woman, and even ran for president of the United States.

Too bad she wasn't elected, Lily thought. *The world might be a different place if she had been.*

Sally Anne's eyes went all glassy as she told Frannie about the woman she wanted to take the torch from when the time came. "And this is what she said, word for word—and I memorized it and believe with all my heart: 'Yes, I am a free lover. I have an inalienable, constitutional, and natural right to love whom I may, to love as long or as short a period as I can; to change that love every day if I please, and with that right neither you nor any law you can frame have any right to interfere.'"

Lily thought Sally Anne might pop down off the table, put one hand on her heart, and raise the other one toward heaven.

"Holy Mother of God!" Frannie swore. "There are really women like that?"

"Yes, ma'am, there are—and I not only believe it, I practice it. I am not a sweet little virgin like Wesley seems to think that I am. I have had lovers, and I'm not so sure I want to settle down to one man," she said.

Daisy gasped.

Frannie giggled.

Lily's mouth made a perfect little O, but no sound came out.

"Maybe you better come clean with Wesley." Lily finally got words to come out of her mouth, and then the imaginary devil that sat on her shoulder and often whispered in her ear reminded her that she should do the same thing with Matt.

"I don't want to break his heart," Sally Anne said. "I have written a long letter to Victoria and am waiting to hear back from her. If she says that she will mentor me, I'm on the next train out of Autrie, and then I'll board a ship to take me to England to help her and her daughter however I can. If not, then I'll count that as a sign that I need to stay in Texas. But if I do, then I'm still stuck between the idea of marriage or going to a bigger place and starting my own newspaper."

"Do you have that kind of money?" Frannie asked.

"My mother and father left me well fixed when they passed away last year. I own a big house at the east end of town and have enough money that I can do whatever I want."

"Have you slept with Wesley?" Daisy asked.

Sally Anne shook her head. "I have not."

"How have you had other lovers? But more importantly, ones that no one in Autrie found out about?" Frannie asked.

Sally Anne shrugged. "I traveled abroad with my parents."

Lily was stunned at how badly she had misread the woman. "Why didn't you stand up for women before we even came to town?"

Sally Anne shrugged again. "Not enough women would follow me, especially when I'm engaged to the judge, who, as you could see, is very traditional in his beliefs."

Lily was still in shock at the way even Sally Anne's expressions and demeanor had changed over the course of a few minutes. "Why did you let him court you?"

"Aunt Edith," she answered. "She knows how I feel about the movement and about Victoria. She thought it would be a good thing for me to settle down and—"

"But she was one of the first ones to stand up for what we are fighting for," Lily argued.

"I'm not stupid," Sally Anne declared. "I know she's doing this for her own rights here in Autrie, but also to appease me. This is just to give me a . . ." She hesitated.

"A little feeling that you've done something, and now you can marry the judge with that behind you," Daisy finished for her.

"Exactly," Sally Anne said. "But all it's done is make me want to fight on a bigger scale. If I get a letter that invites me to England, do you want to go with me, Frannie? Two women traveling together is safer than one going alone. But I will even do that if I need to."

"No, I don't, but Molly reads every newspaper that gets left behind, so I bet she would gladly go with you if she had the money," Frannie replied.

"She won't need to pay for anything if and when the time comes," Sally Anne said. "I'll take care of everything and will even pay her to be my assistant. But please don't tell her until I hear from Victoria."

"You've got my word," Frannie promised. "But why not take Lily and—"

Lily held up both hands in a defensive gesture. "Oh, no, we are happy to stay right here and fight on a local level."

Then she wished she had at least considered the option. Miz Raven was most likely in England by now, and Lily could join her. She wondered if maybe her old madam was even working right alongside Victoria and her daughter, Zula.

"How about you, Daisy?" Sally Anne asked.

"I'll stay with Lily," Daisy answered.

Frannie threw an arm around Sally Anne's shoulders. "Thank you for sharing all that with us. It means more than you'll ever know."

Sally Anne slipped her arm around Frannie's waist. "Thanks for listening, and for not telling me that I'm silly and stupid. We've talked about my dream. What is yours, Frannie?"

"To get out of that saloon. Not to get married again by any means, though," Frannie answered.

"How would you like to be the madam of your own house?" Lily asked.

Frannie laughed so hard that she snorted. "That's not funny, so why am I . . ." She wiped her face with the tail of her skirt.

"In Spanish Fort, there was this very fancy brothel that men talked about," Lily chose her words carefully. "I heard that they only let seven men inside the gates at night. One for each woman who worked there. Staying in the house from seven at night until after breakfast in the morning was very expensive, but the men who got to go inside said it was worth every penny."

Frannie cocked her head to one side and frowned. "What made it so special?"

"The women all dressed like angels, all white dresses with lots of lace, and their hair was clean and shiny, flowing down to their waists. When the client arrived, the woman took him up to her room, gave him a nice warm bath, cut his hair, shaved him, and dressed him in a clean robe. Then she fed him a nice supper at a table for two, let him talk or go to bed with her—whatever was his pleasure. I heard that those angels knew how to please a man so well that he said he had spent the night in heaven. The next morning, the clothing he wore inside had been washed and was ready for him to put on after he had enjoyed a hot breakfast with his angel. The woman walked him downstairs to the porch, and the butler took him and the other men out to the gate in a carriage."

"Was there a doctor to take care of . . ." Frannie stopped.

"The madam there had a special tea that she gave the women once a week. No babies came out of her place," Daisy explained.

"I need the recipe for that tea," Frannie said.

"So do I," Sally Anne agreed with a nod.

"I had a friend who used a tea made with pennyroyal, tansy, and ergot," Daisy said and shot a look toward Lily that let her know she had said enough. "It worked for her when she got in the family way and didn't want children."

"You could make a fortune if you know how to brew that up in bulk," Sally Anne said.

"To have my own house, one like that, would be a dream come true," Frannie said. "It would mean so much more money for all of us than we could earn anywhere else at this point. It'd give us real independence. But even at fifty percent of what we bring in, me and my friends couldn't save up enough in ten years to start up something so fancy."

"If Victoria gives me permission to come to England, and you convince Molly to go with me, I'll *give* you my house in exchange," Sally Anne offered.

"And Daisy and I will make you some white dresses," Lily said.

"You'd do that for me?" Frannie's eyes shifted from one woman to the other.

"You fought tradition and joined us. We vowed to help each other," Sally Anne said. "So yes, I will do that for you—and anyone that don't like it can fall right into hell."

"I can't believe how much I misread you, girl," Lily whispered.

"A good woman can be anything she wants to be, a good lover or an innocent bride—and she learns to bluff if need be," Sally Anne quipped.

"How do you know so much about that brothel?" Frannie focused on Daisy.

"My parents lived on the farm next to it," Daisy lied. "Lily has been my friend for years, and we used to sneak out at night to go over to the gate and stare at the house. There was this big man named Jems who was like a butler or protector or something. He answered our questions."

Some of it was the truth, Lily decided, even if the rest just skipped around the bush, so to speak. "Looks like what we do now is wait for Sally Anne's answer from Victoria," she said.

"If there's even a possibility of that woman telling Sally Anne to come on to England, then me and my girls are certainly not going back to the saloon. We'll stay right here and live off the land until y'all tell us that we can start our own establishment," Frannie declared. "I've got one more question. What did that madam do about drunks in her place?"

"Jems didn't let a man come through the gate if they were drunk, and no liquor was served to them in the house. If they asked for it, the madam would tell them in a sweet voice that they were having a heavenly experience and no liquor was served past the Pearly Gates," Lily answered.

"That's a nice story, but that's all it is," Frannie said. "Things like that don't happen to women like me. I'd best get on up to the camp. You, too, Sally Anne. Edith will need our help getting dinner ready. I promised to stir up some biscuits to go with the venison stew. And she said that she wanted you to learn to make her famous chocolate cake."

When they were out of sight, Lily took a deep breath and let it out slowly. "Well, this was a profitable morning, even though we didn't fire off any rounds or teach anyone how to load and unload a pistol."

"Whew!" Daisy wiped her forehead in a dramatic gesture. "I never saw that coming where Sally Anne was concerned."

"Me either," Lily agreed. "I guess that old saying about not judging a book by the cover is true. You almost got tangled up in the bush as you tiptoed around it when you were telling that lie about living next to the brothel. I thought any minute, you would drop Miz Raven's name or mention the Paradise."

Daisy put her forefinger on her lips and said in a voice barely above a whisper, "Frannie and Sally Anne were hidden so well by the underbrush, we didn't know they were out here. We have to be very careful about what we say anywhere. Do you think we'll be back in town by the weekend?"

"I predict that we will be sitting in the other church come Sunday morning, and Reverend Tobias will be telling us about Adam and Eve and blaming all womenkind for eating that apple," Lily replied. "It will have been two weeks by then. Unless Gertrude and her followers have been busy helping the menfolk, I bet there are some dirty houses that need to be cleaned, lots of laundry piled up, and gardens that need tending, if all the plants aren't already dead."

"I hope that she and her friends didn't do a thing but gather up and gossip." Daisy hopped down from the table. "I don't imagine that a lot will change, but we will have taught the ladies to stand up for themselves, and that's a big start in the right direction. To tell the truth, I'm itching to get back to designing and making dresses, and we haven't even started working on hats. Think we can use the rattlesnake skins some way?"

"I'm planning to twist them into roses, though Fannie had thought hatbands," Lily said.

"Snakes to roses . . . That reminds me of my idea of the rising sun."

Lily eased off the table. "It does, doesn't it? We came out here like snakes, having to crawl on the ground, to be stomped and even killed. But we won't leave until we have turned into roses that will demand to be treated tenderly and loved."

Daisy started down the path to the house. "That's right, and the sun on our mission is just barely showing. Do you think we'll live to see the day that you and I march into the polls and cast our votes?"

Lily fell into step beside her. "If we don't, maybe our daughters or granddaughters will."

"If we even get the privilege of having kids," Daisy said.

Chapter Sixteen

"Hurry!" Beulah yelled at Lily and Daisy when they were still quite a ways from the church. "There's a big storm on the way. Look out at the west sky!"

Lily glanced over her shoulder to see a cloud of red dust coming right at them. It was even bigger than the ones she had seen out in West Texas.

"What *is* that?" Daisy asked.

"We're about to get hit with a dust storm, and we don't have much time," Lily answered. "I figured the snakes were restless because rain was on the way, not a dust storm."

Beulah stepped off the porch and shouted above the roar. "Go get your bedding and bring it to the sanctuary. The barn ladies will be staying in the church tonight. We'll be crowded, but we'll make do. The cooks will stay in whichever house they work in. We don't know how long it will last or how hard it will hit us."

Lily picked up the pace, and somehow Daisy kept up with her. They passed dozens of women running down the path from the barn to the church. Most of them had bundles in their arms and children tearing along beside them. Lily looked over her shoulder, and the giant wall of red dirt coming at them like a mile-wide tornado seemed to be picking up speed. It looked like a hard rain falling down from the sky, only it wasn't water. It was sand and dirt and whatever else a severe wind could pick up and throw at them. If anyone was caught outside, it could easily strip the outer layer of skin right off their bodies.

"Rattlesnakes and now a sandstorm," Daisy yelled and ran into the barn.

Lily could hardly hear her over the growing sounds of the wind already whistling through the trees. "A hard rain right now would be wonderful. Mud balls like we saw in town would be better than what's about to happen. We need to work fast. I can already smell the dust."

"We can't let the horses stay out in this!" Daisy screamed. "We have got to bring them into the barn."

After all Beulah had done for them, Lily owed it to her to take care of the horses before she and Daisy made a mad dash back to the church. The big wooden doors leading out into the corral were stuck, and the hard wind beating against them didn't help.

"Give it all you've got!" Daisy shouted.

Lily pushed so hard that she thought for sure her arms would fall off at the shoulder, but the door squeaked and finally gave way. She grabbed the bridle on one horse, but its eyeballs rolled back, and it reared up on its hind legs. Her muscles ached from pushing on the doors so hard, and she dropped the reins. The dust got thicker and thicker, but she finally got a grip on the reins again and tugged hard.

"Okay, pretty baby," she yelled. "You have to come in the barn or die. This is just the beginning of the storm. When the worst of it arrives, you won't have a chance, so come in like a good girl. In another minute or two, I won't be able to see through all this well enough to get you inside."

"I've got this one headed in the right direction," Daisy shouted. "Follow me."

"I'm trying!" Lily yelled.

As if the animal understood that safety was inside the barn, it bolted. Lily felt like all nearly six feet of her was waving in the wind like a frayed flag. Then the horse stopped dead, and she landed on the floor in a heap. Daisy ran past her and single-handedly closed the door and then slid down the back side.

"Holy hell!" she swore.

"Amen!" Lily gasped.

"Are you all right? Is anything broken?"

"Doesn't seem to be," Lily said between bouts of sucking in air. "But it knocked the wind right out of me. What do we do now?"

"We'll put them in stalls after we can get our legs to work again," Daisy answered. "There's no way we can get to the church in this. I've never seen anything like it before. Have you?"

Lily leaned against a beam holding the roof up and coughed several times. "We'll have to camp out here until it all passes. And yes, I have seen sandstorms, but that was out in the flat country, and what I saw was a baby compared to this thing. I didn't think one would ever hit here with all these trees."

The horse that she'd brought in began to move slowly across the barn toward the stalls at the far end. Lily eased up on her knees and then her feet and got a firm grip on the bridle. "I'm just helping you so your pretty coat doesn't get blasted off your hide. Easy, now." She led the animal back to the first stall and used her free hand to open the gate. "Just take a few steps back. See, there's already hay in the trough, so you don't have to go hungry today."

Daisy stood up and took a step toward the second horse, but it reared up on its hind feet and pawed at her. "I don't think this critter likes me, even though I saved her life."

Lily slowly approached the horse from the side and picked up the reins. "Now, you are going to behave or I'm going to throw you back out into that storm. I don't have the energy to fight with you. Get in the stall and be good or die. It's your choice."

"At least they have hay, but their watering troughs only have an inch of water in the bottom," Daisy said. "I'd rather sink my nose down in that trough than into the pile of sand and dust outside. That's what we'd have to do if we take off in this mess toward the church. It was already blowing so hard that I couldn't even see the outhouse when we ran inside."

When she had the horse in the stall, Lily plopped down in front of the closed gate and put her head in her hands. "That was a close call, but we're safe now." She coughed even more between words. "I guess I sucked in some of the dirt."

"Is there water in any of the pitchers?" Daisy asked. "I'm thirsty, too."

"Yes, there's at least one pitcher of water in here, and a tub full that Amanda hauled in this morning with intentions of giving Bea a bath tonight, but we'll have to save part of that for the horses. But I'm not looking forward to living on a biscuit stuffed with eggs until this blows over."

"You just got one?" Daisy sneezed.

"Two. I brought them with me after breakfast because I didn't have time to eat a full plate, and I planned to come back and eat them after our shooting lessons," she replied. "You don't have to ask. You can have one of them."

Daisy reached over and patted her on the shoulder. "Thank you."

"We'd better both thank"—Lily pointed up toward the rafters in the barn—"someone higher than us that we at least found shelter before that thing hit. Why didn't we see it coming?"

"We were down in a holler with trees all around us. This came from the west, where's there's nothing but lots of dirt," Daisy answered. "It's been a strange year, hasn't it?"

"Yep, rain in July and now this. Think it will hit the sheep farm, or ranch—or whatever Matt and Claude call it?"

"I have no idea, but hopefully it doesn't." Daisy grinned all of a sudden.

"What's so funny? Can't I be worried about two guys who were kind to help us?" Lily's tone was filled with irritation.

"This is another reason I asked about water." Daisy pointed to her own face.

"Good Lord! I thought you meant only for drinking." Lily touched her cheeks. "Do I look like you do?"

"I don't have a mirror, but I would guess we look about alike. Since we'll need water for drinking, we shouldn't take a bath, but we could use some water to clean up a little."

With the doors closed and the one window battened down, the temperature in the barn rose to an unbearable point by midafternoon. Daisy stripped down to nothing but her undershirt and pantaloons. She stretched out on her bed, which consisted of a quilt thrown over a bunch of loose hay, and kept her arms straight out and away from her body.

How Lily could ever sleep through the howling wind and the sound of dirt blasting against the walls of the barn was a total mystery. Daisy ignored her growling stomach and stared at the rafters above her.

"This is *not* going to kill me," she reassured herself. "No one ever died from hunger after only a day, and the storm *will* pass. I'll be a sweaty mess when it does, but I'm made of sass and vinegar, not sugar and spice, and I can draw up a tankful of water and take a real bath tomorrow when the skies are clear again."

She turned her head toward Lily, half expecting her to wake up when she heard Daisy talking to herself, but no such luck. Daisy focused on the ceiling and let her thoughts wander back to when she was married and how miserable she had been. Maybe if she'd been like Sally Anne and had had lovers of her choosing, she might not have dreaded the nights so much. Or maybe if her husband had had a thought about pleasing her instead of simply crawling on and off her body, things would have been better. At least the men at the brothel didn't smell like whiskey and stale sweat.

"Would it be different with someone like Claude?" she wondered in a low voice.

Lily muttered something that sounded like, "Oh, Matt!" Then her eyes popped open. She sat straight up and groaned. "If hell is seven times hotter than this, I don't want to go."

"Start praying," Daisy said bluntly.

"You are in a mood," Lily snapped.

"Yes, I am. I'm hungry, and we shouldn't eat our biscuits until later so we can sleep tonight. And it's hot, and I'm sweating, and I couldn't get all the dirt off, so it's mixing with the sweat and making little balls of mud under my arms and in other places." She stopped long enough to catch her breath and then went on. "And I don't want to think about Claude or about how miserable I was in marriage, but I can't help it."

"I was dreaming about eating one of those horses," Lily said.

"Sounded to me like you were dreaming about Matt Maguire, like you might have been getting all sweaty for a far different reason than you are now," Daisy teased.

"Daisy! Proper women don't talk about bodily functions of any kind," Lily scolded. "We don't sweat—we dew up."

"Proper lady or not, in this heat, I sweat!" Daisy declared.

Chapter Seventeen

"You look like crap—literally," Lily said when she awoke the next morning.

Daisy raised up on an elbow and showed off lovely white teeth when she smiled. "So do you, my friend."

"I think it has passed," Lily whispered, for fear that just saying the words would jinx everything.

"If I look like you, then I would guess that we both need to fill up a trough and clean up a little before we go to the church to see how the rest fared," Daisy grumbled.

"We might have enough water left to—" Lily didn't get the words out before Amanda and Bea pushed the barn door open.

Bea pulled the scarf away that covered her nose and mouth. "Y'all need a bath."

Amanda removed the cloth away from her own face. "I'm glad you survived. We've all been worried about you. Are the horses dead? Miz Beulah has worried about them all night, as well as you two."

"We got them into the stalls just in time," Lily said. "We'll get cleaned up and come to the church. Or maybe we'll just go to Beulah's house for breakfast, if that's where we are eating this morning."

Bea grabbed Lily's hand and tugged. "We're just having hoecakes and jelly this morning. Miz Maggie is making them for us in the church a'cause everyone had to stay there last night. No one could go to the other places. I slept on the floor in front of the altar. Does that make me like baby Jesus?"

Lily kept a straight face even though it was tough. "I think it just might."

"Is everyone all right?" Daisy asked. "No one got hurt, did they?"

"No, we are all safe. Hot and sweaty, but no one is hurt," Amanda said. "As soon as this settles out of the sky, we'll all be taking baths."

"We'll be there as soon as we wash our faces," Lily agreed.

"We'll draw up some water for you from the well so you can wash up properly," Amanda said and looked around at all the dust piled up everywhere. "I guess we will be cleaning this barn and doing laundry all day."

"Looks like it—but there's enough water left in the trough for us to wash up before we come up to the church," Daisy said.

"See you in a few minutes, then, and be sure to put something over your noses and faces before you leave. The wind has died, but the air is thick. I'm going to fill up some buckets to take in to heat for the dishwashing job," Amanda told them. "We'll let you have some privacy."

"Why did everyone gather in the church?" Lily asked. "They could have stayed—"

"Beulah was afraid that the strong wind would blow the houses away," Amanda said. "She's been through a couple of these before, so we listened to her."

"She said that God wouldn't mess with a church," Bea added.

"Miz Beulah is a smart woman," Daisy said.

"Yes, she is," Amanda agreed. "We'll see y'all in a few minutes, then?"

"Soon as we get cleaned up a little," Lily replied.

As soon as the barn door was closed, Daisy stripped out of her dust-covered undergarments and splashed water up from the trough onto her body. "I would love to sink down in a real bath—but if I did, there would be nothing but mud left for you."

Lily drew up two buckets of water, carried them to the horse stalls, and poured some in each of the troughs while Daisy made herself presentable. "What's coming next?" she groaned when she had finished.

"What do you mean?" Daisy asked as she removed clean clothing from the satchel she had brought with her when they left the shop.

"Snakes. Dust storms. Sleeping in a barn."

"That's the downside," Daisy said. "Then there is finding out secrets, bonding with all kinds of women, making friends. Think positive. Your turn to wipe away the dust and sweat."

"And the bad attitude," Lily said as she stripped out of her smelly clothing and squeezed a cloth full of clean water over her body. "That helps a lot."

"Amen." Daisy grinned. "But it's not helping my grumbling stomach."

When Lily and Daisy stepped out of the barn, a strange, uncanny pall had settled over the whole area. Lily had seen gray skies before snow began to fall. She had seen rolling clouds and even lived through a couple of tornadoes, but she had never seen dust still hanging in the air almost obliterating the rising sun.

"This is horrible. The children are going to have to stay inside all day," Daisy said.

"Unless . . . Is that thunder I hear?" Lily cocked her head to one side.

Daisy picked up the pace. "We had better hurry. We'll be caked with mud if it starts to rain."

Elijah held the door to the church open for them and motioned them inside. "Real clouds have covered up the sun, and it's going to rain, for sure. Y'all get on in here."

"What are you doing out here?" Lily asked as she jogged past him.

"Bringing mail." Elijah slammed the door shut behind them. "I'm going to hand it off to you, Lily, and ride like the devil is chasing me to get back to the wagon yard. I figure I've got about five minutes before the mud balls start falling on me."

Lily took a stack of letters from him. "Have you heard anything about our list of demands?"

"I was thinking about how to tell all y'all. I sat in on the meeting, and there was a lot of arguing—some of it even from the women who are following Gertrude. She especially took offense at the idea of women wearing pants and teaching once they were married," Elijah answered as he put a bandanna over his nose and mouth. "The judge is supposed to come out here this evening, but I don't imagine he'll make it until the skies are clear."

"Thank you, Elijah, for bringing this to us and for all your support."

"You are welcome." His eyes crinkled with a smile. "I hope you stand your ground."

"Oh, we will," Lily assured him as he left.

Sally Anne hurried from the front of the church. "Is that letters? Why didn't Mr. Elijah stay with us? Do I have a letter?"

"He needs to get back to the wagon yard," Lily said. "Let's go on inside and we'll see who has mail."

She walked up to the pulpit, flipped through half a dozen pieces, and handed two to Sally Anne. "Looks like this is your lucky day. And here's one for Edith from Maudie and one for Amanda from someone in Oklahoma."

Bea danced around her mother's skirt. "Who is ours from? Will you read it to me?"

Amanda held the envelope to her heart. "It's from your grandma, and yes, I will read it to you."

Lily wanted nothing more than to read her letter, but she needed to eat first—even if it was just hoecake and jelly. The one little biscuit she'd had the day before was long since gone from her system, and she was feeling more than a little faint. Her stomach growled at the smell of fresh bread wafting through the church.

"If I faint, shove food down my throat," Daisy whispered.

"Does that mean you aren't thinking about Claude right now?" Lily asked out the side of her mouth.

"All I can think about is something to eat and a cup of coffee to wash this wretched dust from my throat," Daisy said. "Are you thinking about Matt?"

"Matt who?" Lily answered with a sly grin.

The hard-driving rain settled the dust from the air but left such a mess that the ladies spent the entire day cleaning. Daisy had slept poorly the night before, so by evening, she was ready for supper and to turn in early. But Lily had told the whole group that the judge was coming to discuss the list. Little did he know that Daisy Lindberg was in no mood to negotiate.

Daisy, Beulah, Sally Anne, Amanda, Edith, Maggie, and Lily all lined up on the front pew of the church that evening after supper when Judge Wesley Martin walked down the center aisle and took his place behind the lectern. He held his head high and looked down his nose at the group of women.

Daisy caught his eye and glared at him. He would not intimidate her with his position in town or with that sneer on his face.

Then he held up the petition Daisy had so carefully written up. "This, and the implication of a neglect of wifely duties, is an atrocity."

Daisy folded her arms across her chest and used all her willpower not to storm forward and use words that would bring lightning down through the rafters.

"The majority of your husbands and fiancés have signed it. I did not. I do not have to put my name on a document that says I will respect my wife and not lay a hand on her. That should be a given, and if my fiancée doesn't trust me to honor her, then perhaps she shouldn't be married to me. That said, while we have crossed out the demand that women wear pants and teach school after they are married, we have conceded that families can sit together in church and conceded on the rest of the smaller demands. Otis Ramsey said that he will agree to give the women who work for him in the saloon an eighty-twenty split, but that's as far as he will go. I suppose this means you can all go home tonight."

Daisy could see Sally Anne's spine stiffen when she popped up on her feet.

Frannie stood up from the second pew on the right. "All the rest of the women can go but we won't, not without a fifty-fifty split. We'll stay right here and starve before we take a penny less than that."

Rachael stood up and said, "And I'm staying with them until you sign a petition that says I can continue to teach school after I'm married."

"We will agree not to wear pants in public, but we want to wear them at home. Working in the fields in a skirt and all the undergarments is a hassle," came a voice from the back of the church.

"I suppose you had better take the petition back and talk some more," Sally Anne said. "We will either go together or not at all. And for the record, Mr. Martin, since you are not willing to put your name on that petition"—she marched right up to the lectern and removed the diamond engagement ring from her finger—"you can have this back."

"Sally Anne, don't do something rash," he scolded.

"*Rash* means impulsive. I'm not doing this on a whim. I've given it a lot of thought, Wesley. I wish you all the best, but that won't be me by your side," she said and went back to her place between Edith and Beulah.

"I've said my piece," the judge said and stepped away from the lectern. "I'll leave this here so you can see that it has been agreed upon, and if Frannie and the other saloon women want to stay here and negotiate on their own, then that's between them and Otis. I'm washing my hands of the whole affair."

"Frannie and her friends will be moving into my house with me," Sally Anne called out.

The judge stopped in his tracks and glared at her. "Do you have any idea what you are doing, woman?"

"I do," Sally Anne said.

Wesley turned his gaze to Edith. "You had better talk sense to her. Not only will her reputation be ruined, but so will yours."

Edith turned so white that Daisy thought for sure she would have to send someone for the smelling salts, but she rallied and met Wesley's eyes. "You better go on, now. She has made up her mind and made her own decision."

The judge stormed the rest of the way down the aisle and outside. When the door slammed shut, Edith turned to Sally Anne and said, "What have you done? You will never find a husband now."

Frannie crossed over to stand in front of Sally Anne. "Thank you for being so brave, but we can't let you do this. We appreciate everything all y'all have done for us, but—"

"I got my letter from Victoria, and a second one from Zula." Sally Anne stood up and turned to face the group. "I have been waiting for this mail for weeks now," she said, then told them the story she had already told Lily and Daisy. "I told Frannie she could have my house to run a respectable brothel out of once I left. I've also talked to Molly, who is quite happy to go with me as my assistant, so we will be leaving as soon as I can make arrangements. It will take a few days—maybe even a couple of weeks—to get my affairs in order, but we should be in England and fighting for women's rights all over the world by fall."

Edith fanned herself with her hand. "Why can't you do that right here in Texas?"

"We've made some progress these past couple of weeks," Amanda reminded her. "And we are going to renegotiate the demands. What you did was brave, but—"

"You are right, Amanda. We have made progress, and hopefully we have set an example for other women, but this has been my dream for a long time. Y'all be happy for me."

"We will, but we will miss you so much," Frannie said.

"Okay, then." Sally Anne smiled. "Let's think about the things that we didn't get. It's a long time until school takes up again this fall. What if the two teachers start up a private school? We can look into the law concerning private schools. What if it was a girls' school, where you encourage the young ladies to grow up to be lawyers, doctors, or whatever else they want? All you need is a—"

"You can have my house and barn free of charge," Beulah offered. "You can keep my horses and teach the ladies to ride."

"And shoot a gun, as well as learning to read and write," Daisy added.

"Oh my! That's a wonderful idea," Rachael said. "Start them young to be independent. But who in town would even consider such a thing, or even give us a small salary?"

"I can take care of your salary if I can volunteer to help teach etiquette lessons a couple of days a week," Edith said. "I'm going to be lonely when Sally Anne leaves, and that will give me something to do. I'm sorry that I pushed her towards Wesley Martin."

"Can we see a show of hands from you mothers who might be willing to enroll your daughters in Miz Rachael's new school in the fall?" Sally Anne asked.

Nearly all the hands shot up in the air.

"Okay, then, we are down to the pants issue," she said. "Personally, I own several pair that I intend to take to London with me. There is no written law that says a woman cannot dress as she pleases in her own home. So, what do you say?"

"I say that we can live with that, and Gertrude and the others will feel like they've won a little bone to chew on," Lily said. "That said, anyone that needs a pair of women's pants made to fit them, come visit me and Daisy at the seamstress shop."

"Shall we have supper and pack up our things to go home tomorrow?" Maggie asked.

"Together!" Daisy grabbed Lily's hand and raised both into the air.

"Together!" the echo behind them resounded off the walls.

Chapter Eighteen

Saturday morning brought a bright sun glaring down on a town that seemed to have lost its heart and soul. Not a single wagon, nor horse, was on the street. Even the piano in the saloon was quiet.

A gust of hot wind caught a strand of Lily's red hair and blew it across her face. She tucked it back up under her wide-brimmed straw hat. Even though, at high noon, the heat was already reaching that unbearable stage, she didn't mind. She was going home to sleep in a real bed, take a real bath, and wash what was left of the sandstorm out of her hair. As she walked with the other women behind Beulah's wagon, she wondered whether they had accomplished something lasting or if, little by little, the ladies would all slip right back into old habits and patterns.

"You are frowning," Daisy said. "Are you upset that Sally Anne and Frannie are riding in the wagon with Beulah?"

"Not at all," Lily answered. "They are making a statement."

"Then what is it?" Daisy pressured.

Lily lowered her voice. "I'm hoping that this isn't just a passing fancy. I won't be able to bear it if, in a week, things are right back where they were before we went out to the camp."

"We did what we could," Daisy reminded her. "Now it's up to all of them to see it through."

"You are right." Lily shivered in spite of the blistering heat. "Does the town seem strange to you?"

"Like a ghost town," Daisy said.

"And this is Saturday, when things are usually busy." Lily nodded toward the saloon, where Otis was standing outside with his arms crossed over his chest. "Doesn't look like he's happy."

"Don't look like it," Daisy said with a smile.

When Otis saw Frannie sitting in the wagon beside Sally Anne and Beulah, he shouted swear words harsh enough to cause another sandstorm. That's when Frannie said something to Beulah, and the wagon stopped.

All three women hopped down from the buckboard and stood together in front of Otis. He spit a string of tobacco on the sidewalk at their feet and swore again.

Frannie squared up her shoulders. "You *will* watch your mouth in front of these decent women and children."

"Or what?" Otis snarled.

"Or I will borrow Beulah's frying pan and knock some sense into your thick skull," she answered.

"I can lay my hands on it without even getting back up on the buckboard," Beulah said in a no-nonsense tone. "I'll even give it to you just in case you need it later on down the road. But if you do use it, be sure to wash the blood off the back side before you use it to fry chicken."

When Otis doubled up his fist and raised it toward Frannie, all the women behind the wagon moved forward in a semicircle around her.

"Lay a hand on her and the sheriff will never find your body," Amanda said.

"You are all fired," Otis snapped.

"No, we are not. We quit the day we walked out of here and these women took us in and treated us like sisters," Frannie said. "Thanks for the offer of the skillet, Beulah, but I won't need it. Lily gave me one of the pistols, and it will do a more permanent job."

"You are not to ever walk through the doors of my saloon again," Otis spit the words out like they were poison. He left footprints in the sand that had settled on the boardwalk outside the saloon when he stormed back inside.

"Thank you all," Frannie said once things had quieted. "But y'all don't have to go all the way to Sally Anne's place with us."

"Together!" Amanda called out, and the rest of the women echoed and returned to their places behind the wagon.

"One hurdle jumped over," Lily said, and hoped that what just happened was an indication of the women's determination. Tomorrow, when families were supposed to sit together in church, would tell the real tale.

Daisy went into the shop ahead of Lily and sighed loudly. "I'm so glad to be back. I'm going to draw up enough water for a proper bath in the kitchen and give my hair a good washing."

"I'll fire up the stove and heat up a kettle for you," Lily offered.

Daisy tossed her hat onto the sofa and headed toward the kitchen area. "Thanks, but no thanks. I want a cold bath. If you want a warm one, then you can heat water, but remember that it's going to make the whole place hotter."

"A cold one sounds wonderful," Lily agreed and removed her hat. "I'll help you get the water. We should be finished by the time Beulah comes around to go with us to Hattie's for a hot meal, and then on down to Sally Anne's place to see what kind of house she is giving Frannie. Do you really think those women can make a living in this town? Or that Rachael and her coworker can manage a school for girls?"

"They will survive like we did when we went to the Paradise." Daisy realized that she admired Frannie for giving a fancy brothel a try. It wouldn't be easy, but she and her girls only had to entertain one man each a night. Surely Otis wouldn't mind losing that many men to the new brothel.

She and Lily had just finished having a nice cool bath and getting dressed when Beulah yelled from the front of the shop, "Is everyone decent back there?"

Daisy opened the door between the shop and living quarters. "We are decent, but we had to put our hair up wet."

"So did I," Beulah chuckled. "As dead as this town is, I don't imagine anyone is going to notice. Hattie isn't going to really open the café until tomorrow, but she's whipping up something just for us tonight. She should have it ready when we get there."

Daisy picked up her hat. "I'm starving, but having a bath was worth not getting supper until now."

Hattie met them at the café's door and then locked it behind them. "Elijah shared a slab of cured bacon with me, so we're having that with pancakes, eggs, and fried potatoes for our early supper. I thought that coming home would be . . ." She paused. "Well, I don't know what word to use, but I miss the noise of the camp already. And it seemed strange to cook for four people tonight instead of helping Maggie prepare for an army each evening."

"Same here," Beulah said. "The shelves in my store are pitiful since Elijah brought so much to the camp to help feed the women. I won't starve, and neither will Lily and Daisy, but I won't have anything for you, Hattie, until the train brings supplies."

"Don't need anything more. I've got plenty of staples, and Elijah has said he has a fellow that can keep me supplied with pork and beef." Hattie motioned toward a table set for four. "I don't have ice or even thick cream for your tea, but there's plenty of sugar, and you can sprinkle a little cinnamon on the top if you want more flavor."

"What can we do to help?" Daisy asked.

"You can come on back to the kitchen and help me bring in the platters," Hattie answered. "Lily, you and Beulah go on and take a seat."

In less than a minute, two large platters were on the table, and Hattie and Daisy were seated. "Y'all go on and help yourselves. You've got to be hungry. I've been nibbling the whole time I was cooking. Do you think we really did any good out there, or will things go back to like they were by fall?"

Lily piled her plate fuller than was polite, but she really was hungry, and she was among friends. "I was thinking the same thing. Daisy said that we did what we could. Now it's up to them to carry on. But Daisy and I don't have a wedding to keep us busy the rest of the summer. We may just be making cotton dresses and maybe some hats to sell in Beulah's store."

Beulah loaded her plate even more than Lily had. "She's right, but I'm worried about Edith. Sally Anne was her . . ." She frowned.

"Her princess?" Daisy asked.

"Yes," Beulah said. "Exactly."

"Edith is tough as nails," Hattie said with half a chuckle. "She will survive. Wallace best be careful until Sally Anne leaves or Edith might pack a trunk and go with her."

A wave of jealousy washed over Daisy. She wished that she was going off to England, but when they had all offered to go with Miz Raven, she had agreed that they could do more good right there in Texas than they could in London.

Sally Anne opened the door to her two-story home and motioned for Daisy, Lily, Beulah, and Hattie to come inside. To the left of the wide foyer was an opulent sitting room with a piano in the corner. The whole setup made Lily lonesome for the Paradise.

"The ladies are upstairs checking out the bedrooms," Sally Anne said. "Mama and Daddy wanted a big family, so they built this house in preparation for lots of children, but all they got was me. Come on in the kitchen and let me introduce you to Laverne, my housekeeper, and her husband, Oscar, who takes care of the gardens as well as the ranch and does whatever else Laverne tells him to do."

"I heard that." Laverne smiled at all of them. She was a short, round woman with gray hair done up in a bun on top of her head and had sparkling brown eyes. "And our Sally Anne is right on the button. She has explained what she is going to do and how this house could have some changes."

"I'm Oscar." He held his big hand out toward Lily. He was only a little taller than Laverne and had a full head of snow-white hair.

Lily shook hands with him. "Nice to meet you both."

"We'll take care of Sally Anne's new friends just like we've always done with the whole family," Laverne said. "I'll bring some tea and cookies to the living room. You know, I never did want her to marry that judge. Our Sally Anne has got too much fire in her to settle down to cookin' and cleanin' and takin' care of babies. When she gets to be president of this country, all us women might even have the right to vote and choose how we will make our living and be treated."

"I wouldn't doubt it one bit," Beulah said.

"How come I never met you before now?" Hattie asked.

"We don't have much reason to come to town," Oscar said. "We grow most of what we eat right here on the estate. And Elijah delivers what we don't have for us."

"Not that I'm complainin'," Laverne said. "I've turned into a bit of a hermit these past few years. I want to thank all of you for taking care of Sally Anne out at your camp. If I wasn't so old and wasn't needed here, I would have been right out there with you. I hear the ladies comin' down the stairs. Y'all go on in the parlor."

"Do they really know that this place is about to be a bordello?" Lily whispered to Sally Anne when they were in the foyer.

"They do," she answered. "Short form of a long story is that Oscar and Otis are cousins, and they do not get along. It's probably been years since they've even spoken to each other."

"I see," Lily said. "Is everyone in town related in some way to everyone else?"

"Pretty much," Sally Anne answered. "Wes was about the only man I *could* marry." And then she smiled at Frannie, who was the last saloon girl to come down the stairs.

"I feel like I'm dreaming," Frannie whispered.

Sally Anne sat down on the blue velvet sofa. "Here's the deal: you-all can run a brothel, or you can live here and do whatever else you want. Laverne is getting old and could use some help taking care of this big house and in the kitchen. Oscar manages the hired hands, and she cooks and feeds them two meals a day, but he could use help, too. He could train one of you to take care of the books and maybe another one to step into his shoes as supervisor of the ranch."

"That's quite an offer," Molly chimed in. "If I wasn't going to England with Sally Anne, I would gladly help Laverne in the kitchen."

"Molly and I have already started packing our trunks." Sally Anne's eyes sparkled, and she patted Molly on the shoulder. "It's fortunate that we're the same size and that I have plenty of clothing for half a dozen women."

Frannie swiped a tear from her eye. "We are the luckiest women in town."

Lily laid a hand on Frannie's wrist. "We all are. Sally Anne, do you know when you are leaving?"

"I'm still working on it, but when we do, will y'all come to see us off? I never realized how much planning went into a trip like this. Daddy always took care of that when we traveled abroad."

"Of course we will," Lily answered. "And don't be surprised if there's more than just us four there to wave goodbye."

"I bet all the ladies who camped with us are there," Daisy said.

"Well, I know that I'll be there, for sure," Frannie said. "But right now I want to talk about the ranch. How many hired hands are there?"

"About twenty-five," Sally Anne answered. "We have cattle and grow our own hay for them. It's a pretty big estate. Daddy made a fortune running longhorns from here to Dodge City right after the war."

"That would mean we wouldn't have to entertain men?" Lula, one of the other saloon ladies, asked.

"Only if you want to—and then there's no questions asked. I believe in free love, so whether you choose to sleep with a male friend or not is your business," Sally Anne replied.

"But our reputation will always follow us," Lula said. "Who would ever want to marry one of us?"

"Oscar married me," Laverne said as she set a tray with cookies and tea on the small library table in the corner. "He took me right out of a house even more horrible than the one Otis runs. You are right about the past following you, but I've had a wonderful life."

"I'll work for Laverne and Oscar," Frannie said. "You don't have to pay me. Room and board will be enough."

Lula raised her hand. "Me too."

The other three did the same.

"I would have stood beside you no matter what, but I'm glad you made this decision," Sally Anne said. "And you definitely will each get a paycheck at the end of each month. You will not work for nothing. That's settled."

Frannie held up a palm and shook her head. "Not really. You said that at least one of us will work with Oscar to learn the books and another to learn to be a supervisor. How are the hired hands going to like being bossed around by a woman?"

"They don't have to like it—they just have to obey," Sally Anne answered. "That will be one more step for women's rights."

Life is full of twists and turns, Lily thought. Oscar had to have forgiven Laverne for her past. Would Matt Maguire be that kind of man?

"Don't life turn around?" Daisy said on the way to church the next morning.

"It does have a way of doing just that," Lily agreed. "But what are you talking about?"

"That story that Sally Anne told us about Laverne kind of explains her decision to work so hard for women's rights. I get the impression that Laverne had a big hand in helping raise Sally Anne."

"Could be," Lily answered. "This whole new life that we're trying to live seems like it has all kinds of sharp turns and surprises in the path, don't it? Speaking of which, I expect our new independent women will be in church this morning, but how many husbands and fiancés do you suppose will be there?"

"Every one of them, I hope!" Daisy sent up a silent prayer that all the husbands, fiancés, and young men in town would be there to support their mothers, girlfriends, and sisters. Then she gasped. "What if there's no preacher? Tobias might not even show up. He was pretty mad when he stormed out of the church two weeks ago."

"Then Maggie can preach," Lily answered. "Do you think Frannie and Sally Anne will attend services?"

"Hello!" Beulah came out of her store and joined them. "I heard that last question, and no, they will not be with us this morning. Sally Anne and Molly are busy with their plans. Frannie says that she wouldn't want to cause shame to the very women who were kind to her. Laverne never attends either church. It's been thirty years since Oscar hauled her out to Sally Anne's ranch. But I wouldn't be surprised if she and the ladies don't have a singing, kind of like what we did at the camp."

Lily stopped walking and turned to focus on Beulah. "You knew that story?"

"My mama told me about her before she died. Laverne used to come to the store, but the way the women treated her back then was even worse than folks treat reformed shady ladies today. Mama told me that if the saloon girls came into the business, I was to treat them with the same respect that I showed everyone else." Beulah pulled a lace fan from her purse and changed the subject. "It's going to be another hot one, and there's not a single little rain cloud up in the sky."

Daisy dabbed at the sweat beads collecting on her upper lip. "I still don't know why Sally Anne has to go all the way to England. There's plenty of work to be done right here in Texas."

"She needs to get away from the judge, and she'll learn things over there that will help her. When she feels like she is ready or when she gets homesick, she'll be back, even if it's just for a visit," Beulah replied and kept the fan going as fast as she could. "I hope that Tobias doesn't get too wound up in his sermon and ends up keeping us past noon. Which reminds me, why don't y'all have lunch with me today? It's too hot to fire up the stove, so we can have a cold soup and sandwiches like we did last time. The iceman doesn't come around for a couple more days, so we'll have to drink lukewarm tea," Beulah answered.

"I can live with that—and thank you," Lily said and pointed toward the churchyard when they were only a few houses away.

"It's not ladylike to point," Daisy scolded.

Beulah laughed. "Who says we are ladies?"

"You've got a point." Daisy laughed with her. "It looks like either Tobias or Maggie will be preaching to a crowd." She could hear the normal noise coming out the open door and windows, which meant folks were visiting before the service began. With the heat outside crawling up to the suffocating stage, she dreaded going inside—so many bodies jammed into the pews, and even if the occasional breeze did find a way in, it wouldn't last long.

"I'd rather be at home," she whispered.

"So would I, but we need to go support our little lambs," Beulah told them.

Lambs!

That one word reminded Daisy of Claude, and a vision of him filled her mind. He was lying outside under a big shade tree with his head in her lap. A creek bubbled nearby, and little lambs romped through the tall green grass. She must've been smiling, because she felt both of the other women staring at her.

"What?" She frowned.

"We're talking about heat that would scorch the devil's forked little tail, and you are smiling," Lily said.

"I was mentally preparing myself for the heat by thinking about a pastoral scene with lambs playing in the tall grass," she answered.

They started walking again, and Lily shivered. "How can a cold chill chase down my back in this heat?"

"What were you thinking about?" Beulah used her fan to create a little breeze for her face.

"Daisy mentioned tall grass, and it reminded me of all those snakes slithering out at the camp," Lily answered as she removed her fan from her purse.

"All you are doing is moving hot air," Daisy told them. "I'll be really glad when fall comes, or even winter. I can put enough clothes on to stay warm when it's freezing cold, but I can only take so many off when it's this hot." Daisy walked through the doors into the sanctuary and glanced over the crowd. She couldn't find Elijah, which definitely meant no Matt or Claude. "There doesn't seem to be a place for us except on the front row."

"Then that's where we will sit," Beulah said and started down the center aisle.

"Miz Daisy!" Bea yelled when she passed by the pew where Amanda and her entire family, including her husband, were sitting.

"Hello!" Daisy said. "My, don't you look pretty today."

"Thank you," Amanda mouthed.

Daisy laid a hand on her shoulder and gave it a gentle squeeze. One little step, she thought, had changed Sunday morning, even if it never went past that. She sat down and took her fan out of her purse. Hot air beat no air, and from the look on the good preacher's face, he was about to put more heated words out into the sanctuary.

"Good morning, folks," he said in a calm voice. "I see there have been some changes made in our seating arrangements. Maggie tells me that old dogs can learn new tricks, but I'm not so sure that I can. So, with that in mind, I will be retiring as soon as the deacons find a preacher to take my place. This morning, though, I would like to read the first eight verses from the third chapter of the book of Ecclesiastes." He cleared his throat and glanced down at Maggie, who was sitting on the front row.

"*To everything there is a season, and a time to every purpose under the heaven: A time to be born, and a time to die; a time to plant, and a time to pluck up that which is planted; A time to kill, and a time to heal; a time to break down, and a time to build up; A time to weep, and a time to laugh; a time to mourn, and a time to dance; A time to cast away stones, and a time to gather stones together; a time to embrace, and a time to refrain from embracing; A time to get, and a time to lose; a time to keep, and a time to cast away; A time to rend, and a time to sew; a time to keep silence, and a time to speak; A time to love, and a time to hate; a time of war, and a time of peace.*"

He stopped and wiped beads of sweat from his brow. "These verses have reminded me that God is in control, even of the situation here in this town. The last time I stood in this pulpit, I preached about wives being submissive. I still believe that, but Maggie has reminded me that there is a rest of the story that follows those verses." He opened his Bible to a different place and read, "*Husbands should love their wives even as Christ loved the church and gave himself for it; That he might sanctify and cleanse it with the washing of water by the word, That he might present it to himself a glorious church, not having spot, or wrinkle, or any such thing; but that it should be holy and without blemish. So, ought men to love their wives as their own bodies. He that loveth his wife loveth himself. For no man ever yet hated his own flesh; but nourisheth and cherisheth it, even as the Lord the church.*" Tobias smiled at the congregation. "I see some men wiggling in their seats. Is this landing on your soul? It did with me when Maggie came home, and we had a long talk. I owe you ladies an apology for the way I behaved. It was not with the spirit of Jesus in my heart. And now, with that said, go home and let all of this sink into your hearts. Maggie and I will be leaving soon to make a fresh start somewhere else. We haven't made definite plans, but we will make that decision together. Now I will ask Elijah to give the benediction."

As soon as Elijah's short prayer ended, folks stood up and began to file out of the church, the hum of conversation rising like a swarm of bees. Beulah shook her head slowly. "I bet Tobias has calluses on his knees from praying that Maggie would come back to him."

"I'm just wondering if any of what he said will sink into the men's hearts," Daisy said as she stood up.

"If one powerful man can be changed, then I have hope," Lily said.

Chapter Nineteen

Lily, Daisy, and Beulah gathered with droves of other women to see Sally Anne and Molly off on a bright Monday morning two weeks later. An aura of excitement mixed with a touch of sadness filled the air. When the train whistle blew from a mile down the tracks, Sally Anne grabbed Lily and hugged her tightly.

"Laverne and Oscar could never have children. They are so excited to have a houseful of daughters now," she whispered. "I'm glad the ladies chose to get out of the business they were in, but it was their decision, and I would have supported them either way."

"You do know that your property is tainted now, don't you?" Lily asked.

"It's been tainted since the day Oscar brought Laverne home, and my folks refused to let other people's opinions matter. I was just a newborn baby then. Maybe that's what helped form my own attitude about what others think," Sally Anne replied.

The train came to a loud, screeching halt in front of the platform, and a porter hopped out. "These trunks going?" he asked.

"Yes, sir, and here's our tickets." Sally Anne handed him what the stationmaster had given her. Then she turned to the crowd and raised a fist in the air. "Thank you all for this send-off. Molly and I will do you proud, we promise. Together!" She blew kisses to the women, and then she boarded the train.

Molly hugged Frannie one more time and then took a step back. "I was afraid to leave the saloon that day, but I'm glad we did."

"So are we," Lily told her. "Look what one little decision has caused."

Dozens and dozens of fists went into the air as Molly climbed aboard. The shouting resounded louder than the train's engine. "Freedom for us all!" Frannie said as she raised her hand a second time and started a chant: "Together! Together! Together!"

When the noise died down and the train disappeared, the women headed back to their homes. Almost everyone was gone when Edith turned and grabbed Lily in a fierce hug. Tears flowed down her cheeks and dampened Lily's shirtwaist. "Tell me she will be all right."

Lily patted her on the back and said, "She and Molly will be fine, but I do feel sorry for anyone who gets in her way."

Edith leaned back and looked up at Lily's face. "The judge is really angry. He's threatening to kick you and Daisy out of his store when your month's rent is up."

"I would guess what he's most mad about is the fact that Frannie isn't at the saloon anymore," Lily told her.

The tears dried up in an instant, and Edith's expression changed from sadness to pure unadulterated anger. She turned around and focused on Lily again. "Now, what were you saying?"

"Do you remember the day that Daisy and I went into the bar to buy a bottle of whiskey and Frannie and Daisy got into a fight?"

"Did I hear my name?" Frannie asked from a few feet away.

"Yes, you did," Lily answered and motioned for her to join them. "Tell Edith about the judge."

"He is . . . I mean, *was* . . . one of my best customers. He used to tell me that if I wasn't who I was, that he would take me out of that place and marry me tomorrow," Frannie said.

Daisy's expression spoke volumes when Lily glanced over at her. In that single moment, Lily had no doubts that Daisy was completely over Wesley Martin.

"How could he have said all those words at the church when he was seeing you?" Edith asked.

Frannie shrugged. "We hear . . . *heard* . . . sweet things like that all the time—but we don't have to listen to empty words anymore."

"Why's that?" Edith asked. "And why are you saying *was* and *heard*?"

The women began to walk back toward town in groups, but Edith kept her feet planted on the train platform.

"We will not be working as prostitutes anymore," Frannie said.

"Sally Anne offered us a choice of entertaining men or working for Laverne and Oscar at her estate," Lula answered.

"All of you?" Edith asked.

"Yes, ma'am," Ruby replied with a nod.

"We love it on the ranch," another woman added.

Edith chuckled. "I wonder where the almighty pious judge will go now for his bedroom romps."

"Well, it won't be to my bed," Frannie declared. "I'm done with that life, and men in general."

"Who would have thought that all this change could happen so fast?" Edith started back toward town with the last group—Lily, Daisy, Beulah, Maggie, and the four remaining women who had worked for Otis.

Maggie stopped off at the parsonage. Edith left the bunch when they reached her house.

"We would like to visit with you about making us some clothes," Frannie said in a low voice. "Is now a good time?"

"Absolutely, but don't any of you sew?" Daisy asked.

"I do, but . . ." Lula said. "And there is a sewing machine at our new place, but . . ."

"We don't know how to make pants, and Oscar says that we shouldn't be working with him in the fields in a dress," Frannie finally finished for her. "So I guess we're going from scantily dressed saloon girls that some women won't even speak to, to women wearing pants whom they won't speak to either."

Daisy pointed up at the sky. "The sun is about halfway to telling us that it's noon. Laverne will most likely be needing you soon, so let's get on in the shop and get all four of you measured for your new britches."

"Another step in the rising sun?" Lily asked.

"I would say so," Daisy answered.

"What does that mean?" Lula asked.

Daisy explained the comment. "Our mission is kind of like coming out of darkness and into the light, but it's not all at once. It's like the rising sun that comes up a little at a time. We broke through dawn when we lived at the camp for those few days. Now you are pushing up the sun in the sky even more by putting in an order for pants."

Frannie opened the door and stood to one side to let the other women go in first. "If wearing pants helps the cause, then we will wear them with pride."

Frannie and her friends were barely out of sight when the shop door opened. When Lily looked over her shoulder, a rush of heat filled her whole body.

"Well, hello, Matt," Beulah said. "We weren't expecting you today. The pickin's are slim right now, but I've got supplies on the way."

"Evenin', ladies," Matt said. "We went by the store, but it was locked up. We brought a couple of butchered sheep to help you get through until you can get your store restocked, Miz Beulah. If you don't need the meat, we can let Uncle Elijah have it to deliver to other folks."

"And if you have any left, we need a big sack of sugar," Claude said, but he didn't take his eyes off Daisy. "We're picking apples and peaches to put up pie filling for the winter months. If you don't have it, we can add the sugar later, but the cobblers taste better if the sugar is put in at the time of canning."

"I've got a couple of big bags left, as near as I can figure," Beulah said. "I'll take all that mutton you brought. It will probably be gone before the day is done. For those who fight against sheep farming, our townsfolk sure do like a leg of lamb and mutton chops. How's Alma and the girls doing?"

"Missing you," Matt replied. "Why don't you ride out and see them this week?"

"If it's not raining or another sandstorm doesn't come around the bend, I just might do that," Beulah said. "My next shipment of supplies doesn't come in until Thursday, so I suppose I can lock up the store and spend a day at the farm tomorrow. Lily, why don't you and Daisy go with me? We can take the wagon and make a day of it."

"We should stay here and work on Frannie's order," Daisy said with slight sigh.

Lily laid a hand on Daisy's shoulder. "One day shouldn't make that much difference, and we could sure use a day out of town."

"That's wonderful," Beulah said with a wide grin. "I'll tell Elijah to get my team hitched up and ready. We'll leave right after breakfast. I could maybe help Alma in the kitchen with dinner and supper."

"After we unload the mutton at your store, we're going on down to Uncle Elijah's to see him. We could tell him to have your wagon ready to save you a trip," Claude suggested.

"Thanks," Beulah said. "The store isn't locked, so just put the meat in the kitchen and I'll get it cut up and ready for sale after a bit."

"We can do that," Claude said and tipped his hat toward Daisy. "I'll be looking forward to showing you around tomorrow."

As soon as they were gone, Beulah frowned. "Those are the best of men. Don't y'all go breaking their hearts." She shook a finger at each of them in emphasis. "Now, y'all let me get on back to my place and get word out that I've got mutton for sale."

Miz Raven's voice popped into Lily's head. *Or letting them break yours.*

"We'll be very careful," Daisy promised. "And we'll see you first thing tomorrow morning."

Beulah gave them a curt nod and closed the door behind her.

"Should I clean up the coffee cups or start cutting out pants?" Lily asked.

Daisy sank down on the sofa and leaned her head against the back. "I'll get out the patterns. We'll have to adjust them for women—but, Lily, we've got to be up-front and honest with Matt and Claude tomorrow. We need to nip whatever this is that's going on between us and them in the bud."

Lily plopped down beside her and propped her feet on the table in front of them in a very unladylike fashion. "What if one or both of them is another Oscar?" She picked up Beulah's fan she had left on the wide sofa arm. No matter how fast she moved the air, it did very little to cool off her face and neck. "What if they tell us they don't give a damn what we used to do but that they really like us?"

"You think there's a snowball's chance in hell for that to happen?" Daisy asked. "Women like us don't get those kind of chances."

"Laverne did," Lily argued. "And look at the great situation for Frannie and the others with them now."

"That's a one-in-a-million thing," Daisy scolded.

"But what if—"

"Then I would be on the first wagon train headed north to cooler country with Claude," Daisy said.

"Why do you say that?"

Daisy told her about Claude's dreams and how they matched her own yearning to travel and live in a place that had snow in the winter. "I never wanted to come south from Spanish Fort, but I really didn't have any other choice, and we are such good friends."

"My dream has always been simply to be loved and respected," Lily admitted. "I didn't think that would ever be possible after what we've done. I guess we've both been hiding dreams that can't come true. I can't imagine you not being here with me, Daisy, no matter what happens in the future."

"I feel the same way. Remember when we told Frank we were cousins?" Daisy said. "Look at us. Do we look like we share a single drop of blood?"

"No," Lily giggled. "We do not, but he believed us. And cousins of blood aren't necessarily as close as sisters of the heart."

Chapter Twenty

*P*ure peace. Those were the two words that kept playing through Daisy's mind when she sat down under a massive pecan tree and leaned back against the bark. Just like she had imagined when she couldn't sleep at night, she could hear the river's water behind her as it calmly made its way through the area. Sheep fed on the cool green grass, a pleasant change from Autrie's dusty streets. Claude sat down beside her, close enough that his shoulder brushed against hers and sent little waves of desire deep down in her body.

"What do you think of our little piece of paradise?" he asked.

Why did he have to use that word—paradise? she thought with a silent groan.

To remind you that it's time to come clean with him so that neither of you wind up with a broken heart, Miz Raven answered in her scolding tone.

"Do you still have a dream of striking out on your own and going north?" she asked.

His brilliant smile turned into a frown. "I do, but you didn't answer my question."

"I love it, but if it's paradise, how can you leave it?" Daisy asked.

"To build another one, maybe with cattle instead of sheep, to carve out my own way in the world. I was born right here on this place just before my father went off to fight in the war. And my grandparents,

Uncle Elijah's generation, came here and lived in a covered wagon until they could build a house. I want to see what's out there in the world," he answered. "How about you, Miz Daisy? Do you still want to go on an adventure?"

"Yes, but . . ."

A lamb left the flock and eased its way over to sniff her hand. She sank her fingers into his soft wool and petted the little guy. "Why do you want to deal with cattle when you know all about sheep?"

"Because they'll withstand the cold weather better," he answered. "And what was that 'but' all about?"

She squared her shoulders and got ready to say the hardest words she would ever utter. "Have you been flirting with me?"

Claude picked a couple of wildflowers and handed them to her. "I hope you know the answer to that. But yes, I have. The first time I laid eyes on you, I knew there was something between us, and I think you feel the same. I can see it in your gorgeous blue eyes."

Angst replaced the perfect peace she had known at first. Whatever pedestal Claude had put her on was about to come crashing to the ground. "My name is not really Daisy. When we went to work at the Paradise in Spanish Fort, up in the northern part of the state, Miz Raven loved flowers. So she gave all seven of us a new name: Daisy, Lily, Rose, and so forth. According to her, we made up her beautiful bouquet. My birth name is Ethel Kate Lindberg."

Claude picked a wild forget-me-not and tucked it into her hair. "That's still a real pretty name, but I like Daisy better, so that's what I'm going to call you. Is that all you need to get off your chest?"

"No, it's just the beginning," she answered. "I was married, and my husband died. He wasn't a very nice man, and living with him was miserable." She hoped that would put him off enough that she didn't have to tell him anything more.

"I was married, too," Claude said. "I was very young, and my wife died in childbirth. So did my son. That was five years ago, and I thought I would never fall for another woman until I met you. You've made me feel something again, Daisy." He took her hand in his and brought her knuckles to his lips.

When he kissed them, she fought back tears. She wanted to spill everything about her past, but the words would not come out of her mouth.

"Mama says that life gives us twists and turns when we are traveling down the road to happiness," he said and kissed her knuckles once more.

"Those are lovely words." Her voice cracked a little.

"I've always been a bit of a dreamer," he said. "I love to read anything I can get my hands on, especially about wagon trains and the Idaho Territories."

Time to face the worst part, Daisy told herself.

"Me, too, but remember when I told you that I worked for Miz Raven? She was a madam at a very fancy, exclusive brothel," she blurted out before she lost her courage. "Miz Raven rescued me from having to walk into a place like Otis runs and ask for a job. I had no money and no family when my husband died. We sharecropped the land we were on, and the house was part of that deal. So I had to move out the day after he was buried, and I had nowhere to go or the means to even leave town."

Claude was quiet for a few seconds that seemed to last for three days past eternity. He was a good man, and she felt as if she could trust him not to spread what she had said around town. She fully well expected him to simply stand up and walk away without looking back or saying a word.

He cupped her cheeks in his hands and whispered, "My mama says that not all angels have halos or wings."

"But—"

"There are no *buts* between a man and a woman who are attracted to each other. I can't think of anything but you all day, and then at night I dream about a moment when I can hold you and tell you that I've fallen in love with you." He pressed a kiss to her forehead. "Someday we are going to go on that adventure together, but until then, will you let me court you?"

She nodded, and his lips met hers in a kiss so steamy that the hot sun broiling down on them felt like a nice winter breeze. When the kiss ended, she leaned back.

"Are you sure about this? What your mama said is sweet, but I'm no angel," she informed him.

"I've never been surer about anything in my whole life," Claude answered. "Are you willing to go with me someday to start a new ranch?"

"I am," she answered, and pulled his face to hers for another kiss. One that caused feelings of something more than just simple sexual gratification.

For a brief moment, Lily felt like a queen sitting beside Matt in the buggy. Then she remembered what she and Daisy had both vowed to do that day, and her imaginary crown took a tumble and landed out there in the middle of a flock of sheep.

Over there was where Alma lived now with her two girls. Lily struggled to focus on Matt's idea of giving her a tour. Next to that house was one that belonged to Elijah. He had been born in that place and was the last living one of his generation. On down just a few hundred yards was another empty one. Matt's other cousin had lived in that one, but he and his wife had left a month ago, headed for California.

"And that right there is my house." He pointed to a modest log cabin sitting on a small rise.

"How many houses are on this ranch?" Lily asked.

"I never stopped to count them," he answered. "The big house that you saw when you first arrived on the property is where my parents and unmarried siblings live, and most of the decisions are made around the kitchen table there. You'll meet them at dinner. The place covers several thousand acres, and we all take care of the sheep, moving them from one pasture to another as it's necessary."

"You have cats?" she asked when she noticed a couple sprawled out on the porch.

"Yep, and more than one sheep dog roams around the place. That one belongs to me, though." A dog as big as one of the rams came down the path to meet them.

Matt flicked the reins and made a turn down the short path leading up to the house. "I wanted you to see my place before we continue. Claude and I built it about five years ago when his wife died. He needed something to keep his mind off the grief, and I wanted to move out of my folks' house."

"It's lovely," she said, dreading the upcoming conversation. She blinked away tears at the very thought of telling him.

Just another minute or two, she silently begged, *to be like a normal woman who is being courted by a decent man.*

"What are the cats' names?" she asked.

"The black-and-white one is Midnight, and the gray one is Stormy. The sheep dog is Mozelle because my youngest sister, Abigail, liked the name," he answered.

"How many sisters do you have?" Lily asked.

"Four sisters and two brothers," he answered as he parked the buggy, hopped down from the seat, and held out a hand. "I'm right in the middle with three sisters older than me. Then a sister and two brothers that are younger. The sisters that are older live on the far side of the ranch and have branched out into growing some special breeds of cattle that grow up fast and produce high-quality beef."

She put her hand in his and figured it would probably be the last time he would ever want to help her again. He laced his fingers through hers, and together they walked up onto the porch.

Just like a couple, she thought, and blinked back more tears.

Both cats awoke from their naps and started weaving around their legs.

"They are so cute." Lily bent down, stroked each of them, and enjoyed the last of the idyllic moment.

"Midnight has a batch of kittens out in the barn. You're welcome to however many you can catch." Matt chuckled. "Stormy comes from a previous litter. No one wanted him."

"I don't think a kitten would survive long in town," Lily said. "But thanks for the offer."

"A furry critter that lived in the seamstress shop would have a lot less chance of getting eaten by coyotes than it will here running wild. On second thought, you could move your sewing business out here, and then you can have as many as you wanted," he suggested.

"I reckon we'd better stay in town," she said.

And after today, you won't ever want to see me again.

"Well, the offer is there if you ever change your mind. You saw those two empty houses down the path. You could set up shop in either of them." He opened the door, dropped her hand, and stood to one side.

"That's so sweet, and I will keep it in mind," she said and tried to take in the whole of the big room in one sweep.

"I made the living room and kitchen one big room with the idea if I ever had a wife, she could talk to me while I fixed supper, or I could watch her while she cooked," he said.

"You cook?" Lily was absolutely amazed.

"I love to cook, but I'm not one much for baking. My biscuits are like rocks," he chuckled. "I see you checking out the curtains and the antimacassars. I do not sew or crochet. Abigail helped with those. Come on and I'll show you the rest of the house. There's three bedrooms in case I ever do have a family and, of course, an outhouse out back." He blushed slightly.

Poor darling. If he turned red at the mention of a toilet, his face might burst into flames when he heard what she had to say that afternoon.

"Do you want to sit?" he asked. "I can make us a cup of coffee. We don't use much tea out here on the ranch, so I can't offer that."

"No, but I would like a cup of water." She sat down on the sofa. Just thinking about what she needed to tell him made her mouth as dry as if she'd sucked on a green persimmon.

"Coming right up," he said and went over to the dry sink to dip a long-handled tin cup into a bucket of water.

He poured the water into a glass and carried it over to her. Their hands brushed when she took it from him, and there was that instant attraction again—something she could not deny. She really, really liked Matt, and could so easily find herself falling in real love with him.

But all good things must come to an end.

"Okay, I'm not very good with words, so I'm just going to blurt this out," he said. "I like you a lot, Lily. I would like to court you."

Lily patted the sofa beside her, and he sat down. "My real name is Abigail Carolina Boyle, not Lily."

"Like I told you, I have a sister named Abigail and another who is named Carolina. I think I'll just stick with calling you Lily," he said with a grin.

"I would love for you to court me, but first you need to hear something," she said and went on to tell him the whole story—how she had run away from an abusive fiancé and then landed at the Paradise for five years. "I'm not the sweet woman you think I am."

"I figured that out when you killed a hundred snakes," he said with a chuckle.

How could he laugh at a time like this? She frowned. She had just bared her soul to him and was ready for him to throw something, or at the very least toss her out of his house.

"I also figured out," he said as he took her hand in his, "that you had been hurt sometime in the past, and that's why you want to help all women to stand up for their rights—even those who worked for Otis. By the way, what happened to them? Beulah said they're living in

Sally Anne's house and that she took one of them with her when she left for England."

"They talked about setting up a brothel, but Sally Anne offered them a choice of that or working for her on the estate. They took the latter." She paused. "Did you hear me, Matt? I wasn't any better than Frannie or any of those other girls. The only difference is that I worked in a fancy place and the madam treated her girls with respect and love."

"Yes, I heard you," he said in a serious tone. "I'm not your ex-feller, and I don't give two hoots and a holler about your past. I do care about your future. Now, can I court you or not?"

Lily could hardly believe what she'd heard. "Are you serious?"

"Very much so, and a man like the one you were engaged to would be hanging by a length of barbed wire if he had done something like that on this farm. We take care of our women like they are made of gold and diamonds."

"Then yes, you can court me," Lily whispered.

"You have just made me a very happy man," Matt said.

The first kiss was barely a brush across the lips, but the second one was so scorching hot that it left both of them panting.

"After that, I reckon we should go on and see the rest of the farm." He started to stand up.

She pulled him back down. Her hands shook, and her pulse raced. "I agree, but just one more kiss to be sure that was real."

"Glad to oblige," he said with a grin.

Abigail cornered Lily as she left the outhouse that afternoon. "I read that article in the newspaper. We don't need your kind of rabble-rouser out here on our ranch. I want you to stay away from my brother. He should be with a different kind of woman."

"I'm sorry you feel that way," Lily said past the lump in her throat. She'd thought that she had jumped the last hurdle by being honest with Matt, but evidently not. "You don't believe in women's rights?"

"I do, but not to the extent that you took it," Abigail gritted out. "Stirring up trouble and taking those saloon women into your group wasn't right."

"So you are throwing the first stone at women who are often forced into impossible situations?" Lily asked.

Abigail narrowed her brown eyes and glared up at Lily. "How do you know they were forced?"

Lily shrugged. "I happen to know their stories."

"Well!" Abigail hissed. "I don't care about any of your sob stories. I just don't want someone like you on the ranch."

Lily managed a weak smile. "Maybe when you get to know me—"

"I will not change my mind." Abigail stormed off toward the bunkhouse.

The lovely feeling tried to end right there, but Lily had fought rattlesnakes and lived through a horrid dust storm. She was not going to let a young woman who had been born into the lap of love ruin her day or her life.

When she reached the bunkhouse, Matt motioned her over to his side. "Miz Lily Boyle, I want you to meet my mother, Ruth, and my father, Seamus. Mama and Daddy, this is my lady friend that I've told y'all all about, Lily Boyle."

"So pleased to meet you," Lily said.

"We're happy to finally see you," Ruth said. "Matt said you were beautiful, but his words didn't do you justice." She looked like an older version of Abigail—short, dark hair, and lovely brown eyes. Lily wished that Abigail herself had given her even half as good of a welcome.

"Boyle!" Seamus said with a smile. "As good of an Irish name as Maguire."

Lily smiled. "I don't know about that."

"We won't argue names," Ruth said. "We're just glad to meet you. Matt, take her around and introduce her to the rest of the family. Don't worry about learning all their names right here at first. You'll hopefully be coming to the farm enough that you'll get to know us all eventually."

"Thank you." Did the whole family know about Abigail's position? Lily wondered. If so, how would that affect her relationship with Matt?

"I'll see you soon," Claude said as he lifted Daisy up onto the buckboard. "Matt and I have to come to town day after tomorrow for supplies. Maybe I could take you to Hattie's for dinner?"

"I'll look forward to it," she said, wishing that even the looser rules at the ranch would let him kiss her one more time.

Matt put his hands on Lily's waist and lifted her up to sit on the other side of Beulah. "Y'all be careful. You should be there before dark, but I wouldn't want my girl to get hurt."

"Let's make this a regular thing!" Alma shouted from the bunkhouse porch. "Like tomorrow?"

"Tomorrow won't work," Beulah said. "But it could be a regular thing, like every other week on Sunday?"

"I'll take it, and I'm holding you to it," Alma said.

Beulah waved and then flicked the reins to turn the horses around. They hadn't even left the ranch when she focused first on Daisy and then on Lily. "A dinner date at Hattie's, and Matt called you 'my girl'? You've both got some explaining to do. Daisy, you go first."

Daisy hadn't had time to talk to Lily alone, so she chose her words very carefully. "Claude and I went down to a peaceful place by the river and talked all afternoon. He asked if he might court me, and I said yes." She hadn't said anything to Beulah about her dream to see more of the world and had only recently told Lily about Claude's desire to live in a cooler place.

"Don't hurt that young man," Beulah warned. "He lost his wife and baby about five years ago."

Daisy leaned back slightly and caught Lily's eye. She gave her a brief nod. "We talked about that, and about my previous marriage, plus everything else. How about your day, Beulah?"

"It's been lovely," Beulah said. "Alma and Matt gave me a list of what they'll need from the store, and I can deliver it to save them a trip into town, unless one of them is coming to Autrie for something other than supplies."

"I hope that's true," Lily muttered.

Beulah turned her eyes toward Lily. "Your turn to explain."

"Story is the same as Daisy's," she replied with a shrug. "Matt and I are attracted to each other, and we are going to see where it leads. If it's just a flash in the pan, we'll step back and be friends. If it's more, we'll figure that out later."

"And how is that going to affect the women's rights movement?" Beulah asked.

"Amanda and most of the women at the camp were married," Daisy reminded Beulah. "But you don't have to worry about us for a long, long time. Courting doesn't mean that we're ready to start cutting up that bolt of brocade."

Lily nudged Beulah on the shoulder. "Right now, we have a seamstress shop in town, and they live two hours north of us. They're busy raising sheep. We are sewing pants for Frannie and the others. The courting might be a hit-or-miss thing."

"Well, you could see them every two weeks if you go with me," Beulah suggested. "I do hate this drive with no one to talk to."

"Count us in," Daisy said without hesitation.

"Very well." Beulah steered the horses to the left down a rutted path that could hardly even be called a road. "We'll talk about something else now. I told Alma all about the camp and how we did some good. I can see how happy she and the girls are there at the farm. Did you know that every so often, a wagon train parks out on the back side of their place by the river? The people buy a sheep or two from the shepherds, and they always invite the ranch folks to come to their camp for an evening. I guess it's a big thing. Alma said that she baked a bunch of pies to take to the gathering last week. She wants me to stay a couple of days next time another one comes and go with her and the girls. I told her that I would. We can close up both our shops and take a little break. Maybe you could bring some of the premade day dresses."

"Sounds great," Lily agreed.

Daisy could hear the other two talking about the ranch, and she caught a word or a sentence every so often. But she got lost in her thoughts about Claude's dream of going north by wagon train. Would she really go with him on a trip like that? Days on end of traveling across what could be rugged land, only to start all over again in a new place?

Yes, I would, she thought, and sealed her silent answer with a nod.

Chapter Twenty-One

The setting sun was throwing out a beautiful array of colors when Beulah stopped the wagon in front of the seamstress shop. "What the hell?" She spit out the swear word like it was a nasty taste in her mouth. "The window is broken, and there's something nailed to your door."

Lily hopped down off the buckboard and didn't need a light to read "Eviction Notice" written in big letters across the top of the paper that had been fastened to the door with a huge nail.

"What the hell?" Daisy echoed Beulah's words in an even harsher tone. "Why are we being evicted? The rent isn't even due for a couple of days."

Lily marched over to the door and ripped the paper away. She removed a key and unlocked the door, went inside, and lit a lamp. Holding the notice close to the light, she paraphrased the words.

"Because we have been unsavory tenants and created havoc in the town, we will no longer be allowed to rent this building. When the rent is up, Judge Wesley Martin will take possession of the place and everything that is left in it."

Daisy balled up a fist and slammed it against her other hand. "I'm so mad, I could chew up railroad spikes. He will pay for this."

"He owns the building," Beulah reminded her. "Where is your contract? Does it say that as long as you keep things in good repair that you can continue to rent?"

"We didn't sign anything. It was verbal." Lily felt as if she had lost the paddle to her small canoe that was out in the middle of the ocean, and the tiny boat had just sprung a leak.

Frannie rushed into the shop. "Hey, one of the hired hands came home and said the men in the saloon are all riled up, and he's afraid there's going to be a riot."

Lula followed close behind her. "He said that it had something to do with y'all, so we borrowed the buggy and came to see if you need us."

"We are being evicted, and we have to get out in two days," Lily said in a voice she hardly recognized as her own. "Why are they throwing such a fit over us being put out of a building?"

"You ever hear of a man named Cooter Wilson?" Frannie asked.

"Sweet Jesus!" Daisy gasped.

"No!" Lily raised her voice. "There's nothing 'sweet' or religious about Cooter showing up here. This is a *holy hell* situation!"

"Our hired hand said that he has fired up an angry crowd at Otis's place, and some of them are getting ready to come over here and demand that y'all own up to who you really are. He's the one that put the rock through the window. What is going on?" Frannie asked.

"The guy who was in town said that Cooter is so drunk, it was a miracle he even hit the window when he threw the rock," Lula added.

"He's yelling that you two and five more worked at that brothel you talked about," Frannie said.

Lily's heart tumbled down to her toes. "He's right about all that, and we will gladly explain . . ." She plopped down on the sofa. "Y'all better have a seat. Daisy and I will tell you the truth."

"I can't believe he's followed us down here," Daisy whispered and began to pace the floor.

"Me, either, but it's happened." Lily was glad that Matt and Claude hadn't had to hear the news from anyone else.

Everything was quickly falling apart, and all because of one man who'd gotten turned away at the Paradise gate more than once because he was so drunk that he could hardly walk. Who had yelled obscenities at them when they were in town one morning, and who swore he would get even with them no matter what. Evidently that day had arrived, just in time to ruin the most perfect day Lily had ever known. She wondered if any of the many women who had gone to the camp with them would stand by her and Daisy now. They'd stood by Frannie, but neither she nor any of the saloon women had lied.

"The truth will out, and it has," she whispered, feeling as if the other women, including Beulah, stared at her and Daisy like they had horns and a spiky tail. All she and Daisy needed was a pitchfork and some red paint to wallow around in, or maybe a big red *S* to hang around their necks—for *Shady Ladies* or even *Soiled Doves*.

"I guess y'all better start talking," Beulah said.

"I'll go first," Lily said. "Let me begin by saying that I'm sorry we haven't come clean with you, Beulah. You've done so much for us. You deserved the truth from the beginning, but in our defense, we really were trying to make a new life here in Autrie. Remember that story I told at the first women's meeting? The one about my abusive fiancé? We've all got similar stories, I'm sure, but that's the one that drove me to Spanish Fort. And that town is where I ran out of money and went to work at the Paradise, which was a brothel. It's no longer in business, but yes, I was just like you, Frannie, and the saloon girls, except the Paradise was pretty fancy and we didn't have to put up with anyone like Otis."

"And," Daisy picked up the story, "like we told you before, we were paid well, and we didn't have to entertain more than one man a night. We didn't lie to you about how it was run, although we did beat around the bush a little about Jems."

"He is a real person, though, and he's on his way to England with Miz Raven," Lily added. "We lied about either of us living next door, and for that, I apologize. I wanted you ladies to have a better life than you had working for Otis, but it looks like we just made things worse."

Frannie pursed her lips together. "So, Cooter is telling the truth?"

"Yes," Daisy answered, "and we will probably lose most of what we have here. We'll have to pack our trunks and get on the train to go to Nechesville or Jacksonville, where our other friends are. That rock through the window is most likely just the beginning."

"No one else is going to rent to us, even if there were a vacancy." Then Lily remembered what Matt had said about putting in their seamstress business at the ranch, and her mind began to run in circles like a dog chasing its tail. "I have a question for Beulah . . ." She finally grabbed a thought long enough to hang on to it. "Will you still be willing to put our creations in your shop?"

"Hell yes," Beulah swore. "I don't give a rat's behind about what you did to survive. We've all done what we had to do to stay alive. I just wish you would have thought I was trustworthy enough for you to tell me the truth."

Elijah poked his head in the door. "I hear there's been some trouble. Anything I can do to help?"

"What do you know about this?" Lily held up the eviction notice.

"That judge is taking his anger about Sally Anne out on y'all, and some guy named Cooter is over at the saloon shooting down whiskey like it was water and spouting off stuff about you and Daisy," Elijah answered. "Any of it true?"

"Most of it," Daisy said.

Lily paced around the room a couple of times and then asked, "Think you might ride out to the sheep farm and take a message to Matt and Claude?"

"I reckon I could," Elijah said. "But why would I do that?"

"Matt asked me today if I could do my seamstress work out there," Lily answered, and handed the eviction notice to him. "If you would go ask him if he was serious, and if we could rent one of those empty houses on the ranch, maybe that would be a place for us to go. We've only got two days. We don't even have a formal rental agreement. The judge said that his word was good enough, but I guess his isn't, because he's now saying that anything left will belong to him when our rent runs out."

"Well . . ." Elijah rubbed his chin. "My old house is sittin' empty now. My last tenants left with the wagon train that came through back in the spring. They told me when they moved in that it wouldn't be forever, that they were just stopping over until they could join up with another train going to California. They both worked on the ranch, but they had the wandering fever and moved on when they got the chance."

"Could we rent it?" Lily asked.

"No, but you can live in it," Elijah answered. "I'll ride out there and tell Matt and Claude to each bring a wagon tomorrow. And I'll add mine if we need more room to get you moved."

Tears began to flow down Daisy's cheeks. Alma might not even want to be friends with a couple of reformed soiled doves. "What if the women out there shun us and treat us like this?" She waved her arms toward the broken window.

"Honey, don't you be worryin' none about that. Shepherds are a different breed of people," Elijah assured her.

The short argument with Abigail came back to Lily's mind, and she wondered if even asking Matt for such a big favor was the right thing to do.

"My wagon is available, too," Beulah said. "If you need it, I'll drive it out back to the ranch tomorrow afternoon. Seeing Alma two days in a row would be a treat."

"And we'll help pack," Frannie said. "It's the least we can do after all y'all did for us—but the way the town seems to be backing Cooter, it might be best if some of us stand watch tonight."

"But aren't you mad at us?" Daisy asked.

"Maybe a little—especially with you, for looking down your nose at me in the saloon when you wasn't no better than me," Frannie answered. "But we are past that now, and I don't turn my back on friends."

"Let's load up my wagon with all we can. He can take it out to the farm and bring it back in the morning. No telling what might happen if that crowd over there turns violent. They could burn down the place or vandalize it," Beulah said. "Damn that Cooter feller to hell and back."

Why did he have to come to town and ruin things? Now y'all will be gone, and I'll still be here."

Frannie gave Beulah a sideways hug. "You can come out to our place anytime you need company. We'll be itchin' for some gossip, anyway."

"Thank you all," Daisy murmured. "Let's load up the sewing machine, too, and as much fabric as we can. Other stuff can be replaced if things go south."

"You will still make our ladies' pants for us, won't you?" Lula asked.

"Of course we will, and we'll send them back to town with whoever comes out to see us," Daisy promised.

Lily wiped a tear away with the back of her hand and said, over the lump in her throat, "Or you can all pile up into Beulah's wagon and come spend the day with us, maybe on a Sunday when you don't have work to do."

"Okay, then, let's get busy and load what goes tonight. I will spend the night at the ranch and be back first thing in the morning," Elijah said.

Lula stood up and gave Lily a hug. "We'll miss y'all."

Frannie followed behind her and hugged Daisy. "After we help fill up Beulah's wagon, we will go on home, but we'll be back tomorrow morning to help any way we can."

Daisy broke into sobs the minute the wagon was loaded with the sewing machine, the worktable, and as many bolts of fabric as they could stuff into the extra spaces.

"Y'all be on watch, now," Elijah called out as he hitched his own horse behind the wagon and drove away.

Lily slipped an arm around Daisy. "We can't help what's happening. Thank goodness we both came clean with Matt and Claude today. Some higher power has been looking after us this whole time."

Daisy wiped the tears away with a hankie she'd pulled out of her sleeve. "How can you say that after coming home to find a broken window and an eviction notice?"

"Think about it," Lily answered. "We find a place to set up shop just days after we get here because you kind of blackmailed the judge. Then we meet Beulah, who is ready to fight for women, and Edith and Sally Anne, who want us to make a wedding dress. We were saved from even starting to cut the brocade by the women all going to the camp with us. Fate or God, one is working for us."

"But we have to move. As much as I like Claude, it doesn't seem to me like anyone is looking over us," Daisy snapped. "Why would this 'higher power' you are talking about let Cooter Wilson turn up here in Autrie instead of just sending him to hell?"

"Everything happens for a reason," Lily said with a long sigh. "Even old drunk Cooter. Moving to the sheep ranch must be where we are supposed to be, and we have friends to help us get there. We can be seamstresses anywhere that we have a place to set up our sewing machine and cutting table."

Daisy didn't seem to have an argument, but Lily could see the wheels turning in her head.

"You are right, but I don't like that we're being thrown out like trash," Daisy grumbled.

"Neither do I, but—"

Before she could finish her sentence, the shattering noise of glass breaking and flying through the air—and a rock bouncing across the floor—caused both women to cover their eyes.

"Come out, you liars!" a male voice that sounded a lot like Otis's yelled.

"Or let us in and take us to bed like you did other men in Spanish Fort," another man demanded.

"We should go before . . ." Daisy took a couple of steps toward the back.

Someone rattled the door, and then another person kicked it in.

Daisy grabbed her pistol and fired off a shot into the ceiling. "That's a warning!" she shouted. "The whole bunch of you had better leave."

Lily hurried across the room and picked up her loaded pistol from a shelf under the counter. She held it with both hands and aimed right at Otis's face.

Otis motioned toward the angry mob. "First one in—"

"Gets shot in the heart," Daisy finished for him and took aim.

He stopped right inside the door and growled, "You can't shoot us all."

Lily pointed the gun below his waist. "I don't need to shoot all of you. We each have six bullets. It will be like shooting fish in a barrel. Twelve of you should fill up that door and keep the rest out. If not, Daisy and I will reload and work on the next dozen."

Cooter was right behind Otis, but he couldn't take his eyes off the two pistols. "You'll hang from the gallows if—"

"You are trespassing on private property," Daisy reminded him, "and you threatened to assault us. We are simply defending our honor."

"There's a lot more of us than you," Otis said. "And it's your word against ours. We'll all say you invited us in and that we left money over there on the counter to pay for what we got."

Beulah came through the back door with a sawed-off shotgun in her hands and set a box of shells on the counter with a thump. "I can load this faster than you can bleed out on the floor, and I do not miss, either. I would suggest that you get on out of here. I also just heard what you said about your intentions, and I will testify in a court of law if these two women are brought to trial. Jimmy Holt, does your wife know where you are tonight? Didn't you sign a paper promising to respect Amanda if she came home? Is threatening to assault these women keeping your word? How about you, Danny Larson? You've got three teenage daughters. Would you like them to be treated like this? We're having a women's auxiliary meeting this next week. Right now, I'm taking names, and later I will be saying them loud and clear if y'all don't change your minds and get out of here."

One by one, the men slunk away into the darkness like whipped dogs, leaving only Otis and Cooter in the doorway. Then Frannie and

Lula, each holding a pistol, pushed past them and into the room to stand on either side of Beulah.

"We are here to take care of any rats in the shop that need to be taken out," Frannie said.

"Big old ugly rats too big to be stomped. Guess we're gonna have to shoot 'em," Lula added as she pointed her pistol at Cooter's head. "'Course, Lily here taught me not to waste ammunition. I believe between the bunch of us, we could just pistol-whip him and send him back to whatever rock he crawled out from under. Saves us some bullets. Your call, Lily. What do you want us to do with these stinky critters?"

Lily didn't take her eyes off the men. "If they move, shoot 'em."

Otis threw up his hands. "We're leaving, but this is not over. Come daylight, I'm going to the judge."

"Please do," Daisy said. "And tell him that Daisy Lindberg from the Paradise in Spanish Fort says hello, and that she will be out of this place tomorrow."

As soon as the two men were gone, Beulah slammed the door and propped a chair under the doorknob to keep it shut. "We'll take turns keeping watch tonight."

Lily sank down on the nearest church pew and slowly let out the breath she had been holding in. "I hate to admit it, but I'm scared."

"'O ye of little faith,'" Daisy said as she sat down and laid her pistol on the table.

"And what does that mean?" Lily asked.

"Who was just up on a soapbox preaching at me not even an hour ago about everything happening for a reason?" Daisy shot over at Lily. "Maybe this happened to show everyone that we can stand up for ourselves, even against a bunch of rowdy, drunk fools."

Frannie took a bottle from the shelf and held it up. Lily didn't need the dim light from the oil lamp to know that Frannie was holding the whiskey that she and Daisy had waltzed into Otis's saloon and bought. That night seemed like it had happened years and years ago, but in reality it was only weeks.

"We could all use a shot of this right now," Frannie said. "And then we're going to put on our stompin' boots and get to packin'. Seems fittin' that Daisy and I share the bottle that caused us to fight in the beginning." She opened the whiskey, took a swig, and passed it over to Beulah.

"Stompin' boots?" Beulah asked, then turned the bottle up.

"That's the ones that we imagine we are wearing when we need to stomp a rat," Lula explained as she took the whiskey from Beulah and swallowed two big gulps. "If you don't kill 'em dead, those varmints can find a way to sneak back into the house."

Lily was last in line, and she finished off what was left in the bottle, which had been full when they'd started passing it around. Drinking out of the same bottle seemed like a sign that they were all sisters of the heart. Kind of like the seven women who'd left the Paradise that hot summer day. She looked around the room and counted to five, but Ruby and Betsy would be there if she needed them. It had to be a sure sign that she would be happy surrounded by sheep, and maybe even a kitten or two.

"Well, now!" Beulah said. "That little nip settled my nerves, but I still intend to keep my shotgun close by. I vote that we take shifts standing guard."

"And those of us who aren't guarding will begin to pack. I saw a bunch of crates in the kitchen." Frannie headed that way and dragged two into the shop.

"If we run out, you could get what is stacked up in back of my store. Elijah usually gathers them up to use at the wagon yard, but he hasn't gotten the last couple of weeks' worth," Beulah offered.

Daisy glanced over at Lily. "Maybe you are right about a higher power. But I'm not really believing it until we are safely at the farm and there's not a rain cloud in sight tomorrow morning."

"How about if we don't get rained on but a hailstorm hits Otis's place after we are gone?" Beulah giggled.

"And the hail knocks some sense into the judge when he sneaks in right after noon," Frannie said.

"Why noon?" Lily asked.

"That's when the almighty judge comes to the saloon for his midday drink and a romp in the sheets with whatever new girl Otis gets to work for him," Frannie answered.

"Why, darlin'," Daisy said in her sweetest voice, "that can't be true. Judge Martin is a fine, upstanding man in Autrie. He's so hurt by losing Sally Anne, who was the love of his life, that he just needs a little comforting."

"But, darlin'," Frannie grinned and drew out the endearment, "he was needing comfort before she left. Methinks maybe he's one of those men who is a wolf in sheep's clothing."

"I agree," Daisy said. "And I'm speaking from experience. He will have to face the truth one of these days."

Chapter Twenty-Two

Daisy wiped her brow on the hem of her apron and stared at the roomful of loaded crates. "How did we accumulate so much stuff in such a short time?"

"With one trip to the wagon yard," Lily reminded her. "We haven't bought a single thing since then. It came to us in two wagons. Think we can take it away in only that many?"

Daisy waved an arm to take in the whole room. "All this only had to come less than a quarter of a mile. Leaving is a different matter. We will have to travel several miles over rough ground. We'll have to pack things a lot differently than merely piling it up. We'll need Beulah's and Elijah's help, too."

"Maybe the trip will cure you of wanting to join a wagon train and light out on an adventure," Lily teased.

"Or make me more determined," Daisy shot back. "But will you-all want to come back to town once a month for the women's auxiliary meeting? There's men in town that wouldn't want their women to associate with us."

"Can we come to the meetings, too?" Frannie asked.

"Of course you can," Beulah told her. "We stood together at the camp, and we will do the same here in town."

"I plan to come back," Lily answered. "That will be a good time to take whatever we create to Beulah's store and to keep the ladies encouraged."

"Think they'll even come around if they know we are there?" Just asking the question put a lump in Daisy's throat.

Lily went over to the broken window and looked out. "Here comes the judge—and the way he's strutting, it looks like he's on a mission."

Frannie and Lula crossed the room, moved the chair away from the door, and met Wesley on the boardwalk outside the store.

"Judge?" Frannie tipped up her chin. "What brings you to the seamstress shop this morning? Are you going to help load the wagons?"

"Frannie?" He stopped and stared at her. "No, I'm not. I'm here to tell these two women that this window has to be fixed before they can leave."

Daisy stomped outside, crossed her arms over her chest, and went nose to nose with the man. "All repairs on any rental property fall on the shoulders of the owner. We will be out of this place before dark, which means you actually owe us a couple of days' refund on the month's rent we paid. We don't want the money, so you can use it to have the window fixed."

"Birds of a feather . . . ," he started.

Frannie held up a palm. "Before you go any further, remember that Sally Anne flocked with us. I didn't say a word to her that you were cheating on her, but she had enough sense to fly away."

Wesley squared his shoulders and narrowed his eyes. "You may have won a small battle, but you will never win the war. Women don't have the staying power to ever get to vote."

Daisy took a step forward. "Women kept the home fires going during the last war, and we will win this one—one victory at a time. Someday women will be running for politics and winning elections. We might even be working right next to the president of the United States, or maybe even holding that office. Never underestimate the power of all of us when we stand together and set our minds."

"You're just a bunch of . . ." He hesitated, and then the corners of his mouth turned up in a mocking smile. "Y'all are all—and I do mean *all* the women who joined you in your little campaign—are just a bunch of cackling blue jays. You make a lot of noise, but soon you'll find out that's all you can do."

"Blue jays also rob other birds' nests, like we did yours, and they certainly scare predators away," Frannie told him.

"What's that got to do with anything?" Wesley asked.

"We robbed y'all of your will, didn't we? And we made enough noise to scare most of you into signing the petition," Frannie said.

Men, right along with Gertrude's little group of women, had begun to gather and line up across the street, blocking Matt's and Claude's wagons. When they were close enough, both sides brought out pistols, and the sheriff took a step forward. "You boys turn around and go on back to your sheep."

"I don't think so," Amanda called out as twice as many women marched down the street and began to push their way into the crowd.

"Go home, the bunch of you," Wesley called out as he joined the men. "Daisy and Lily can leave with these men if they're willing, but they won't take one thing off my property."

Beulah stepped out of the store with her shotgun in her hands. "We're not going anywhere."

"You don't have the firepower that we do. We're just running a couple of bad women out of town. They are lucky we don't tar and feather them," Otis yelled.

"Ladies?" Beulah said in a calm voice.

Fists raised into the air, and they all shouted, "Together!"

They lowered their hands and clasped them as they moved forward, letting go only to push or shoulder their opponents out of their way as they broke up the line that had been formed. Gertrude stumbled and fell. Amanda stopped and helped her up, then looked her right in the eye and said, "Shame on you!"

Maggie whipped around and faced the crowd so fast that her skirt stirred up the dust. "He among you without sin can shoot the first bullet at whichever one of us you deem to be the worst of the lot."

In groups, the other women made it through the line the men had formed, and Amanda said, "Either Daisy and Lily are allowed to leave with *all* their belongings or else we are going back to our camp."

"And we will stay there until their things are delivered out to the sheep farm—and then maybe until Christmas, to show you that we mean business. There will be no clean houses, cooked meals, or women to warm your beds," Beulah declared.

"And no Thanksgiving dinner or Christmas celebrations, either," Amanda added.

"And shame on you in particular, Wesley Martin." Edith shook her finger so close to his nose that he took a step back. "You have not been setting a decent example for the office you hold. Hanging out in the saloon, drinking, playing poker, and taking the women upstairs for a romp in the sheets. No wonder Sally Anne left you—and someday, when women can vote, men like you won't even be hired to clean outhouses."

His jaw worked like he was trying to spit something out, but he didn't say another word.

Matt flicked the reins, and the women parted to allow the two wagons through, then closed up their ranks again.

Elijah drove Beulah's wagon in behind them and nodded at the women on either side of him. He brought the team of horses to a halt and hopped down off the buckboard to face the crowd of men. "Y'all need to remember something," he yelled. "A wagon yard is an important part of the town, and I can close it down before you can blink if you don't do right by these women."

"Yes, but—" the judge started.

Elijah butted in before he could finish. "As acting judge, if this case was between any other two people in town, would you rule for the owner or the renter?"

"Daisy blackmailed me, and that's against the law," Wesley muttered.

"Did she?" Elijah asked. "You made no attempt to hide that you were visiting the girls at Otis's saloon on a regular basis. What would any of you men do if your wives"—he waved his hand to take in the line of women behind him—"visited the saloon and went upstairs with one of the poker players or drinkers there?"

"There's different rules for men and women!" Cooter shouted, slurring his words.

"You don't even have a woman! Here's the deal . . . ," Beulah said. "You either get on back out of here or shoot us. We are going to stand right here until these three wagons are loaded, and if there's anything left after that, Elijah will get another one of his wagons to help out. There will not be a hairpin or a speck of dust left when Daisy and Lily have left Autrie."

Total silence filled the town, and then a blue jay lit on the barrel of Beulah's gun and squawked for a full thirty seconds before it flew up to the broken window and entered the seamstress shop.

"Judge Martin, do you think that bird might be a sign?" Daisy asked with half a giggle.

"I'm glad to be a pretty blue jay. Seems like the judge liked my blue saloon dress better than my red one," Frannie said.

"I'll be a blue jay if it gets things done for all of us," Maggie said.

"Me too," Edith added. "And someone better haul Cooter off to the jail to sleep off his drunkenness."

One at a time, the men began to slip away, and Matt climbed down off his wagon and went into the shop, loaded a crate onto his shoulder, and carried it outside. Claude followed him and brought out another one.

"Judge Martin, you can watch us all morning if you want to, but I promise we are only taking what we brought to the place. We don't need a broken window or a—" Lily ducked when the blue jay suddenly flew right over her head and landed on top of Wesley's hat.

He slapped it with his hand, and it flew away, but not before it left a splat of bird crap on the brim. "See what you caused?" he accused Lily.

"It wasn't me that referred to all us women as just a bunch of blue jays, but that one just proved what we think of you," she countered. "I guess the birds don't like it when you use them to try to annoy us."

He glared at her for what felt like a full minute, then stormed back to Otis's saloon, grumbling the whole time. Cooter staggered along behind them, weaving as if he might fall on his face any minute.

Lily started down the row of women. She hugged Amanda first, and then each one as she went up to them. "Thank you all so much for supporting us. That could have ended a whole different way."

"I vote that we are no longer the women's auxiliary club, but the Blue Jays," Maggie announced. "We can make money for our cause instead of giving it to the churches since we can't be pastors or deacons or even have a voice in those places."

All hands raised in agreement, and tears flowed down Lily's cheeks. She swiped them away, determined not to be a big softy in the moment.

Daisy threw her arm around Lily and whispered, "And the sun rises a little more."

"Together! Blue Jays forever!" the ladies all chanted later that morning when four wagons left in a line headed out of town.

"I can't believe that you are actually doing this," Matt said when they were well on their way.

Lily leaned over and kissed him on the cheek. "Thank you for letting us move onto the sheep farm—or is it a ranch? I never know what to call it."

"It can be anything you want it to be," he answered. "Claude and I are glad that you are joining us."

"Are you truly all right with this, Matt? How do the ladies who live there all the time feel about us?" She thought of what Abigail had said.

"Several years ago, a whole big wagon train of a hundred women stopped to rest awhile on our land. They were mail-order brides on their way to the California gold mines. I wasn't born yet, so I'm telling you what I heard about that time," he said.

Lily was about to ask what that bit of history had to do with her and Daisy being accepted, but she kept quiet, and after a few seconds he went on. "The women had come from all walks of life, but most of them were poor folks just looking for a second chance, for a new start. That's when the wagon master had a big party out there for the folks who lived on the farm to thank them for letting the women camp there."

"That's when the celebrations began, right?" she asked.

"Most likely. A few of the women had been saloon workers in Houston. Two of them decided to stay on the farm and marry Uncle Elijah's younger brothers. One of those women is my mother. The other woman is Claude's mama. They never hid what they did in the past, and they've been good wives and mothers. No one is going to throw stones at you, darlin'. If I love you, then they'll love you like family. Does that answer your question?" he asked.

That sure enough explained why Elijah hadn't turned his back on Lily and Daisy, and why, even after she'd told Matt, he hadn't thrown her out the door with a good solid cussing. But knowing what family meant to him, she could never come between him and them. If she couldn't win Abigail over, then she would simply have to move on to another place.

"Well?" Matt prompted.

"Now, I'm both humbled and excited to be moving out there, but I do have a question."

"Anything, darlin'." He grinned.

"When you drove the wagon into town and the mob had gathered, you just sat there and didn't confront them," she said.

"I don't hear a question in there."

"I expected you to come off that buckboard, pull out your pistol or maybe grab your rifle, and demand that they leave. Why didn't you?"

"Were you disappointed?" he asked.

"I'm not sure how I felt," she replied.

"From the buckboard, I could see the women forming a line and pushing the men," Matt said.

"But why didn't *you* do something?"

"Darlin', you are the slayer of snakes, the leader of women, and the strongest woman I know. It's not my job to protect you, though I will when you need me to."

"Then what *is* your job?" she asked.

"To tell you how beautiful you are every morning and evening, to make you feel safe at the farm, and to support you—but most important, to let you handle things in your own way," he whispered.

Lily scooted closer to him. "I can live with that."

Chapter Twenty-Three

"Miss Lily, Miss Lily!" Alma's daughter Elsie squealed as she ran through the tall grass between the two houses.

Lily dropped her pincushion on the floor and ran outside just as the sun had begun to slide down the western horizon. All kinds of thoughts shot through her mind: Alma had fallen and needed help. Abbie had climbed a tree—again—and couldn't get down. Or worse yet, something was wrong with Daisy.

"Well, don't you look pretty with the sun on your lovely red hair," Matt said as he followed Elsie to the house.

"Did I hear yelling?" Daisy rounded the end of the house with Claude right behind her. "Is everything all right?"

Elsie danced around like she heard music in her head. "Mama sent me and Matt to tell you and Daisy to come to supper at the bunkhouse. It will be ready in a few minutes, and I get to sit by you, and Mama says Abbie can sit by Daisy."

"Everything is fine," Lily told Daisy. "It just looks like we have a supper invitation."

"Yes, Claude just told me. Beulah is here, too, and we can send Frannie's pants and those four housedresses we made back to town with her," Daisy said.

"Shall we?" Matt offered Lily his arm.

"Is this a big thing? Should I change into something fancier?" she asked as she slipped her arm through his.

"You look great," he told her and then whispered, "Claude and Daisy have a big announcement to make, but I can't tell anyone."

According to Lily's mother, she'd inherited her red hair, height, and quick temper from her grandmother on her father's side. The Boyle family had come to America from Ireland along with their worst traits. That very Irish anger shot up through her body like a blast of pure fire. That Claude had to tell someone his secret was understandable, but why hadn't Daisy confided in her?

She did back before you moved out here to live among the sheep, but now she has a man in her life and she's in love, Miz Raven's voice scolded.

Tears welled up in the back of Lily's eyes, but she blinked them away. Daisy and Claude were about to announce their engagement, or else that they were engaged and leaving on the next wagon train that came through the area. Either way, Daisy would not be living in the same house with her anymore, and if the latter was the news, Lily might not ever see her again.

"You are awfully quiet," Matt said. "Did you have a hard day?"

Not until right now, Lily thought.

"Kind of," she said. "But I'm glad to get to spend the evening with you."

"Me, too, because it will be our last one for a week," he said. "It's my turn to take part of the sheep to the far pasture to graze. I'll be out there alone, but I'll be thinking of you every single minute."

"Do you do this often?" she asked.

He nodded. "My turn to be a shepherd and take the sheep to one part of the farm or the other comes around once a month. Mozelle and I live in whichever shepherd's shack near where we herd the sheep for that week."

"I'll miss you coming by in the evenings," she whispered.

Elsie had been skipping along ahead of them, but she stopped and looked back over her shoulder. She put her finger over her lips and pointed to the ground. "Come and see what I found."

All four adults eased up on the spot and looked down at a beautiful butterfly sitting on a wild forget-me-not flower. Matt leaned over and kissed Lily on the cheek. "The color on its wings and the little flower are both the same color as your eyes."

"Isn't it pretty?" Elsie whispered.

"Yes, it is," Daisy answered.

The butterfly was still for another few seconds; then, in a fleeting moment, it took flight and disappeared into the thick foliage of a nearby tree. Lily was reminded of how quickly things had changed since she and Daisy had arrived in Autrie. Had someone told her back in those days what the future would hold, she wouldn't have believed a single word. A memory surfaced of that first night when they'd arrived in the hotel–dining room. Elsie and Abbie had been so sweet, but then Joshua punished them for what he'd considered rudeness. Who would have thought those little girls would ever have so much joy in their young lives now?

"A penny for your thoughts?" Matt said as they walked on toward the bunkhouse.

"I'd rather have a good-night kiss tonight," she said.

Matt grinned. "Gladly."

"I was thinking about how fast things can change. We've only been in this area a few weeks and . . ." She was annoyed that those precious children had had to endure hardships, and also that her world had been turned upside down so quickly. Her mind was spinning in circles, but she couldn't seem to slow it down.

They walked up on the bunkhouse porch, and Matt opened the door for her. "I'm glad for the way things have worked out in that time. Are you having regrets?"

"Not a single one," she answered, but she wondered if she truly meant what she had said.

Daisy was nervous, not about her decisions, but because she had been on the fence all day about whether to tell Lily the secret or not. She and Claude had talked just that morning, and she had almost blurted everything out to Lily several times that day.

"Come in," Alma said with a bright smile on her face. "Supper is on the tables and ready for us all to take a seat."

Beulah crossed the room and hugged both Lily and Daisy. "I've got some news that's going to shock both of you—but first, we eat. Alma has fixed up a wonderful mutton stew, and we don't want it to get cold."

"Save your forks," Alma said when everyone was seated. "We have apple pies with whipped cream for dessert."

Lily nudged Daisy on the shoulder as they sat down at the long table for eight. "Have you been keeping secrets from me?"

"Only for one day, and it's about to come out," Daisy answered. "I wanted to tell you, but Claude and I agreed to keep it to ourselves until we could share it with everyone."

Lily turned slightly to focus on Matt. "How did you find out?"

He leaned over and whispered, "They had no idea I was in the loft of the barn when they were . . . well, you know."

Daisy frowned and drew her brows down. "Then Claude didn't actually tell you?"

Matt shook his head. "I was eavesdropping—but then, in my defense, I could have spoiled the moment if I had come down from the loft."

Now Lily was both relieved and jealous at the same time, and wishing that she had snuck off to the barn with Matt. She had been so busy putting the final touches on the pants that she hadn't even realized Daisy had left the house.

Beulah stood up at one of the other tables and tapped her spoon on a pint jar filled with sweet tea. "Maggie and Tobias have bought a rig from Elijah, and they will be joining a wagon train coming through the area real soon. Most likely their first stop will be right here on the farm for at least one night before they head on north. They plan to leave the group in Dodge City, Kansas, and retire there to be close to Maggie's sister. Maggie assures us that she will continue to work for women in that area."

"I hope he's sincere," Daisy said, "and not just leaving Autrie because of families being able to sit together."

"He does, and he seems to be happy about the move," Beulah said. "And a new one started preaching in Joshua's old place last Sunday. He came over from Nechesville. That reminds me, I have a letter for Daisy and Lily postmarked from there."

"Changes are happening," Matt whispered in Lily's ear.

"Constantly," Lily replied.

Daisy took Claude's hand in hers, and together they stood up. "We had no idea about Maggie and the preacher," she said, "but we'll be joining Maggie and Tobias on that same journey."

"I asked Daisy to marry me this morning, and she said yes, so we'll be having a wedding between now and next Sunday. Uncle Elijah is bringing us a covered wagon rig tomorrow, and then we will begin getting it ready to travel," Claude announced.

Lily gave Daisy a hug, but tears flooded her cheeks the whole time. "You deserve happiness, but I'm going to miss you so, so much."

"You and Matt could come with us," Daisy suggested.

Matt raised an eyebrow at Lily. "Do you want to do that?"

"Do you?" she asked.

"Not in a million years, but I won't stand in your way if you want to go," Matt answered.

Abigail stood up and brought another basket of bread to the table. When she set it down, she leaned in between Lily and Matt to whisper softly for Lily's ears only. "You should go with Daisy. With what we know now, you sure aren't worthy to be in the family."

"But Matt told me—"

"And it's the truth," Abigail said. "But those were different times. We won't ever accept you, Lily Boyle—or whatever your real name is."

"What makes you think it's not Lily Boyle?"

"Most women like you cover up their real identity," she hissed.

"Is everything all right?" Matt asked from her other side.

"Just fine," Lily lied.

That evening, Lily paced the floor, back and forth, from the living room to the kitchen and on into her bedroom, and then started all over again. Midnight had come and gone, and Daisy was still on the porch with Claude. Lily washed up, put on her nightgown, and stretched out on her bed, but she couldn't sleep. Finally, she heard the hinges on the front door squeak and Daisy tiptoeing across the floor.

"It's about time," Lily called out.

"You're not my mother," Daisy teased, and then added, "Thank goodness!"

Lily slung her legs over the side of the bed and stood up. "But I've waited up for you so we can talk about you leaving. You've only known Claude for a little while. What happened to courting? Isn't that supposed to last a year?"

Daisy leaned against the doorjamb. Both of her eyebrows shot up halfway to the ceiling. "Spare me any more of the lectures. My gut tells me this is what I want."

"Your gut can only tell you when you are hungry or need to make a run to the outhouse," Lily countered.

"Okay, then, I'll listen to my heart instead of my gut," Daisy shot back. "I'm going to do this, Lily. I can't wait to be married to Claude. I want to make this trip with him and start all over in a brand-new place. Be happy for me. I couldn't stand it if you weren't—and please drag out your trunk and go with us. I heard Matt tell you that he wouldn't get in your way if you want to go."

"And get in the middle of a couple on their honeymoon?" she growled. "No, thank you."

"Did you read the letter from Nechesville yet?" Daisy asked.

"You are trying to change the subject," Lily accused. "And no, I have not. I wanted to read it when you were here with me, and you stayed out half the night."

Daisy crossed over to the bed and sat down. "Well, then, I'll turn up the lamp and we can share it right now."

Lily got out of bed and picked up the letter from the tray in her opened trunk. "We should both write to the others and send the letters back with Beulah."

"We'll have lots to tell them," Daisy said. "I'll already be gone when they read them, and if I can sweet-talk you into it, you'll be with me."

"Keep dreaming, sister!" Lily said before she opened the envelope and began to read:

> Dear Lily and Daisy,
>
> We were glad to hear from you, and to know that you have made a few strides toward our goal, but oh, so sorry to know that things have turned bad for you in town. We have run into quite a problem here. Cooter Wilson turned up in Nechesville. Holly was fired from her teaching job, and the ladies here are not supporting us like they did you. We are selling everything and boarding a train to come over to Autrie. Hopefully, you will welcome us to stay with you until we can figure out what we can do next. We have bought tickets for August 26 and should be there in the afternoon.
>
> Love,
>
> Holly, Iris, and Jasmine

Lily folded the letter and carefully returned it to the envelope. Daisy beamed. "This is wonderful."

"What makes you say that?" Lily asked. "We don't have room for three more in this house. And what if Matt says that he doesn't want them out here? And what if they hate living on a sheep farm?"

"Evidently you don't know Matt Maguire at all, girl," Daisy scolded.

"I can wholeheartedly agree with that," Lily shouted.

"Did y'all have a fight after supper tonight?"

"I don't know if we did or didn't," Lily said. "I'm not good at this courting business. I only ever really dated one man, my ex-fiancé, and you know how that turned out."

Daisy frowned. "But why wouldn't you know if you had a fight?"

"After what he said about not stopping me, I got to thinking that maybe it's his way of telling me that this courting business isn't working for him. Maybe he wants to get rid of me, and after moving me out here, he doesn't want to—"

"Hush!" Daisy chided. "If you aren't sure where you stand with him, don't second-guess yourself. Go ask him first thing in the morning. Don't make yourself sick by wondering what he meant. I'm going to bed now. We've got to plan a wedding. I'm planning on wearing my white dress, so we don't have to make new ones, and I'm glad that Holly, Iris, and Jasmine will be here to celebrate with us. Good night."

"Good night," Lily said.

Daisy blew out the lamp and left the room. Lily threw herself back on her pillows. Only a sliver of the moon still hung in the sky, but when clouds shifted back and forth over it, there was enough light to make strange shapes on the ceiling. She was wide awake and trying to figure out how they would accommodate three more in their house when it dawned on her that there was another empty place down the road from where Alma lived. Daisy would be gone, so one of them could stay in her old room, and the other two could live in the empty house if Matt was willing to rent it. The thought of Matt brought tears, and she silently scolded herself. She was a tall, independent, mostly Irish-blooded woman with a hot temper. She had had the fortitude to leave her ex when she couldn't stand the man another minute.

"I cannot wait until tomorrow to find out exactly what he meant," she whispered, and threw back the thin sheet covering her. She stuck her feet down into her work boots, wrapped a shawl around her shoulders, and slipped out the back door.

Twice during the half-mile walk, she stopped and turned around to go back. No self-respecting woman would ever knock on a man's door in the middle of the night, but each time, she shook off the feeling and went forward.

She stopped in the yard long enough to pet Mozelle, then knocked on the door. It opened so fast that it startled her. Matt stood in front of her, shirtless. Dark hair covered his chest and extended down his muscular chest into the top of his trousers. She felt a rush of heat shoot through her body.

"Lily," he muttered. "Is everything all right?"

She took a deep breath and blurted out, "No, it is not. Can you come out here on the porch and talk to me? This can't wait a whole week while you are out with the sheep."

"Give me time to put on a shirt," he said.

He left the door open, and she could hear him rustling around in the house. She sat down on the top porch step and swatted at a mosquito the size of a buzzard that landed on her arm. She was very aware of him even before he sat down beside her and took her hand in his. She wondered if the gesture meant that he loved her or if it was one that said he wasn't interested anymore but maybe they could still be friends.

"What's on your mind, darlin'?" he asked.

"I couldn't sleep," she said.

"Me either," he admitted. "I don't want you to leave, but I also only want you to stay if you want to be with me. You didn't have anywhere else to go when things went down like they did in Autrie. Maybe you really want to be off somewhere like Sally Anne and Molly, or even on an adventure with Daisy. I know you will miss her, and I don't want to stand in your way."

His shoulder brushed against hers when he turned to look deeply into her eyes. The same heat that had always been there when he touched her rose up from the depths of her heart and soul.

"Am I right?" he asked.

"No, you are not," she answered. "I am not here because I have no other place to go. I want to be on this farm with you. I do not want to go on an adventure with Daisy and Claude, and I can do some good for my cause from right here."

"Thank God!" He tipped up her chin and kissed her—not once, but half a dozen times.

"But . . ."

"I don't like that word," he said.

She quickly told him about the letter she had received from her friends. "I wouldn't feel right about bringing them to the farm without asking you and your parents."

"Of course they can live here," he said. "Who knows? Maybe they'll even be as happy as we are. I'll send one of the hired hands into town tomorrow to tell Uncle Elijah to meet them at the train and haul them out here. I would offer to do it myself, but I expect that Claude will want me to help with his and Daisy's wedding. Is there anything else before I put on my boots and walk you home?"

"Not one single thing," Lily said, but she thought, *Except your sister hating me.* Maybe with enough time, she hoped, Abigail's mind could change.

Chapter Twenty-Four

Daisy stood back and looked at herself in the cheval mirror that had been left behind when the last renters moved out. Her white dress might not be fitting in some folks' eyes, considering her past, but it did look like something straight out of *Godey's* anyway. "This is far more beautiful than the dress I wore to my first wedding," she whispered. "But whatever am I going to do with it after today?"

"You are going to pack it in your trunk and wear it for Claude every year on your anniversary," Lily told her, then gave her a hug. "I'm going to miss you so much. Write to me often and let me know how things are going. I can't believe that you are really leaving."

"I will," Daisy promised. "Do you think the others will make it in time for the wedding?"

"I do," Lily answered. "Mainly because I hear a wagon coming right now."

Daisy swung the door open and squealed, "They're here at the farm! They really are, Lily. Elijah, bless his heart, got them here before the wedding."

"Did I hear there was a bride needing a ride to the church?" Elijah called out.

"Yes, you did, and thank you," Lily answered. "But y'all stay in the buggy. We've got to be at the church in just a few minutes."

Elijah hopped out of the driver's seat, opened the door into the back, and helped Daisy and Lily inside. "I'll get the whole bunch of you there. Not to worry, Lily. I can see you are wondering where their things are, right?"

"I am worried that they might change their minds about staying and decide to go somewhere else," she said as she sat down on the seat in front of the other three.

Holly adjusted her hat and tucked a strand of light brown hair back behind her ear. Her brown eyes sparkled when she said, "Not a chance. We already love this place better than Nechesville. We looked for a letter from you right up through this morning when we boarded the train, so we just prayed that you would take us in."

"I wrote to you the very next day after we got your note," Lily said. "I suppose that letter saying we were glad you were coming to the farm is somewhere between here and there."

Daisy smoothed the front of her skirt. "But since it didn't arrive, then count this as a welcome."

"Thank you, but—"

Daisy reached over and took Holly's hand in hers. "No *buts* today. Just be happy for me."

"Okay, but would you please tell us what was in that letter?" Iris asked. She was the only woman of the seven with jet-black hair and clear blue eyes. Miz Raven used to say that Iris was the dark red rose in her bouquet of flowers, and with her short fuse, no one had better mess with her.

"That you are welcome to stay here with us," Lily answered. "That we have a house for two of you, and the other one can move in with me since Daisy is—or rather *has* moved out. That she is getting married today and joining a wagon train going north tomorrow morning. And that we are having a party at the campsite tonight as her reception."

And I really don't want to go and deal with Abigail on Daisy's special day.

"Now, please tell me you were not run out of town without even your personal things," she said.

"Another wagon is bringing our trunks. We didn't expect to be picked up in a fancy buggy," Jasmine added. "I want to hug both of you, but I'll wait until we are at the church."

"This is a lot to take in. Until Mr. Elijah told us that we were going to a wedding, we had no idea that . . ." Holly paused and focused Daisy. "You are a beautiful bride. But are you sure about this? You can't have known this man very long."

"I'm very sure," Daisy answered.

"Does he know?" Iris whispered.

Daisy nodded and shifted her focus from one woman to the others. "He knows . . ." She went on to tell them the story that Matt had told Lily. "We kind of fell into a pile of fresh horse manure in Autrie when Cooter Wilson stirred up all that trouble. But then we were welcomed out here, and all that was washed away, and we came out smelling like roses without even the first thorn on the stem. Lily and I both feel like a higher power has led us to where we are."

"Well, then, I hope that higher power is still working for us," Jasmine said.

The buggy came to a stop, and Elijah opened the door for them. "Ladies, I believe we are at the church, with five minutes to spare. Do all y'all, except our bride, want to go on inside and find a seat?"

"I've got to get out and give my friends a real hug before I go into the church," Daisy said and followed the rest of the women out of the buggy. "And, Lily, you can't go in just yet. You and Matt are walking in together since he's the best man."

"This is really happening, isn't it?" Holly asked as she used her hand to wipe the dust from her dark green skirt.

"It is," Lily answered, "and I'm going to miss her something fierce."

Daisy gave her a hug. "These three will help keep you busy."

Claude's sister, Mary, and her family parked their wagon right behind the buggy, and she hurried over to hand Daisy a bouquet of yellow roses. "A bride needs flowers," she said with a smile.

"Thank you. That is so sweet," Daisy said.

Evidently Mary had a sweet, forgiving nature and wasn't at all like her cousin Abigail.

"You are beautiful. My brother is going to be speechless. Now, we've got to get on in the church. One little girl is tougher to get dressed than all four of her brothers. We'll see all y'all at the reception," Mary said and then turned to whisper in Lily's ear, "Abigail told me how she felt about you. Don't pay any attention to her. She's the baby of the family, and quite spoiled."

Easier said than done, Lily thought, but she said, "Thank you."

"What was that all about?" Daisy asked when she was waiting outside with her friends.

"She was just wishing me well," Lily lied. "Your dream is coming true in a few minutes, isn't it?"

"Yes, it is." Daisy's eyes sparkled. "I never thought I would find this kind of love. Be happy for me?"

"You know that I am," she replied. "But we've been like sisters so long."

"No, darlin', we are cousins," Daisy said with a nervous giggle.

Miz Raven's British accent was back in her head again. *No dark clouds in the sky to warrant a bad sign. A lovely breeze is blowing, so everyone in the church won't be scorching hot in their best finery. A party awaits the new bride and groom. Don't be sad for yourself. Be glad for them.*

Exactly what I want for Daisy, and I won't be sad, Lily promised.

"All seven of us will forever be more than just cousins. We are sisters of the heart," Daisy whispered. "I hear piano music. That means you and Matt are supposed to walk inside now. I will be right behind you in a few minutes."

"You ladies look so beautiful," Matt said when he reached them. "Are we ready, Lily?"

"I am if you are," she answered and kissed Daisy on the forehead. "See you on the other side."

Daisy grinned and blew her a kiss as she walked away; then she turned to Elijah. "I have a favor to ask."

"Anything for you," Elijah said.

"I'm a little nervous and could sure use an arm to lean on as I walk down that aisle. Would you please give me away?" she asked. "You've been so good to me and Lily, and supported us when very few others would, especially after you knew our background."

Elijah looped her arm through his. "I would be very honored. I'm going to miss you and Claude both, but a person has to find his own path, even if it leaves loved ones behind."

She rose on her tiptoes and kissed him on the cheek. "Thank you for this and everything else."

Elijah straightened his back and put a broad smile on his face. "Let's get this over with so I can dance with the pretty ladies from the wagon train."

Lily had only been to a couple of weddings, but never one where the church was packed and where she was the maid of honor. Her hands trembled as she let go of Matt's arm and took her place on the other side of the pulpit. She locked eyes with Matt and wished that she was the bride that day, or maybe that she and Daisy were having a double wedding.

Then there was Daisy and Elijah in the doorway. Her best friend looked radiant, and it seemed so fitting that Elijah was playing the part of the father who gives away the bride.

Trust. That was the only word that Miz Raven had to say to her during the whole ceremony.

Then the preacher pronounced the bride and groom *husband and wife*, and said, "What God has joined together, let no man put asunder. You may kiss your bride, Claude."

Claude cupped Daisy's face in his hands and kissed her—long, lingering, and passionately—and the whole congregation clapped and whistled for them.

When the noise died down, the preacher said, "Now, let's all go out to the wagon train camp for the reception. Claude and Daisy will be leaving with them tomorrow morning, so bring out the bagpipes, the fiddles, and the flutes, and let's give them a good old Irish send-off. I know Uncle Elijah loves to dance."

"Yes, I do!" Elijah shouted from the front pew, then rushed outside.

Claude and Daisy got into Elijah's buggy in a hailstorm of rice, and Elijah drove away with them.

Matt slipped his arm around Lily and said, "You and your friends can ride in my wagon. I should have brought a buggy, but I didn't know how many we would be transporting. We have to go slow, though. Mama made the wedding cake. I'm in charge of getting it out to the camp, and even if I am twenty-six years old, she will take a switch to me if I ruin it."

"We'll ride in the back," Holly said. "I will protect that beautiful cake with my life."

Matt helped each lady into the back of the wagon and then rounded the side and hopped up on the buckboard beside Lily.

"You are even prettier than the bride," Matt said. "When are we going to do this?"

"Someday, when the man who is courting me does the asking," she answered with a sly wink. But hidden deep within her heart, a small doubt lingered when Abigail's words came back to haunt her.

Chapter Twenty-Five

The aroma of campfires and food cooking floated out to meet the folks coming out to the circle of wagon trains. Even though it was late August and still hot, a nice little breeze seemed to promise that fall was on the way. A few wildflowers poked their colorful heads up through the tall grass on either side of the rutted pathway. When they were close, Lily could hear the laughter of children and musical instruments being tuned.

"Sounds like the party is getting ready to start," Matt said as he parked his wagon behind Elijah's buggy. He tied off the reins and got off the buckboard and helped Lily down first. "Save the last dance for me."

"Just the last one?" Lily asked.

He took her hand in his. "I'd like to have all of them, but the last dance means you go home with me."

"Always," she assured him. "But aren't you forgetting something?"

"The cake!" He dropped her hand and took a couple of steps toward the back of the wagon.

"We've got it under control." Holly had already gotten out of the wagon. "Just show us where to put it."

"Mama can take care of where it needs to be, but for now we'll just set it wherever we can find a place," he said. "Just follow me and Lily. And thank you for handling it for me."

"You are very welcome," she said.

Maggie met them and motioned for Iris to set the cake in the middle of a long table made by setting a couple of boards on two water barrels off to one side of the center circle. "Just set it right down there in the middle of the other two cakes. One for the bride"—she pointed to one decorated with yellow roses—"a chocolate one for the groom, and this one for the couple."

"That is so sweet," Iris said.

"The Irish do things up right," Maggie whispered. "If they had a general store and a post office out here, they would have their own town and wouldn't even need Autrie."

Lily glanced over at Matt and could tell that the wheels in his mind were spinning round and round as fast as hers were. She wondered just what it would take to turn the sheep farm from a community into an actual town.

"That was such a sweet ceremony, and I'm so glad that Daisy is going along with us as far as Dodge City," Maggie was saying when Lily left the future behind and came back to the present. "We haven't had time to get acquainted with the other folks on the train, so it's comforting to have her close by."

Had someone told Lily that she would ever hear words like that from a preacher's wife, she would have thought they had cow patties for brains.

"Did I hear that woman right?" Iris whispered as she set the cake in the middle of the makeshift table. "Isn't she the preacher's wife you told us about in a letter?"

"Yes and yes," Daisy answered from right behind the four of them. "It's like we're living in a different world."

Claude took Daisy's hand in his. "Thank you all for joining us today in the celebration of mine and Daisy's wedding," he said in a loud voice. "We are starting off our marriage tomorrow morning by joining all y'all on this wagon train."

Everyone, including Lily, applauded, but she felt like a hypocrite. She really wanted Daisy and Claude to stay right there on the sheep farm—or ranch, or whatever it was called. She had visualized them raising their children together. If they were ever able to have any.

Matt drew her close to his side and whispered, "Are you having second thoughts about staying or going?"

"Are you?" she fired back.

"Not in the least, but you looked sad right then."

"I am sad that I'm losing the best friend I ever had in my whole life, but I wouldn't be much of a friend if I made her feel guilty. She is happier than I have ever seen her, and part of me is glad for her," Lily tried to explain.

"And the other part?"

"Is a pure hypocrite," Lily answered. "I told her to go, but . . ."

"'The mind says one thing, the heart says another,'" Matt said. "'It's only when they agree that things work for the best.' Those are Uncle Elijah's words, not mine."

"He's a smart man," Lily said. "But now I have to go find my friends. I've been neglecting Iris, Jasmine, and Holly. They don't know anyone. Daisy is the new bride, so she's got things to do, and here I am, not introducing them to the folks that live here."

Matt pointed toward the table where all three of the ladies were visiting with Claude's and Matt's sisters—Abigail included, who shifted her gaze over to Lily several times as she talked to them.

Lily had shared the comradery of those three friends for a long time, and they wouldn't tolerate anyone saying negative things about her.

"Looks to me like they're all getting along, so you don't need to worry," Matt said.

As soon as Claude and Daisy finished feeding each other a bit of cake, the women stepped up to help serve lamb chops, beef steak, and all kinds of fresh vegetables, right alongside thin slices of the cakes—chocolate with chocolate icing, white with buttercream, and spice with burnt sugar.

Everything looked to be going well. Not even Holly's expression had changed when she was talking to Abigail, so evidently the young woman knew to bridle her tongue at a wedding reception.

"I'm so glad folks are making them welcome." She glanced over her shoulder at the "Just Married" sign tacked to the side of the rig that Daisy and Claude would be living in until they reached their dream place. And she wished that she and Matt were sharing a bed that night in the back of a wagon—or anywhere else, for that matter.

You want to go on a journey after all? the voice in her head asked.

No, I just want to sleep with Matt, she answered.

Iris nudged Lily's shoulder and startled her. "It's hard to believe that all these people are so nice to us."

"Not just these women, but the ones in Autrie, too," Lily told her. "I will be going into town when they have the women's meetings to help out. Y'all will go with me, right?"

"Absolutely," Iris answered and nodded toward the musicians. "What are they doing?"

Matt gave Lily's shoulder a gentle squeeze and answered, "They're fixing to dance in a circle around the bride and groom to bring them good luck and happiness. Uncle Elijah started the tradition years ago, and he's beckoning to me."

Lily took a step back and said, "Then go show me how it's done."

He jogged over to the men and women gathering around the bride and groom and nodded toward the musicians. The fiddles whined, and the two bagpipe players created a haunting sound. Abigail left the table and came over to stand beside Lily, and she did not look happy.

"Matt likes you a lot and is a lot like our father," she said.

"I like him, too," Lily said.

"I'm not as forgiving as my father," Abigail said bluntly. "I know what my mother did before she married, but I want better for my brother. I want him to have an untarnished bride."

Abigail never took her eyes off the dancers, who were now doing all kinds of fancy steps and moving around the bride and groom at the same time. Lily's eyes kept darting from Matt out there having a wonderful time to Abigail, who had pasted on a fake smile.

Had she heard Abigail right? Had she really said that the family would accept her living within the community, but not if she married Matt?

"Does everyone feel like you do?" she finally asked.

"Matt and Claude have been the heads of the farm since my dad got hurt, and Seamus wanted to step down. Now Matt will make the decisions," Abigail answered.

"But he's out there dancing and doing a fine job of it," Lily argued.

"This is a big ranch," Abigail said, like that was important.

"What does that have to do with anything?" Lily asked.

"Think about it. Now that Claude is gone . . ." Abigail let the sentence hang and walked away from Lily to join the ring of dancers.

Lily finally got the drift of what she was saying, and her own Irish temper rose up from her toes. Abigail thought she was out to get a stake in the business—nothing more than an opportunist. In Lily's mind, that was even worse than being called a soiled dove. She had been a fool to believe that everything would turn out to be all peaches and cream for her. Maybe she *should* change her mind at the last minute and crawl up on the buckboard of Daisy and Claude's covered wagon. She was strong and could help out on the trip, and she didn't mind sleeping out under the stars at night. Perhaps Elijah had another wagon up for sale and she could buy it from him. Then she and all four of the others could start over somewhere in a faraway territory.

The dancing stopped, and the next song the musicians played was much slower. Claude took Daisy in his arms and began to waltz her around one of the many open fires in the middle of the campsite. Lily couldn't be upset with her, not even for a single second, not when she looked so happy.

Matt appeared in front of her and held out a hand. "May I have this dance?"

"Yes, sir, you may," she answered.

Every nerve in her body told her to ignore Abigail, but her heart was a different matter. Finally, she looked into his eyes and asked, "How much does family mean to you?"

"Everything," he said and held her closer.

When the dance was over, he led her over to a quilt and waited for her to sit down before he eased down beside her. "Someday I hope to have sons to pass this business on down to. I want to teach them all about sheep farming."

"What if all you get are daughters, or if you don't get children at all?" She could almost feel her heart breaking.

"Then I'll teach my daughters the same as the boys—and if I get none, there's lots of nephews and nieces on the farm for me to train up to take my place when I am old," he said with a grin. "Why are you asking this?"

Lily wasn't sure if she would ever be a mother. That was another reason for her to walk away now: to give Matt a chance to find an untainted wife—a pure woman with no sordid past who would give him a houseful of sons.

She forced a smile. "I just wondered. You love your sisters and brothers very much, don't you?"

"Yes, I do. Even though you haven't seen them in years, don't you love your family?"

"No, I don't," she replied. "They didn't stand by me when I needed them. My brothers were all older than me and left home when I was just a baby. My mother didn't really want another child, but . . ." She couldn't bring herself to say the words—that her mother had often whispered in the presence of other women that she'd done her wifely duty and wound up with another squalling kid.

"Well, look around you," Matt said. "You have a big family now that loves you. But out of all of them, I love you the most."

"I love you, too," Lily said.

And that's the very reason why I have to end this relationship, she thought. *It will break my heart, and I will write you a long letter tonight. You'll be better off without me, and you will find a woman who deserves a good man like you. One whose past does not hinder your dreams.*

Chapter Twenty-Six

It was well past midnight when Lily carefully eased out of bed and tiptoed to the front room. She sat down at the table, lit a lamp, and started writing. She wrote *My Dearest Matt* and then couldn't go any further. Tears rolled off her cheeks and left big smeary splotches in the ink. She tore the page off the tablet, dipped her pen once more, and started again.

"What are you doing?" Iris asked, so close behind her that Lily jumped and smeared ink all over the new page.

"I'm writing a letter to Matt because I can't tell him what he needs to hear without crying," Lily said on a sob.

Iris went to the kitchen and brought out a plate with slices of leftover wedding cake and two forks. She handed one to Lily and said, "Tell me what that sweet man needs to hear."

Lily put the pen in the holder beside the inkwell. "I'm not sure I can put it in real words. I can't even write down how I feel, but my heart says that I cannot cause a problem with Matt and his family."

"Eat. Food cures everything, even broken hearts. Miz Raven told us that, and I believed *every word* she said." Iris accentuated *every word* by jabbing her fork toward the plate. "What makes you think there's a problem, anyway? He seemed smitten with you at the party tonight, which was a pretty nice welcoming event for all of us. We weren't sure how we would be received, and we were greeted with a wedding and a big reception."

Lily ate one bite of cake and told Iris about Abigail being so determined not to accept her. "I thought I could change her mind by being kind and nice, but evidently that is not going to happen. I asked him what family meant to him," she said with a sigh, then went on to tell her what he had said. "After what we have all done to keep from having kids, I may never be able to have children, and he wants a big family. I can't leave, but I *can* free him from being with me."

"You are a fool!" Iris said. "You came through a horrible experience and have led women to fight for their rights."

"Oh, sure," Lily argued. "They get to sit by their husbands in church. Some big victory that is."

"Come on, now," Iris scolded. "That gave them confidence to stand beside you when you moved out here, didn't it? A little backbone and support from one another will give them what they need to take another step for their rights."

"What has that got to do with today?"

"Anything worth having is worth fighting for," Iris said, reminding her of what Miz Raven had said the night before they all left the Paradise. "Do you love Matt Maguire?"

Lily nodded and swiped a tear away. "I do."

"Then change his sister's mind," Iris said.

"I've tried but it won't work. What more can I do?"

"By doing what you're already doing," Iris answered. "And then ask Abigail to go to the meetings in town. That will show her that we are all strong women and we don't back down from a fight."

Lily started to say something, but a soft rap on the door stopped her. Who would be coming around the house in the wee hours of the morning?

Iris was on her feet and slinging the door open before Lily could even collect her thoughts. "Well, hello, Matt," she said. "Is everything all right? Nothing has happened to Daisy or Claude, has it?"

"Everything is fine—or at least, I hope it is. I need to speak to Lily."

Lily could hear the anguish in his voice and figured she didn't need to finish her letter. Abigail, and perhaps even his other sister, had convinced him that Lily was not a suitable woman for him to court. She pushed back her chair, picked up a shawl from the sofa, and wrapped it around her shoulders.

"Matt," she said.

"I know it's late and this isn't appropriate, but I can't sleep until I get things straightened out," he blurted out.

"I'll see you in the morning," Iris whispered and left the room.

"Will you come sit on the porch with me?" he asked.

"Yes—and I agree, we do need to talk." She closed the door behind her and sat down on the top step of the porch. Mozelle flopped down close by when she stretched her long legs out and sank her bare feet into the green grass. Her heart felt like a rock in her chest, and she held her hands tightly in her lap to keep them steady.

Matt sat down beside her, and even in that moment, the touch of his shoulder against hers sent her emotions into a whirl. She wanted to snuggle up in his arms and have the right to put her hand on his chest—to feel his heartbeat and know that it was keeping time with hers. But that privilege had passed.

"I could tell something was wrong at the reception after Abigail talked to you and then walked away. I've been over at the house, and she came clean about all the ugly things she has said to you. I came to apologize, and she will do the same tomorrow. What she said is unforgivable, and I won't hold it against you if you can't let her off the hook. I love you, Lily Boyle, and—"

She butted in before he could finish. "I love you, too, but I can't cause problems with your family."

"Remember what my uncle preached about last Sunday in our little church here on the farm?" he asked.

"I'm sorry, but I don't—and what does that have to do with all this?" she asked.

"Leave your mother and father and cling to your wife, is the basis of what he said." Matt took Lily's hand in his and placed it on his chest. "That's my heart. It will shatter if you let anything come between us—Abigail or anyone else."

"What if I can never have children?" she whispered.

"Then we'll love all the ones that are already here on the farm, and all the ones that will be born from now until the end of our days, when we are holding hands in eternity," he answered. "You are more important to me than anything else in this world. Please don't leave with that wagon train tomorrow morning. Without you, there is no us."

"I won't leave," Lily said. "I just want your promise that if you change your mind, you will be honest and tell me."

"I promise, but it won't happen." Matt moved away from her and got down on one knee. "Lily Boyle, I believe I fell in love with you the first time I laid eyes on you on that train platform. It just took my mind longer than my heart to realize it. Will you marry me? We don't have to rush, but I want to know that you will be in my life forever."

"Yes, Matt, I will," she said, and sealed their engagement with a kiss.

The rattling of pots and pans in the kitchen woke Lily later that morning. She'd only had a couple of hours of sleep, and that was stretched out on the sofa so that she wouldn't disturb Iris. She sat up and rubbed her eyes and then looked around the room. Holly had cleaned off the table and was busy peeling potatoes. Jasmine was whipping eggs in a bowl. For a brief moment, she thought she was back at the Paradise. Then she felt the warmth of Matt's kisses still on her lips, and she realized where she was.

"Yes!" she exclaimed.

"Yes, what?" Iris poked her head around the doorjamb separating the front room from the kitchen.

"With all of you here, for a minute there, I thought we were back at the Paradise," she answered, stretching the kinks out of her back.

"But the 'yes' means you want to be back there?" Holly asked.

"No, it means that I'm glad to be here and that I said yes when Matt proposed to me last night. We worked things out—so thank you, Iris, for reminding me that I'm a strong woman."

"Anytime," Iris said and disappeared back into the kitchen. "Lard is melting and is almost ready for those potatoes, Holly, and biscuits are cooking."

Lily ate a couple of bites of cake on her way to open the windows. "There's no stopping that ball from rolling, now that it's got a good running start. Let's get breakfast done and go wave as the wagon train passes by. I can't believe Daisy is leaving, but thank God y'all are here."

"Amen!" Jasmine said. "After the horrible reception we had in Nechesville, this is like leaving hell and landing in heaven. But what are we going to do to support ourselves?"

"We can all sew," Lily assured her. "Beulah has offered to put as many garments as we can design and make in her store, and with four of us working, we might even be able to ship them to other places. I'll ask her before she leaves this morning if she has some connections in surrounding towns."

Holly kneaded the biscuit dough a few times and then cut out the biscuits with a glass. She placed them in a cast-iron skillet and laughed.

"What's so funny?" Lily frowned. "We might end up with our designs and clothing all over this part of Texas. We could sew labels in the back and folks would think that they're getting something special. Holly, you are good at embroidery. You can design and make our tags."

"That was my happy laugh, for all the good fortune we have had. I will gladly make tags for our creations. What will we put on them?" She stopped for a breath.

"A little blue jay," Lily suggested, then told them the story.

"Sounds fitting," Iris said from the kitchen. "When is the food going to be ready? And yes, yes, yes, we are excited for you and Matt."

They had just sat down at the table, made up of three crates and covered with a cloth, when Daisy poked her head in the back door. "I couldn't leave without getting another hug from each of you. I don't feel so bad about leaving Lily now that you are all here with her."

Lily was the first to wrap her up in her arms. The other three hurried over and made it a four-way hug. Tears flooded Daisy's eyes when they broke away. "My wedding was beautiful, and . . ." She blushed.

"I bet you didn't think you would ever do that again," Iris teased.

"What? Go to bed with a man?" Daisy asked.

"No, turn scarlet at the thought of what followed all the fun last night," Holly answered.

"Y'all are right on both counts—and now I have to go. I hear the wheels of the first wagon coming this way. Claude is second in line, and he's picking me up when ours gets to your house," Daisy said.

Lily and the other three followed her through the house and out onto the porch.

"I hate goodbyes." Lily's voice cracked.

"This is so fitting," Daisy said. "I'll cherish this image forever of y'all all wearing white nightgowns, just like we did every morning at the Paradise."

Claude stopped the wagon and jumped down to the ground. "Are you ready, darlin'?"

"I am."

He scooped her up in his arms and set her up on the seat. "Goodbye," he called out.

"Be safe and write!" Lily yelled.

"I promise I will!" Daisy shouted.

The four waved for a full five minutes and then went back into the house. "What's on your mind?" Iris asked Lily as she sat down and passed her plate over to Holly for a biscuit.

"Everything happens for a reason," Lily said around the huge lump in her throat. "Daisy has found her happiness. I've found mine. Y'all are next."

"Oh, no!" Iris declared. "There were a lot of good-looking men at the party last night, but the only one that really took my eye was the wagon master, and now he's gone."

But according to Matt, he comes through here a couple of times a year, Lily thought, but she didn't say a word.

Epilogue

Christmas, 1883

Lily eased out of bed, leaving Matt snuggled down in the covers. She stoked up the embers in the fireplace, added a couple more logs, and pulled her shawl tightly around her shoulders. Yesterday had been her wedding day—nothing elaborate, just a simple ceremony at the church. Matt had asked her where she wanted to go on the honeymoon, and she'd chosen the old shepherd's shack at the far reaches of the farm.

The place was one room, with a bed in one corner, a cookstove in the other, and a small table with a couple of mismatched chairs. She wrapped her shawl even tighter around her body and stared out the window at the white fields in front of her. The snow wasn't as deep as what Daisy's latest letter had told her about in Nebraska, but the sight was still so beautiful that it took her breath away.

Her reflection in the window showed the same tall, red-haired woman who'd gotten off the train almost six months ago, but so much had changed. She'd watched the events play out from then until that very day. Daisy was happy in Nebraska, having just gotten there in time for the first snow in November, and they had already found a small sheep farm to buy and were settling in when she wrote.

Holly had landed a job helping Alma in the bunkhouse kitchen. In the evenings she kept busy embroidering labels for all the garments the other three were making. Beulah had reached out to a couple of folks she knew in Austin and Houston, and they were stocking their stores with Blue Jay creations that sold as fast as they got a shipment.

Abigail was engaged to one of the hired hands and planning a spring wedding. That was one of the reasons why Lily wanted to keep things simple. She and Abigail had mended fences and were becoming good friends. Lily didn't want to overshadow her new sister-in-law's wedding and had even offered to use that lovely bolt of white brocade to design and create a beautiful wedding gown for her.

"Someday," she whispered.

"Someday what?" Matt walked up behind her, slipped his arms around her waist, and pulled her back to his chest.

She turned and wrapped her arms around his neck. "I hope that someday Holly, Iris, and Jasmine will be as happy as Daisy and I are."

His lips found hers in a passionate kiss. When he pulled away, he looked deeply into her eyes and said, "We could be at my house . . . I mean, *our* house now," he corrected himself. "Why did you want to come all the way out here for a honeymoon?"

"Because I get you all to myself for my Christmas present." She smiled. "No one will come out here in this kind of weather, so we are alone for three whole days—or maybe longer if the snow doesn't melt off. So, Merry Christmas to me and to you. We have everything we need right here."

He scooped her up into his arms and laid her gently on the bed. "You are so right. Now, tell me one more time."

"I love you, Matt Maguire," she whispered softly in his ear.

Acknowledgments

Dear Readers,

I would like to thank each and every one of you who asked me to write a book about what happened to the ladies who worked at the Paradise when it was a brothel. Miz Raven closed the place and sent her seven women off to South Texas in hopes that they would work toward the women's rights movement in the booming towns of Autrie, Nechesville, and Jacksonville.

I'm so excited to give you my first historical novel in almost two decades. I hope you enjoy going back in time to 1883 and reading Lily and Daisy's story. Life was not easy for women in those days, and we, as women, owe a lot to our ancestors who were willing to go to battle so that we can have the freedoms we have today.

From a single idea to the book you have in your hands, writing this took a lot of work, and many thanks are due. First of all, a huge thank-you to the fans who asked for this story, and then to Montlake for giving me the opportunity to write a historical book. A big thanks to Krista Stroever, my developmental editor, who continually takes a lump of coal and helps me shine it up to be a diamond. Thanks to my agency, Folio Management Literary Agency, and to my agent, Erin Niumata, who has continued to believe in me for more than twenty-five years. And to my family, who has helped me stay on track after losing my precious Mr. B last December. He was my best friend and biggest supporter during all our fifty-seven years of marriage.

Happy reading to all y'all!

Carolyn Brown

About the Author

Photo © 2015 Charles Brown

Carolyn Brown is a *New York Times, USA Today, Washington Post, Wall Street Journal,* and *Publishers Weekly* bestselling author and RITA finalist with more than 140 published books. She has written women's fiction, historical and contemporary romance, and cowboys-and-country-music novels. She lives in the small town of Davis, Oklahoma, where everyone knows everyone else, knows what they are doing and when, and reads the local newspaper on Wednesday to see who got caught. She and her late husband, Mr. B, are parents to three grown children and too many grandchildren and great-grandchildren to count on the fingers and toes of one person. For more information, visit www.carolynbrownbooks.com.